S0-AZC-894

No Tears for Hilda

by Andrew Garve

"I enjoyed the story very much for its combination of a simple straightforward style and a taut, exciting story line. The characters are real people and that is so rare in a story of this type."   —John McCloy

"... a solid work, which can be reread at intervals with the greatest pleasure. The detection is adroitly divided, or doubled (as one may want to look at it), so that the business of being on both sides of the hunt does not produce the usual disintegration of suspense. The hero and heroine are likable, and so is the murderer. Garve writes with economy and color...."
   —Jacques Barzun and Wendell Hertig Taylor,
   in *A Catalog of Crime*

Other titles by Andrew Garve available in Perennial Library:

The Ashes of Loda
The Cuckoo Line Affair
A Hero for Leanda
Murder Through the Looking Glass
No Tears for Hilda
The Riddle of Samson

No Tears for

HILDA

BY
ANDREW GARVE

PERENNIAL LIBRARY
Harper & Row, Publishers
New York, Hagerstown, San Francisco, London

This book was originally published in hardcover by Harper & Row, Publishers.

NO TEARS FOR HILDA. Copyright 1950 by Andrew Garve. All rights reserved. Printed in the United States of America. No part of this book may be used or reproduced in any manner without written permission except in the case of brief quotations embodied in critical articles and reviews. For information address Harper & Row, Publishers, Inc., 10 East 53d Street, New York, N.Y. 10022.

First PERENNIAL LIBRARY edition published 1978

ISBN: 0-06-080441-6

78 79 80 81 82 10 9 8 7 6 5 4 3 2 1

No Tears for

HILDA

❦ ONE ❦

GEORGE LAMBERT sat huddled in his greatcoat in the sitting room of his Finchley home, waiting for the police to come. He looked the personification of lonely misery. The air of a raw November night swept through the open front door and out through all the open windows, but the smell of coal gas still hung about the house.

At the first sound of a car he roused himself and went into the hall. The police party consisted of a plain-clothes officer, a uniformed constable and a man with an attaché case.

"Mr. Lambert?" inquired the plain-clothes man, briskly.

"Yes—come in," said George, in a low voice. He stood back to let them pass. "In the kitchen—straight through."

The C.I.D. man was sniffing the gas. "Better leave the door open," he called to the fresh-faced young constable.

The doctor had already made his way to the kitchen. On the red-tiled floor the body of a large fleshy woman was stretched full-length on a settee cushion beside the gas oven. A dented pillow inside the oven showed where her head had rested. The eyes were closed, the cheeks and lips cherry pink, the dark hair tightly waved and slightly incongruous. At one corner of the mouth was a trace of froth. The doctor lifted an eyelid, felt for a nonexistent pulse, and shook his head. "Quite dead, I'm afraid."

George nodded. The plain-clothes man laid a firm but kindly

hand upon his arm. "Better come into the other room. It'll take Dr. Roberts a little time to make his examination."

George turned obediently and led the way back into the sitting room. His rather chubby face was ashen; his brown eyes were clouded with worry.

"What you need, sir, is a drop of brandy."

"I'm afraid we don't keep any in this house, Inspector."

"Just Sergeant, sir—Detective Sergeant Green. We're short-handed this week. Constable!"

The young policeman put his head in at the door. "Sir?"

"Ask the doctor if he's got a drop of brandy."

"Yes, sir."

George looked grateful. "It's all this gas," he said.

"More likely the shock," said Green. "You're bound to feel a thing like this."

They sat in silence for a few moments, and then the constable returned with a stiff shot of brandy. George drained it.

"That better, Mr. Lambert?"

"Much better, thank you, Sergeant."

Green cleared his throat and got down to business. "Have you any idea why your wife did it? Did she seem depressed?"

"I wouldn't have said so."

"Was she all right when you left her this morning?"

"Perfectly. At least, she appeared to be. She's had rather a trying time lately—we both have. Our daughter had a bad nervous breakdown a little while ago and had to go into a mental hospital."

"Ah," said Sergeant Green. "That must have been a great worry to her. Did she ever talk of suicide?"

"Never. As a matter of fact, I thought she was bearing up astonishingly well. I wish to God she'd told me how badly she felt. I might have done something."

"I shouldn't worry myself on that score, sir. When people start getting suicidal, there's no stopping them. She didn't leave any message, I suppose?"

"Nothing at all."

"H'm. She must have done it on impulse. They usually do."

"It must have been a very sudden impulse, Sergeant. Did you notice her hair?"

"Can't say I did, sir. Why?"

"She always wore her hair straight, in a bob. It was like that when I left her this morning. It seems an odd way to prepare for suicide."

Green gave a little shrug. "You never can tell with women. I've known a woman to dress herself up in her best clothes, jewels and all, and then throw herself out of a window. Brainstorm or something."

"I suppose so," said George, wearily. "When do you think it happened, Sergeant?"

"Difficult to say, sir. Dr. Roberts'll give us an idea, I expect."

George stared into the empty grate. "If only I could live this day again . . ." he murmured.

"What's that, sir?"

"Eh? Oh, nothing, Sergeant. How long's this business of yours going to take?"

"Not long. It's just a routine checkup. As soon as the doctor's finished, we'll get the body down to the mortuary. You'll feel better when the place is cleared up. Roberts'll give you some sleeping tablets before he goes, if you ask him. He's a good chap —lucky he was in the station when you rang."

A voice suddenly called from the kitchen, "Sergeant!" and Green said, "Excuse me, sir," and went out. He seemed to be away a long time. When he came back, there was an odd look on his face, and his tone was a little more official.

"I'm afraid we're going to have to worry you a bit longer than I thought, Mr. Lambert. Dr. Roberts tells me that your wife has bitten her tongue."

"Bitten her tongue!"

"Yes, rather badly. She didn't have an accident of any sort before you left home this morning?"

"Of course not. I'd have told you."

"You can't account for it?"

"No, I can't. Do people who gas themselves usually bite their tongues?"

"They don't, sir—not usually."

"Could she have had a fit or something?"

"It's impossible to say at the moment." Green looked hard at George. "Dr. Roberts has also found what may prove to be a bruise at the back of your wife's neck."

"She must have fallen. . . ." A look of incredulity sprang into George's face. "Good heavens, you don't think . . . ?"

"I don't know, sir," said the sergeant, gravely. "We shall have to look into it. May I use your telephone?"

"Of course," said George. Green went out into the hall, closing the sitting-room door behind him.

It seemed no time at all before another car drew up outside the house, and a second police invasion occurred. George decided that there was nothing to be gained by curiosity. He was clearly not wanted. The atmosphere was now free from all but a lingering smell of gas, so he closed the sitting-room windows and switched on the electric fire. He was evidently in for a long session and might just as well be comfortable. He lit a pipe and sat before the glowing fire reflecting somberly on the turn of events. Presently the door opened, and Green said, "Inspector Haines would like to ask you a few questions, Mr. Lambert."

George waved the inspector to a chair. He was a plump, burly man, fiftyish, with thick gray eyebrows and good-humored wrinkles around eyes and mouth which gave him a deceptively paternal appearance. He settled himself into the easy chair, stretched his legs out to the fire, and said, "I'm sorry about all this disturbance. We'll be as quick as we can. You must be very upset already."

"Naturally," said George. "But I suppose you must do your duty, whatever it is."

"Exactly. You see, Mr. Lambert, it looks as though some violence may have been used upon your wife."

"So I gathered from Sergeant Green. I think it's fantastic."

"Why?"

"I can't think of any reason why anyone should want to harm her."

"I see. Well, we'll go into that later. Now I wonder if you'd tell me exactly what you did and saw when you got in—let's see, around nine-thirty, wasn't it?"

"That's right, Inspector." George gathered his scattered thoughts. "Well, the house looked just as usual from the outside. There was a light in the sitting room. I let myself in at the front door, and of course I smelled gas. In fact, the gas was so strong I had to go out again. I ran round and opened the back door. The kitchen was dark, but I could hear the gas hissing out of the oven. I took a deep breath, rushed in, and switched on the kitchen light. I saw my wife lying on the floor, but the room was absolutely full of gas and I couldn't stay. I turned off the gas taps and dashed out again to breathe."

"Just a moment. You say you turned off the gas taps. Were they all turned on—the rings as well as the oven?"

George thought for a second. "Yes, all of them—I'm pretty sure."

Haines nodded. "And then?"

"I went in again straight away and opened the kitchen door and the hall door so that a draft would blow right through. Then I opened all the kitchen windows. I knelt down beside Hilda, but I felt dizzy, and I had to go out for a couple of minutes while the gas cleared. I went in to her as soon as I could, I swear."

"There's no need to defend yourself, Mr. Lambert," said the inspector, smoothly. "Just tell me what happened."

"Well, she looked so natural I thought she must still be alive. I—I pulled her away from the oven—I thought I might be able to bring her round. I tried, but she had no pulse, and her body was getting cold. I went to the telephone and rang our own doctor, but he was out. So then I rang the local police, and they said they'd bring a doctor."

"Did you move or touch anything in the kitchen, apart from the body?"

"I don't think so. Only the taps, of course, and the doors and windows. I didn't feel like hanging about there."

"What did you do after you'd rung the police?"

"Nothing much—they were here in five minutes. I went upstairs and opened all the doors and windows. I looked in all the rooms to see if there was a note or anything, but I didn't find one."

"Were there any signs of disorder or struggle—in here, for instance? Any furniture out of place—anything knocked over?"

"On the contrary," said George, "everything was very tidy." He seemed to recollect something. "Of course, I remember now —it's Wednesday. Mrs. Biggs must have been here."

"Mrs. Biggs?"

"The char. She always comes on Wednesdays."

"How long does she stay?"

"I think she usually stays all day. She's always gone when I get home, of course."

"She might help us a lot. Do you happen to know where she lives?"

"I'm afraid I don't, Inspector. My wife may have kept her address somewhere."

"We must try to find it. As a matter of fact, we'd like to have a good look over the house anyway. Have you any objection?"

"None whatever. Look anywhere you like."

"Thank you," said Haines. He went to the door and gave some instructions which were inaudible to George.

"Of course," said the inspector, resuming his seat, "we mustn't jump to conclusions. We don't know for certain that your wife didn't commit suicide. We shall be able to judge better after the autopsy. But if there *was* violence . . ."

"I can only say again, Inspector, that I can't believe that."

"I understand. But supposing there was—can you tell me anything that would help me to find out who was responsible? Did your wife ever quarrel with anybody? Did she make enemies? Do you know of anyone who had a grudge against her?"

George made a gesture of impatience. "My wife hardly ever saw anybody," he said. "She wasn't very sociable. She rarely went out. We all led a very regular sort of life—she and I and our daughter. Quiet and domestic. She was the last sort of person to get caught up in any sort of violence. I tell you it's absurd—unless, of course, you're suggesting that some maniac came in from the street."

The inspector said, "H'm," and seemed to be hesitating on the brink of a question. Then he said, "Mr. Lambert, I don't like asking things like this, but I've got to. Were you at home all through the war?"

"No, Inspector. I was overseas for three years. In the army."

"Ah! Many women, you know, became involved with other men while their husbands were away in the forces. What do you say about that?"

"Only that you didn't know my wife. She was a highly moral woman. She'd never have got involved with another man."

"That's a big claim for anyone to make," said Haines.

"Oh, don't misunderstand me, Inspector—it hadn't anything to do with me. It's just that she was brought up that way. Her people were very strict. Besides, my daughter was with her all through the war—I don't think they were apart for a single night. You're barking up the wrong tree there."

"I dare say. You'd be surprised how many trees we policemen bark up. Anyway, while we're on this topic would you care to tell me about your own relationship with your wife? Did you get on all right together?"

George looked moodily at his feet. "I suppose as well as most people who've been married twenty years. We never quarreled, if that's what you mean. My wife wasn't a quarrelsome sort of woman."

"Her death is a great blow to you, of course." The inspector's voice held a note of inquiry.

George flushed. "Aren't you exceeding your duty, Inspector?"

Haines raised an eyebrow but didn't pursue the subject. "Tell me about your daughter," he said. "I hear she's in the hospital."

"Unfortunately, yes. She's at Swan Park. She's been there about a month."

"What's her trouble, Mr. Lambert?"

"Well, they call it manic-depressive insanity. My wife said it was just 'nerves.' I'm afraid I'm not much good at this psychological stuff—you'd better ask the hospital if you're interested. Anyway, Jane's getting better now. The hospital's done a very good job."

"I'm glad to hear that. How old is your daughter?"

"Nearly seventeen."

"Was she fond of her mother?"

"They were devoted. My God, Inspector, you're not suggesting . . . ?"

"Easy, Mr. Lambert. I'm not suggesting anything. I'm quite certain that your daughter was safely in the hospital all day—but I shall check up, all the same. That's my job."

The door opened, and Sergeant Green looked in. "Can we go over this room for fingerprints? We've done everywhere else."

"If Mr. Lambert doesn't mind," said the inspector.

"Go ahead," said George. "Get it over." A man whom he hadn't seen before began methodically to go over the room, dusting here and there. Another man took some photographs. They paid particular attention to the door handle, finger plate, and various movable objects, including the poker in the grate. They seemed extremely thorough.

"What exactly are you looking for, Inspector?" George asked.

"Anything unusual. We naturally expect to find your wife's

prints, and your own, and Mrs. Biggs's, pretty well all over the place. If we find others, then we shall have to try to identify them. It's just routine, you know. We've taken your wife's prints, for purposes of elimination, and we shall have to get Mrs. Biggs's. It would help us if we could have yours. There's no compulsion, of course."

"I don't mind," said George.

"Good. We'll take them now." Haines watched quietly while the operation was performed.

As soon as the others had left the room, the inspector said, "Well, it looks as though we're nearly through. By the way, Mr. Lambert, you mentioned earlier that Mrs. Biggs had always left by the time you got home. What time do you usually get home?"

"It varies," said George. "If I'm lucky, about half-past six. If we're very busy, it may be seven or eight. I'm a civil servant—Town Planning."

"But tonight you were detained—you didn't reach home till nine-thirty?"

"That's right."

"What were you doing?"

There was a barely perceptible pause before George said, "I was at a lecture."

"What lecture?"

"Oh, it was a departmental thing on 'The Community Center and the New Town.' Part of a series—we have them every fortnight."

"I see. Did you go to the lecture straight from work?"

"No. I had a meal first in the canteen, and then went upstairs to the lecture at seven-thirty. It finished about nine."

"And you were in the building the whole time?"

"Of course."

The inspector nodded. "I'm glad to hear it. I shall have to get confirmation from your colleagues, of course—a pure formality. Don't worry—it'll be done very discreetly."

There was a loud silence. The inspector seemed to have run out of questions. George was sunk in thought. Presently, his face a dark red, he said, "I'm sorry, Inspector, but I misled you just now."

"Oh?" said Haines, quietly.

"Yes. I didn't go to that lecture. I—you got me flustered. I intended to go—that's what I should have said. I actually told my wife I was going. But when the time came, I was a bit tired, and I felt I just couldn't face it, so I—I went to the cinema instead."

The inspector's gray eyes were stern. "Mr. Lambert," he said, "your wife is lying dead in the next room, and the odds are piling up that someone murdered her. Surely you can see that this is no time to tell childish lies about how you spent the evening. Misled me, indeed! Where *were* you?"

"I've told you—I was at the cinema."

"Alone?"

"Yes."

"Which cinema?"

"I've forgotten the name. It's in Leicester Square."

"What was the picture?"

"A thriller—*Ten Seconds to Go.*"

"What time did you go in?"

"I don't know exactly."

"Roughly, then. Did you go straight from work?"

"Yes."

"About what time? You must have some idea."

"About six."

"Was the main film showing then?"

"Yes," said George, desperately.

"And what were the other features?"

"The usual—news and so on."

"What was in the news?"

"Fighting!" said George. "Fighting all over the world."

"What else?"

"I can't remember now—it wasn't very interesting. Women's fashions, politicians making speeches—all sorts of things."

"Was there a second feature?"

"No," said George, "one of those cartoon things." Sweat stood out on his forehead. "Inspector, I'm tired out. How can you expect me to remember all these details now?"

Haines snorted. "It shouldn't be difficult. You know, Mr. Lambert, you're not being very wise."

"Oh, confound your lectures! I tell you I was at the cinema. That's all there is to it."

"Very well," said Haines, softly, "we'll leave it at that—for the moment. I see you have a garage. Have you a car?"

"Yes," said George.

"Do you drive to business in it?"

"Sometimes."

"Did you today?"

"Yes."

"Where did you park it while you were in the cinema?"

"In Leicester Square."

"What sort of car is it?"

"An Alfa-Romeo."

"Really! Aren't they very expensive?"

"It's an old one—1932."

"Saloon?"

"No, coupé."

"I see. Perhaps you could let me see your registration book before I go. You like distinctive cars, do you?"

"I don't like the modern mass-produced junk, if that's what you mean." George got up and went over to the bureau. "Here's the registration book, Inspector."

"Thank you." Haines made a few notes. "I'll see the car on my way out."

The door opened, and Sergeant Green came in again. "We're all through, sir."

"Right," said Haines. "I'll just have a last look around myself before you move the body. Did you find Mrs. Biggs's address?"

"Yes, sir. Will you go and see her tonight? She lives quite near."

"No, it'll do in the morning. You might send a man along early to detain her till I come."

"Very good, sir."

The policemen went out. George stayed in the sitting room, brooding. He could hear the inspector pottering about in the kitchen. A car drove up—or was it the ambulance? Once again the house seemed to be full of tramping feet. George went to the door and watched, his feelings numbed, while they carried the remains of Hilda away.

Haines came in. "Well, that's all, Mr. Lambert. The house is yours again. It would be convenient if you could arrange to be here all day tomorrow. I'm sure your office will understand. Good night."

"Good night," said George, wretchedly.

Inspector Haines dropped in at the local station early next morning on his way to see Mrs. Biggs.

"Any developments, Sergeant?"

"No, sir. We kept an eye on the house but Lambert didn't go out or telephone. I suppose there's been no report on the Alfa yet?"

"Not yet, Sergeant, but we shall get something, I'm sure. I've got a fingerprint report here that will interest you. Just look at this."

Green ran his eye down the document and gave a low whistle. "I say—no prints on the taps except Lambert's, eh?"

"That's right. Lambert's thumb and index finger on each tap. Just the one impression. The chromium took the prints perfectly. No smudging and no other prints. That makes you think, doesn't it?"

"It seems queer," said Green. "But at least it proves it was murder. If Mrs. Lambert's prints weren't on the taps, she couldn't have gassed herself."

"I think that's a fair conclusion," said Haines. "What puzzles me is *why* the taps hadn't any old prints on them, including hers."

"I suppose the murderer must have wiped them all off at some time," said Green, without any great conviction. "Somebody must have."

"Yes, but why the murderer? Put yourself in Lambert's place, supposing he did it? He'd want to make it look like suicide. He'd know that various prints would be on the taps, mostly his wife's, and that would just suit him. By wiping them all off, and leaving nothing but one set of his own prints, he'd destroy the very suicide theory he was trying to build up. It doesn't make sense."

"Lambert didn't strike me as a very seasoned sort of criminal, sir. He might have lost his head and hardly known what he was wiping. Look at the way he lied to you. That cinema story's complete eyewash—we checked up this morning. He's got almost all his facts wrong except the name of the big picture, and he could have read that on the hoardings. He doesn't seem to have any grip on the situation at all. Just a bungler, if you ask me."

"I can't make him out at all," said Haines. "How did he behave at first, when it seemed like suicide?"

"Well," said Green, "I must say he seemed very badly cut up."

"That's what I gathered. Then, when it began to look like murder, he seemed to lose some of his depression. I don't mean he was cheerful or anything like that, but he talked more and answered back a bit—just as though a weight was off his mind. If he'd murdered her, you'd expect just the opposite."

"There's insanity in the family," said Green, hopefully.

"Not good enough, Sergeant. There's another thing. From what you tell me, he didn't seem to agree with the suicide theory at first. He thought it was improbable. He insisted that his wife wasn't depressed in the morning—he drew your attention to her newly waved hair. Would he have done that if he'd murdered her and wanted it to look like suicide?"

"He might have, sir. Sort of double bluff."

"Look, Sergeant—one moment he's so hopelessly dumb he wipes off the taps, and the next he's so bright he's two jumps ahead of us. You can't have it both ways."

The sergeant pondered. "Come to think of it, he couldn't very well pretend his wife was depressed if she wasn't. Mrs. Biggs was coming in, and she'd know. He had to tell the truth about that."

"He'd forgotten about Mrs. Biggs."

"So he said, sir. How do we know?"

The inspector sighed. "That's true. All the same, he didn't strike me as a guilty man—not until he began to lie at the end. Look at the way he pooh-poohed the idea of her having an enemy. He could at least have left the question open—or was that another double bluff?"

"I think *you're* being a bit too subtle now, sir, if I may say so. Stick to the evidence, that's what I say." Green pointed to the fingerprint report. "His prints were on the poker."

"And why not? It's November. Ah well, we're only just beginning. We should have the medical report this afternoon, and p'raps there'll be something about the Alfa as well. There's his weak spot. Right, I'm going along to see Mrs. Biggs now. Back before lunch, Sergeant."

"Okay, sir."

"Well, Mrs. Biggs, I'm sorry to have kept you waiting," said the inspector, settling himself down in the neat front parlor.

"So I should think," said Mrs. Biggs. She was dressed for the street, and the cherries in her black toque bobbed with impatience. "Nice to be a 'tec, I must say, startin' the day at ten o'clock."

Haines smiled. "Not as bad as that, Mrs. Biggs." He noted

the old lady's neat black shoes and black stockings, the brooch at her neck, the hairnet keeping in place the abundant light brown hair that could scarcely have been her own. The last of the old-fashioned charladies! "Anyway," he said, "we'll see you're not out of pocket."

She looked a little mollified. "Well, what's it all about, eh?"

"It's about Mrs. Lambert. You work for her, don't you?"

" 'Course I works for 'er. I was there yesterday. Wednesday's always me day for Mrs. Lamb."

"You'll be sorry to hear she's dead. She was found gassed last night."

Mrs. Biggs's bright little eyes opened wide. "Well, what do yer think o' that? The pore lady! Gassed 'erself, eh? Well, I never. It don't seem possible."

"Did she seem all right when you were there?"

"Bless yer, yes. Cheerful as anythink, she was. Brighter than usual, I'd say. Why, she went off to 'ave an 'air-do in the afternoon. 'You don't mind me goin', Mrs. Biggs,' she says, 'do you?' Made me larf! As though I'd mind. Precious little use she was around the place anyway—not got the knack of 'ousework like us old 'uns. Liked to put 'er feet up and read a book. 'That's right, Mrs. Thingummy,' I says, 'you go and 'ave your 'air-do,' I says, 'it'll do yer good.' An' off she goes as 'appy as anythink while I puts the 'ouse ter rights. 'Much better out o' the way,' I thinks ter meself."

"You got on with her all right, eh, Mrs. Biggs?"

"With Mrs. Lamb? Lor' yes, an' why not? She was a nice enough lady. Left me alone, she did. Not like some o' them— tellin' yer what to do when they don't know themselves. Mind *you*, she 'ad a funny way of puttin' things sometimes. Always liked to pretend she was doin' you a favor. Only last week she says to me, 'Oh Mrs. Biggs,' she says, all smiles, 'I've bought you a lovely new 'oover,' she says." Mrs. Biggs made a clicking noise with her tongue. "Now 'ow d'yer like that? 'You 'aven't bought it fer me, Mrs. Thingummy,' I says, 'you've bought it fer yerself.' But that was just 'er way. She was a kind lady. She'd give me a bit extry now an' again, an' I'd take 'er a few heggs or a few honions. Tell yer the truth, I was sorry for 'er, with 'er girl put away, pore thing. Mind yer, she didn't let on what she was feelin'. 'I certainly 'ave to 'and it to yer, Mrs. Thingummy,' I says, 'yer do know 'ow to 'ide yer sorrer.' 'I try not to think about it, Mrs. Biggs,' she says, cheerful as yer like."

As Mrs. Biggs stopped for breath, Haines managed to say quickly, "And what about *Mr.* Lambert?"

"Oh, I 'ardly ever saw 'im. P'raps just a ' 'Mornin' Mrs. Biggs,' if 'e was late startin' for 'is office. 'E's a nice-spoken gentleman, I will say that."

"Was he on good terms with his wife?"

Mrs. Biggs looked shrewdly at the inspector. "Now 'ow would I know? I tell yer I didn't see much of 'im. They was friendly like in public, but yer can't go by that. Men'll kiss their wives goodbye in the mornin' even though they 'ates the sight of 'em. 'Abit, that's what it is—just 'abit."

The inspector plodded on. "Can you tell me what time you left Mrs. Lambert's last night?"

" 'Arf-past five, same as I always do. Not a minute sooner, not a minute later. Takes all day, that 'ouse does. It's not what yer'd call a *big* 'ouse, but there's a lot o' work in it. Bit ole-fashioned, yer know. . . ."

"Lot of corners to collect the dust, eh?" said Haines, sympathetically. "Did anybody call or telephone during the day?"

"There wasn't any callers—not as I can remember. Now telephone, yes. 'Ow I 'ates the thing! 'Orrible noise it makes. I don't answer it, meself. But Mrs. Lamb was talkin' on it in the mornin'."

"Do you know who to?"

Mrs. Biggs shook her head vigorously. "None o' my business. P'raps it was the 'orspital what rang—she does sometimes talk ter the 'orspital. I just gets on with me work. Finished it up a treat, I did yesterday. We 'ad a cup o' tea at five o'clock—now she *could* make a cup o' tea—an' then I finished the kitchen an' orf I went."

"What exactly do you do in the kitchen, Mrs. Biggs?"

"Do in the kitchen? Now ain't that just like a man! Why, I tidies up, washes up, cleans the sink, scrubs the floor, cleans the stove—it's like a new pin when I'm done."

The inspector suddenly had an idea. "You forgot to polish those chromium taps, Mrs. Biggs, though, didn't you?"

The cherries began to bob. "What taps? You mean them gas taps? Well, I likes your cheek. I'll 'ave yer know I give them taps a good rub the very last thing. Always do, *and* the water taps. Why, they shines somethink lovely. I couldn't leave a nice bit of cronium like that. 'What counts in a kitchen, Mrs. Thingummy,' I always says, 'is keepin' things *bright*,' I says. 'When things is bright,' I says, 'it makes you 'appy ter look at 'em.' "

"Ah, well," said Haines, soothingly, "I must have been mistaken. I wish I could have you to do my kitchen, Mrs. Biggs. Oh, there's just one other thing. I've got a chap outside who'd like to take your fingerprints." He went to the door and made a signal. "You don't mind, do you?"

"Me fingerprints? Well, I dunno." She looked at the pad with distaste. "Yer don't want me ter get meself all messed up with that dirty stuff?"

"Oh, now, come on, Mrs. Biggs. It'll wash off."

"What do yer want 'em for?" asked the old lady, suspiciously.

"It's just routine," said Haines. "Same as with you. You clean everything in the kitchen; we take everybody's fingerprints." He leaned forward confidentially. "As a matter of fact," he said, "there's a bit of a mystery. You'll be helping us to solve it."

"Well," said Mrs. Biggs, "if yer puts it like that, I can't say no, can I? Dirty, messy thing! It'll take me all mornin' ter clean meself up, let alone the 'ouse I oughter be doin'." She went on grumbling, but she watched with interest while the pad was inked.

"There you are," said Haines. "Just press firmly. That's right. Now the next one."

"So you see," said Haines, "it wasn't the murderer who wiped the taps after all—I knew it couldn't be." He was back in the office with Green. "It looks as though Lambert took it for granted that the taps would have his wife's prints on them, and he was just unlucky. He forgot Mrs. Biggs. That seems, after all, to have been one of the few truthful things he said."

"It was a bad break for him," said Green. "Anyway, we're all clear now about the prints."

"Well, not quite, Sergeant. Put yourself in Lambert's place again. He wants to make it look like suicide. He assumes that his wife's prints are on the taps, and that a few extra prints of his won't matter. He turns the taps on and gasses her. Later, as he told us, he turns them off. Why is there only one set of his prints? Why not two?"

Green scratched his head. "He could have used gloves, the first time. Or he might have flicked them on with his fingernail. They're not very stiff."

"I dare say he *could*, but why should he?"

"P'raps he thought if he left two lots of prints, his wife's would be covered up. I can see his point of view. The less there were of his about, the better."

"H'm. I suppose that could be it," said Haines, doubtfully. "Pity we can't make up our minds whether he's dumb or not! Well, any other news?"

"Oh, yes, sir, the medical report's in. More or less what we thought."

Haines ran his eye down the paper. "Ah!" he exclaimed. "So that *was* a bruise at the top of the spine."

"Yes, sir—no doubt about it. It came out quite clearly under infrared treatment. And it *could* have been done with the poker —quite a light blow just there would have caused unconsciousness. You see it was inflicted before death—there's very little carbon monoxide in the contused blood. And the bitten tongue's consistent with a blow on the neck."

Haines laid the report down. "Time of death probably between six and seven. H'm—the evidence is piling up. Nothing on the poker, was there, except prints—no hairs or anything?"

"Nothing, unfortunately. But there wouldn't be—the skin wasn't broken."

The telephone rang, and Green answered it. As he listened, his face brightened with interest. "At the Bull, eh . . . ? Yes, I know it. . . . Is he quite sure . . . ? Good. . . . Right, we'll ring you back." Green dropped the receiver back into place with a melodramatic gesture.

"Well," said Haines, "something about the Alfa?"

"Yes. It was parked outside the Bull on the Great North Road last night. Lambert had dinner there. The innkeeper recognized him from the description. He's quite certain. Lambert was with a girl."

The inspector sighed. "I thought that would be it. What fools these chaps are! All right, Green, you see if you can trace the woman. I'll have another word with Lambert."

"She may give him an alibi of sorts," said Green.

"Of sorts, yes. We'll see." Haines got up, a little stiffly. "You know, Sergeant, I think I'm getting too old for this manhunt business. I don't relish it the way I used to. What I can never understand is why men have to *murder* their wives just because they prefer somebody else."

"Don't ask me, sir," said Green. "I'm not married."

"I suppose killing them saves a lot of argument!" said Haines. "Well, see you later. You might try to trace any telephone calls made to or from Lambert's house yesterday. I don't suppose you'll get anything—they were probably local calls anyway. And it might be as well to find out if any of the neighbors heard a car at the house at about six-thirty. A long shot, but if we don't ask, somebody's sure to raise the point. When's the inquest, by the way?"

"Day after tomorrow, sir—ten o'clock."

Haines nodded. "We should be ready by then."

George's nerves were the worse for wear. He looked as though he hadn't slept. As soon as the inspector entered the house, he said, "Well, I suppose you've found out I wasn't at the cinema?"

Haines regarded him, thoughtfully. "It wasn't a very good story, was it?"

"No, it wasn't. It was damn silly."

"Perhaps you've had time to think up a better one?"

"No," said George. "I've simply decided that I can't tell you where I was."

"But we know, Mr. Lambert."

"Oh," said George. "Then why bother me about it?"

"I'm giving you a chance to tell your own story, whatever it is—to come clean, as the Americans say."

"You mean you're giving me a chance to put a rope round my neck."

"That depends on what your story is."

"Well, I've nothing to tell you."

"We know that you were at the Bull last night with a woman."

"What do you expect me to do? Tell you who she was?" George pointed to a pile of newspapers. "And have her picture splashed all over the front pages of those filthy rags?"

"It'll happen anyway," said the inspector. "We're bound to find her."

George's lips tightened.

"I warn you again, Mr. Lambert, that you only harm yourself by this attitude."

"I can't help that. I deny everything—you understand? You think I murdered my wife because of a girl. Well, you're wrong."

"I hope so," said the inspector. "While I'm here, do you mind if I have another look round the house?"

"You can tear the place down brick by brick for all I care," said George, savagely.

Haines was still at the Lambert house when a call came through to him from Sergeant Green.

"We've got a line on the girl," Green told him. "The waiter at the Bull says he's seen her there in uniform once or twice with some nurses from the mental hospital."

"Oh, so that's it? Swan Park, I suppose?"

"Yes. The waiter says he couldn't mistake her."

"Right. I'll go straight along to the Bull and pick up the waiter, and we'll get her identified right away. Warn them at the Bull, will you?"

Twenty minutes later the inspector's car was racing up the Great North Road. The Bull proved to be a solid and comfortable hostelry of considerable size. A constable was standing by the reception desk with a young man of sleek appearance. "This is the waiter, sir," said the constable. "Name of Spicer."

"Good. Will you both come along? I shan't keep you long, Spicer."

"That's all right, Inspector. Pleased to be of service." Spicer had a slight cockney accent.

"I suppose you know quite a lot of the girls at the hospital," said Haines, as the car moved off.

Spicer grinned. "Quite a few, sir. Enough to make a change."

"But you don't actually know this girl?"

"No, Inspector. She's not my fancy. One of those dames with big solemn eyes—makes you feel uncomfortable. Nice-looking, though. Good figure. Just not my type."

"I see," said Haines and fell silent.

At the hospital they were shown into a bare waiting room while an orderly went off with the inspector's card to find out if the matron was free. Ten minutes later he was conducted into her presence. Matron was a commanding woman of fifty-odd, and she seemed to fill the large room. Haines felt like a naughty schoolboy as she turned a gimlet eye upon him.

"Well, Inspector, what do you want? I hope none of my girls has been getting into trouble?"

"I *am* interested in one of them," said Haines. "Unfortunately, I don't know her name. She was having dinner at the Bull last night."

"That's regrettable, perhaps, but hardly a crime." Matron glanced at a paper on her desk. "Three nurses had evening passes last night. Nurse Draper, Nurse Brown, and Nurse Grant."

"Can I see them?"

"All of them? Really, Inspector, we can't close the hospital because of some trivial inquiry. They're on duty."

"Well, Matron, perhaps we can manage without that. The girl I'm looking for is attractive, with—er—big solemn eyes and a nice figure."

A wintry smile hovered for a moment on Matron's lips. "I think there can be no doubt that it's Nurse Grant you want. She's an excellent nurse—most reliable. I'll send for her. Perhaps you'd be kind enough to see her in the waiting room, and I hope you won't keep her long. Good afternoon."

"Good day, Matron, and thank you."

A few minutes later there were quick footsteps in the corridor, and a girl pushed open the waiting-room door.

"Come in, Nurse Grant." Haines turned to Spicer. "Well?"

"Yes, Inspector, that's the lady."

"Certain?"

"Positive."

"Right—you two can go. Sit down, Nurse. My name is Haines, Inspector Haines. I'm a policeman."

"Yes," said the girl, quietly.

"May I know your first name?"

"Lucy."

Haines looked at her for a long moment. She was certainly very attractive. Large blue eyes, set wide apart, gave her face a candid expression. The dark wavy hair escaping from the nurse's cap set off her pale complexion. She sat upright on the hard chair, her hands loose in her lap, looking competent but slightly apprehensive.

"I understand, Nurse, that you spent last evening with a man named George Lambert?"

A trace of color came into the girl's cheeks, but she made no reply.

"Well?" said Haines, sharply.

"I—I don't want to say anything."

The inspector said gravely, "Nurse, Mrs. Lambert was found dead last night."

"I know," said Lucy. "I saw it in the *Mirror* at lunchtime."

"It's possible that there may have been foul play."

"Oh, no!" Horror—or was it fear—leapt into her eyes.

"It's possible. I must warn you that if you know anything at all which might help the police, and you deliberately withhold that information, you may make yourself liable to severe penalties. I realize this is very unpleasant for you, but the best thing you can do—for yourself and for every innocent person who may be concerned—is to tell the truth."

"Did Mr. Lambert tell you that he was with me?"

The inspector smiled a little sadly. "No, Nurse—he was very loyal to you—but rather foolish. We found out without his help. I hope you'll be more sensible."

She hesitated. "What do you want to know?"

"First, what time did you meet him, and where?"

"I met him about seven—he picked me up in his car near the hospital gate."

"About seven—you're sure of that?"

"Yes—I'd just come off duty."

"Did you drive straight to the Bull?"

"We stopped on the way for a little while. I can't remember how long. We were talking."

"A bit cold for parking by the roadside, wasn't it? What were you talking about that wouldn't wait until you got to the Bull?"

"Mainly about Jane—his daughter. She's here in the hospital, you know. I help to look after her."

"I see. So it was a purely professional discussion?"

"Well—not quite. We've been friends for—for a week or two."

"Friends—nothing more?"

"Nothing more."

"He didn't make love to you?"

"No."

"He didn't even kiss you? Be careful, Nurse."

"Well . . ."

"So he *did* make love to you?"

"He needed me," Lucy burst out. "His wife didn't understand him."

"Really! Is that what he told you?"

"He didn't have to. I know—I saw her here. She didn't *try* to understand him. She didn't care."

"And you did care. You and George Lambert are in love with each other, aren't you?"

"Yes, we are, if you must know."

"All right, Nurse, calm yourself. Did he talk of marrying you?"

"How could he—he was married already."

"He isn't married now," said the inspector, quietly.

"That's a dreadful thing to say. . . ." There was no mistaking the alarm in her face now. "*Surely* you can't think . . . Oh, you're wrong, you're quite wrong. He could never do a thing like that. He couldn't possibly. You don't know him. He's so kind. . . ."

The inspector got up. "Well, I don't think I need detain you any longer, Nurse. We shall probably want a statement from you later. That's all."

Once more Haines sat with Green in the office, puffing at a battered pipe. He looked depressed.

"I wish I'd sent you, Green," he said. "I don't care for interviews like that. She's a rather nice girl."

"I don't think you need worry, sir. She'll be much better off free of a chap like that. Always supposing she wasn't in on it herself. What do you think?"

"How do I know, Sergeant? There's no evidence, anyway. I've been through everything at the house with a fine comb. And Lambert certainly won't talk."

"P'raps something will turn up, sir."

"You're a ghoul, Sergeant. Personally, I don't feel too happy about the whole case."

"Why's that, sir? It seems to me as tidy a case as I've struck. Look at it. Lambert's in love with an attractive girl. He's carrying on a surreptitious affair with her. His wife is murdered, and it's made to look like suicide. By his own admission Lambert was practically passing the house at the time of the murder—he'd have had to do that on his way to the Bull. He has no alibi for the time of the murder. His fingerprints are on the gas taps and no one else's. His fingerprints are on the poker. There isn't a hint of anyone else in the case. Finally, he lied black and blue about what he was doing. If that isn't a good case, I'm Jack the Ripper!"

Haines smiled. "It's a good summing up, anyway. The case for the prosecution. I wonder what the defense will be. I agree that the circumstantial evidence is just about as strong as it could be. I'm still not happy. It's one of those cases where everything fits except the people. I think I'll keep working at it for a bit."

"They're bound to bring it in as murder at the inquest," said Green.

"No doubt about that," said the inspector. "Better keep a close eye on Lambert until the arrest."

❦ TWO ❦

A SIGH of contentment came from the deep lounge chair where Max Easterbrook was relaxing after his journey, his long legs stretched out to the imminent danger of passers-by, a cocktail glass in his hand. It was a relief to be on solid earth again—he had never been fond of flying, and the trip from Germany that morning had been bumpy. He caught a glimpse of his lean face in one of the lavish hotel mirrors. Definitely travel-worn. Still, a spot more to drink and a good lunch would soon put that right.

It was grand to be back in London. The place might be shabby and a bit bleak, but at least there was nothing neurotic about it. A good place to spend a month of leave. He dwelt on the prospect with acute pleasure. A solid month! Ample time to get rid of that feeling of strain that seemed inseparable from work in the camps. He'd be able to revisit his old haunts and see if any of the people he used to know were still around. He'd see George again—gosh, it would be good to see old George after all this while. He glanced at his watch. There was still time to give him a ring and say hello before lunch.

He finished his Martini, flicked over the pages of his diary, then went to the telephone and dialed Whitehall 55114.

"Ministry of Town Planning," announced the girl at the switchboard.

"Extension 54, please."

26

There was a click, and a man's voice said, "Hello."

"Is that you, George?" asked Max, eagerly.

"Who do you want to speak to?"

"George Lambert, please."

"Oh!" There was an awkward pause. "I'm afraid Mr. Lambert isn't here. Who is it speaking?"

"My name's Easterbrook. I'm a friend of his. Perhaps I can leave a message?"

"Well—no—it's a bit difficult . . ."

"What's the trouble?—he still works there, doesn't he?"

"I think you'd better have a look at the midday papers," said the voice. "I'm sorry." The man hung up.

Max replaced the receiver with a puzzled frown. The midday papers! Good Lord, that sounded as though George had had an accident or something. Why on earth couldn't the fellow have said so straight out? A fatal accident, perhaps! Oh, no! He strode across to the porter's desk and seized a paper from the pile on the counter. His anxious eye scanned the main headings. MORE MILK AND EGGS IN THE SPRING. CIVIL SERVANT CHARGED WITH WIFE-MURDER. JET FIGHTER BREAKS RECORD. Nothing there! He looked down the page but could see nothing about an accident. He was just going to turn over when a name started out of the text under a subhead, *Sent for trial*. He skimmed through the first few lines and suddenly exclaimed, "Good God!" in a horrified voice. He read through to the end of the long report, incredulous yet fascinated. He studied the picture captioned, *Nurse Lucy Grant*.

The porter was observing him with interest. "Anything the matter, sir?"

Max stared at him as though he suddenly personified the whole unreasonable world. "I know this chap," he said.

"What chap, sir?"

"Why, this man George Lambert—charged with murder."

"That so, sir?" said the porter, from his comfortable chair.

"Well, it looks as though 'e done it, all right. Nice-lookin' girl, that nurse."

Max leaned against the counter, feeling slightly sick. It seemed somehow important to convince this man. He said, "George Lambert wouldn't do a thing like that. They must have made a mistake."

"Looks like *someone's* made a mistake, sir."

Max took the paper into the lounge and read through the account again. There seemed to be a great deal of evidence, and it sounded horribly definite. But it *must* be wrong. It was monstrous that a thing like this should be charged against George —the gentle, loyal, reliable George. Max was swept by a wave of indignation.

George *couldn't* have changed to that extent. True, it was nearly two years since Max had seen him, and no doubt he'd altered in some ways. There might have been postwar strains, problems of readjustment he couldn't cope with—though it was odd he'd never mentioned them in his letters. The nurse certainly looked attractive. George might easily have fallen for her —there was nothing unlikely about that. It could happen to anyone. But murder, and a coldly calculated murder at that— bashing your wife and putting her head in a gas oven to make it look like suicide!—George wasn't capable of that. He just wasn't capable of it, and anyone who said he was didn't know him.

Max lit a cigarette and ordered another drink. What a *mess*, what a bloody awful mess! He wondered who George's solicitors were—the paper didn't say. Perhaps if he rang the police . . .

He might write to George at Brixton, of course. He toyed un-happily with phrases. "Dear George: I'm terribly sorry to hear you're charged with murder . . . !" "Dear old George: Can I do anything to help . . . ?" No, that wouldn't be any good—sym-pathy through the post. George wouldn't have done that if Max had been up against it. The thing to do was to see him—if only to shake him by the hand and tell him the charge was a lot of damned nonsense.

Surely they'd allow visitors. After all, a man was innocent until he was proved guilty. How did one get into a prison, as a visitor? If it had been a D.P. camp, now, he'd have known the drill.

It began to look as though he was going to have a busman's holiday. Still, he'd obviously got to stand by old George. He walked over to the telephone and turned up *Prisons, H. M.* in the book.

At three o'clock that afternoon he was shown into one of the visitors' rooms at Brixton Jail provided for the use of prisoners on remand. Getting permission had been less difficult than he'd expected, when he'd explained who he was. He sat down at the table, feeling nervous and wishing he might smoke. Now that he was actually about to see George in these surroundings, the whole thing seemed more preposterous than ever.

In a few minutes George appeared in the doorway, with a warder close behind him. He looked a little embarrassed, but as Max came forward to greet him, the old slow smile lit up his face. "Max, old man!" he said, and there was a note of thankfulness in his voice. They gripped hands. George said ruefully, "It's not quite what we planned, I'm afraid. Damn good of you to look me up. When did you get in?"

"This morning," said Max. He looked searchingly at his old friend, but there was no obvious sign that George had turned into a villain overnight. No sign of any change at all, in fact. The same old George—big, solid, and slightly shaggy about the clothes, with kindly eyes and a dependable look about the mouth and chin. Max smiled his relief. "It's good to see you again, old fellow—though I wish to God it were anywhere else but here. What *have* you been getting up to?"

George sighed. "It's the devil of a business, isn't it?"

"You're in touch with your solicitor, of course?"

"Yes—he was here most of the morning."

"Is he good?—what's his name?"

"Perkins. He's a partner in Perkins, Perkins and Watson."

Max nodded. "I seem to have heard of them. What about counsel?"

"That's going to be one of the problems," said George. "Perkins wants to get the best, but they're devilish expensive. It'll be a bit of a squeeze."

"Don't worry about that," said Max. "We'll fix something. . . ." He gazed anxiously across the table. "George, how on earth did you manage to get yourself into a jam like this?"

George's face had the puzzled, hurt expression of the man who isn't quite sure what has hit him. "It just happened," he said. "I can still hardly believe it. I didn't *do* it, you know."

"You don't have to tell me that," said Max.

"But it *looks* as though I did. Have you read the evidence?"

"All that I could get hold of."

"Then you know things look pretty black. I can't understand it, Max. It's just as though a trap has closed on me." For the first time a look of resentment crossed his face. "I feel so helpless in this place. How can a man fight for his life when he's shut up in a cell? It's worse than the old Oflag—at least there was a chance to break out there."

"If you've got a good lawyer," said Max, "he'll put up the best fight possible. These chaps know what they're doing. Look, George, is there anything I can get you or do for you? Have you got everything you need?"

"I think so, thanks. Some relatives of mine have been very kind—well, of Hilda's, really—her brother and his wife. It's amazing how people have rallied round. Chaps at the office who hardly knew me at all . . ."

Max smiled. "You always were a modest cuss." His thoughts went back to the newspaper report. "George . . ." He hesitated. "You don't mind talking about what's happened, do you?"

"Not a bit."

"Well—I suppose it is absolutely certain that it wasn't suicide?"

"Absolutely, I'm afraid. You never met Hilda, of course. She just wasn't the type to kill herself—she was always able to look on the bright side. I don't think I've ever seen her really de-pressed—not even when we had to pack Jane off to hospital. She must have had inner resources or something. And she certainly wasn't at all upset last Wednesday." George told Max about the visit to the hairdresser. "Besides," he added, "there's all the other evidence. If her prints weren't on the taps, she obviously couldn't have turned them on. There's no getting round that. And then there's the blow on the neck. No, Max, it was murder all right."

"And you haven't any idea at all who might have done it?"

"Not the faintest. That's what everybody asks. I've racked my brains, but I haven't the vestige of a clue. Perkins this morning asked wasn't there anything in Hilda's past life. I told him she hadn't had a past life—only with me. We married pretty young, you know, and I've been with her ever since, except for the war. The police had an idea she might have had an affair while I was away, but how could she have had with Jane around all the time? Anyhow, it's a fantastic notion. She had the most rigid scruples about that sort of thing, as I told the inspector. Caesar's wife had nothing on Hilda. I ought to know—I've lived with her half a lifetime. Frankly, I just can't see that anyone could have had a motive."

"She *was* killed," Max reminded him. "Somebody must have done it, and there must have been a reason." His thoughts dwelt speculatively on Hilda. "What was she like, George? I've heard you talk about Jane often enough, but you've never told me much about Hilda."

"She was all right," said George, slowly. "Quiet, you know—easygoing—not at all the sort of person anyone would want to kill. A bit humdrum, perhaps, but we got on moderately well."

Max regarded him thoughtfully. "Oh, well," he said after a moment, "I'm sure the police will get to the bottom of it. Something will turn up—and I'm not just being a Micawber."

"I hope you're right," said George, unhappily. "You know,

Max, it's Jane I'm really anxious about—Jane and Lucy. . . ."

"Has Lucy written to you?"

"No, and I'm worried about her. I'm afraid she may be having a bad time herself. Everyone knows about her—I seem to have pretty well ruined her life." He looked at Max in deep distress. "I'd have done anything to save her from all this. I tried to keep her out of it, but the police were too smart. I've even wondered if they'll suspect her of being involved—a sort of Thompson-Bywaters case in reverse. If they do, I'll have to plead guilty. . . . The awful thing is that she may believe I did it. I can't bear the thought of that."

"I think you're imagining things," said Max, gently. "You may still hear from her. I dare say she's written to the house—or she may be afraid of making things worse for you by writing. Look, would it help if I were to see her?"

"Do you think you could?" asked George, eagerly.

"I'll try. What shall I tell her?"

George was silent a moment. Then he said, "Just tell her I didn't do it. That's all. What else can I tell her now?"

Max looked curiously at his friend. "How did she happen, George?"

"Lucy?"

"Yes."

George stared at the table. "She just happened," he said in a low voice. "It was soon after Jane went into Swan Park. Hilda and I visited the hospital together the first time, and then they thought it would be better if Hilda didn't go again, so I went by myself. Lucy was the nurse in charge of Jane. She was very good with her—kind and sensible and friendly. We talked a bit and—well, I don't know—I just fell for her. I wasn't consciously looking for an affair. I—I just fell in love with her. I couldn't get her out of my mind. The next time I went to the hospital I was late leaving—I'd been having a long talk with the doctor—and as I drove away, I passed Lucy walking toward the gate. She'd just come off duty. I stopped and offered her a lift. She was going to the pictures, but she didn't seem very keen, so I suggested we should go and have a drink instead. And that's how it started."

"Did you see her often?"

"Only three or four times, but that was enough—we both felt the same way about each other. It wasn't all fun, of course. I was in a frightful turmoil. I felt disloyal to Hilda, and yet I couldn't have stopped seeing Lucy to save my life. I felt—I felt as though I'd begun to live all over again. Honestly, it was just like being in a new world. You've no idea . . ."

"I've heard about it," said Max, with a smile.

"Well, perhaps you do know. I'd never imagined it—it was something quite new to me. Damn silly at forty-two! Sitting in a drafty car, in the dark, in November, without a thought in my head except how wonderful she was! Oh, blast!"

"What were you going to do, George? Get a divorce?"

"I don't know. We hadn't got as far as that. Being together for an hour or two now and again still seemed good enough. I really don't know what I'd have done. I suppose I was being a selfish swine. I don't see how I could ever have left Hilda. She hadn't got anyone except me and Jane. She relied on me. When I went home last Wednesday and found her dead, and it seemed like suicide, I felt ghastly. I wondered for a moment if she could have found out about Lucy. I had a fearful sense of guilt, just as though I *had* killed her. I felt I'd let her down—that I ought to have been with her. Then when the police started talking about murder, I was almost relieved."

"You don't think she *could* have known about Lucy?"

"I'm sure she didn't."

"I wonder what she'd have done if she had known."

"She wouldn't have believed it," said George. "In her world, people simply didn't do that sort of thing."

"It must have been a curious world," said Max. He got up. "Well, I'll have to go, old boy. I'll see Lucy, and I'll let you know what happens. Is there anything else I can do?"

George looked at him with troubled eyes. "I wonder if they'd let you see Jane?" he said wistfully. "She'll be wondering why I've stopped visiting her. The hospital isn't too keen on anyone going except me, but if I tell them about you I think they might make an exception."

"I'll talk to the doctor. What's his name?"

"Challoner. He's the medical superintendent there—a first-rate fellow. Max, it's darned good of you. I'll write and tell him you're coming. . . . I'm afraid all this is going to mess up your leave."

"Oh, don't bother about that. I haven't made any hard and fast arrangements, so it won't matter if I lie low for a bit. Good-bye, George. Keep your chin up. Worrying won't help, you know."

George smiled sadly. "You sound like Hilda. That's what she used to say about Jane."

Back at the hotel Max obtained after a little trouble the telephone number of the nurses' hostel at Swan Park Mental Hospital, and as soon as he thought Lucy would be off duty, he put in a call. For a long time there was no reply, and he was about to hang up when a woman's voice answered.

"Hello," said Max. "Is Nurse Grant there, please?"

"I'm afraid not," said the voice.

This, thought Max, is where I came in. "Is that one of the nurses?" he asked.

"Yes."

"Well, look, Nurse," he said earnestly, "be an angel and tell me where she is. It's very important."

"Is it about . . . ?"

"Yes. I'm a friend of hers. I've got to get in touch with her. Where is she?"

"She's gone—she's been suspended."

"Don't you know where she's gone to? Surely she must have told somebody."

"Hold on—I'll try to find out."

Max waited anxiously. It would be very awkward if Lucy had just disappeared into the blue. He heard a voice shouting, "Anyone know where Grant's gone?" and the background noise of other voices. Then the nurse came back. "She's gone to stay with her sister at Beckenham. Number 944 Maybank Road."

"Thank you *very* much" said Max. "Bless you!"

He looked at his watch—it was half-past seven. He was tired and hungry, but he would never forgive himself if he missed her. He could get a sandwich at Charing Cross.

Ninety minutes later his taxi drew up outside a three-story Victorian house in Maybank Road. Judging by the number of lighted windows, it was divided into flats. Max struck a match in the porch and saw that the ground-floor flat was marked with the name "Angela Grant." He rang once and waited. A girl came out of the room on the right and opened the door. It was too dark to see her face.

"Good evening," said Max. "Are you Miss Lucy Grant?"

"No. If you're another reporter . . ."

"I'm not."

"Not the police again!"

"No, no. I've got a message for your sister. I'm a friend of George Lambert's."

"Then I don't know how you dare come here. Hasn't he done enough damage already? She doesn't want any messages. She's not well."

"I'm sorry," said Max. She was beginning to close the door when another girl came into the hall.

"Who is it, Angela?"

"Oh, you're hopeless, Lucy. He says he's a friend of George Lambert's. I'm sending him away."

"No, wait." Lucy came to the door and looked at Max. "You'd better come in," she said. He followed them into the room.

"Well, I give up," said Angela. "Don't say I didn't warn you." She was dark, like Lucy, but plumper and a year or two older. "I'll go and make some coffee." She bustled away.

"Please sit down," said Lucy. She had been crying a little,

Max thought, and there were dark smudges round her eyes. Even so, she looked more attractive than her picture. Her soft, wavy hair was too nice to be hidden under a cap.

"My name is Easterbrook," Max said. "I saw George this afternoon."

"Oh," said Lucy, in a subdued voice. "How is he?"

"He's bearing up. He sent a message. He asked me to tell you that he didn't do it."

Lucy was silent.

"Don't you believe him?"

"I want to," said Lucy. "Oh, God, I want to."

"But you can't?"

"I don't know what to think. I go over it again and again in my mind . . . I can't decide. Angela thinks he did it."

"Oh, but come," said Max, "she doesn't know him."

"She says *I* don't really know him. It's true, I suppose—I was only just beginning to when this happened. I tried to write to him, but I got stuck. . . . I couldn't believe it, it just didn't seem like him. He was so kind and gentle, always. But when I started to write, I thought of his wife and what an awful woman she was, and then I thought he might easily have wanted to get rid of her. . . ."

Max looked up. "I didn't realize you knew his wife."

"I didn't *know* her. I only saw her once—the time she visited the hospital. But that was enough."

"Why, what was so awful about her?"

Lucy hesitated. "It's difficult to describe, somehow. She was one of those large, gawky women, and she seemed to sweep everything along with her, including George. And she was so silly with Jane."

"How do you mean—'silly?'"

"Well, the girl needed stiffening—she'd lost confidence in herself. Mrs. Lambert just covered her with sloppy emotion—'Darling this' and 'Mummy that,' all over her, while George stood by looking worried. I felt so sorry for him."

Max said gently, "Don't you think perhaps you're being a bit unfair to Mrs. Lambert? After all, you were in love with George—later on, I mean."

"I still am," said Lucy. "I can't help it."

"I'm glad. He needs to believe that now. . . . What I was trying to say was that if you're in love with George, you'd naturally tend to be critical of his wife. It's human nature. You'd *look* for things to dislike about her. She seemed a managing sort of woman to you, but, after all, she'd run George's home for twenty years. As for Jane—well, you can't expect mothers always to treat their children as sensibly as nurses would. I expect she was very fond of Jane. . . ."

"I'm not so sure. I don't believe she was fond of anybody except herself."

"Isn't that prejudice?" asked Max.

"No," said Lucy, stubbornly. "There was something about her—I could feel it. Something—horrible."

"And that's why you think George may have killed her?" Max shook his head. "Did George talk about his wife as you do?"

"Oh, no. He hardly talked about her at all."

"I didn't get the impression that he disliked her."

"He felt a—a responsibility."

"A responsibility—nothing more?"

"Loyalty, I suppose. I know it sounds odd. . . ."

"I don't think so. I think that's just what he did feel. I think you're all mixed up, Lucy. You didn't like her because you were in love with George; you knew he got on with her fairly well and you didn't want him to. You're making *your* dislike a reason why *he* should have murdered her. But according to that reasoning, *you* had more motive than he had."

Lucy looked startled. "You don't think I did it? I was on duty at the hospital all the time. The police asked about that yesterday."

"Of course—silly of me. One gets so suspicious. You see how easy it is, though—if you'd been off duty all afternoon, it mightn't have been at all simple to prove what you were doing. That's more or less how it is with George."

"Yes—I see that now. Oh, you've made me feel so much better."

"Poor Lucy! You must have had a wretched time. Was Matron very difficult?"

"No—she was wonderful. I think I could have stood it better if she *had* been difficult. She was always so severe about little things. She didn't lecture me or anything. She just said she was very sorry, but she had no alternative, and . . . she hoped that I shouldn't be too unhappy."

Max said, "George will be glad about that, anyway. He's terribly worried about you—more than about himself, I think. He blames himself for having got you into all this. If you *could* write to him . . ."

"Oh, I will. I'll write tonight."

"Your letter will be read, I expect. I shouldn't say too much about—well, your feelings. If you just say you believe he didn't do it, that'll cheer him up no end."

"All right."

"I know it needs a lot of faith, but you have to believe in spite of the evidence. I believe in him myself because I think I know him, and I just can't imagine him doing—well, that sort of murder anyway, unless there was some absolutely overpowering reason which had sent him clean off his rocker."

"Do you know him very well?"

"I know him in a rather special way. You remember Christmas, 1944, when the Germans broke through in the Ardennes? There was an awful flap, of course. I got cut off with a bunch of chaps from a lot of different units, and George happened to be one of them. We were all taken prisoner, and I got to know George pretty well in the camp. He was one of those fellows who show up best when things go wrong—always cheerful and optimistic—everybody liked him."

Lucy nodded, her head turned away.

"That wasn't all, though. We were always full of ideas for

escaping—we didn't see why we should wait till Germany collapsed. He and I worked out a plan together, and after a couple of months we made a break for it. I was unlucky—a more or less random shot in the dark got me in the foot. George could have got away easily, but he wouldn't go. He stuck around with me until we were picked up—and afterward, of course, he had to pay for it. When you've been through that sort of experience with a bloke, you have a sort of instinct about him that counts more than evidence. The trouble is that instinct doesn't carry any weight at a trial."

The door was pushed open, and Angela came in with a tray of coffee. She gave Lucy a searching look. "Having a nice cozy chat?" she asked.

Lucy said, "Angela, I'm going to write to him."

Angela sniffed. "I *thought* so. You've let this smooth Romeo talk you into it." She gave Max a glance that was not wholly disapproving. "I only hope it won't mean more heartbreak later, that's all. Sugar, Mr. Easterbrook?"

Max gave her a complacent smile. "Just three lumps," he said.

Eleven o'clock was striking on the following morning when Max found himself looking across an opulent desk at Mr. Perkins, of Perkins, Perkins and Watson. The lawyer, who was dapper, precise, and younger than Max had expected, studied his visitor with shrewd, appraising eyes.

"So George Lambert is a friend of yours, Mr. Easterbrook?"·
"Yes."

"I'm glad you got in touch with me. He needs friends badly just now. Have you known him long?"

"I met him during the war. I knew him—intensively. We went through some rough stuff together."

"Ah. I've been going through his war record. Quite creditable. If the charge were one of passing a worthless check, it might save him from prison. Unfortunately, this is murder. . . . Were you in the same unit?"

"No. I was in Intelligence."

Perkins nodded. "You haven't seen Lambert recently?"

"Not till I saw him yesterday. Not for two years."

"That's a long time, of course. Well, Mr. Easterbrook, what exactly had you in mind when you telephoned me?"

"I wondered if I could do anything to help."

"In a general way or specifically?"

"In any way at all. If it's necessary, financially—up to a point. I gather George is in fairly low water."

Mr. Perkins seemed to unbend a little. "We may be glad to take advantage of that offer. This is the sort of case where first-class counsel is absolutely essential. Perhaps we can talk about it again when we see what sort of expenses have to be met."

"Certainly. Any time you like."

Mr. Perkins studied Max's clean-cut features as though trying to decide how much he should say. "Of course," he remarked after a slight pause, "the evidence is purely circumstantial and, I would think, not conclusive. But there's a lot of it, and the effect is cumulative. In a case like this, almost everything depends on the caliber of the jury and on what they choose to consider a reasonable doubt. The English system of jurisprudence, as you know, is the best in the world . . ." a faint smile flickered on Mr. Perkins' thin lips ". . . but I still haven't a very high opinion of juries. However, we shall have to do our best with the material provided. At present we cannot hope to prove that Lambert *didn't* murder his wife. It seems clear that he could have done so. There was, in fact, opportunity. Our hope must be that the prosecution will fail to clinch its case. We shall hammer away on the theme of reasonable doubt."

"You should have plenty of material," said Max. "Lambert doesn't seem to me to have behaved like a guilty man—not consistently, at any rate. If he'd plotted a murder beforehand, he'd surely have been more careful. At the very least he'd have tried to give himself an alibi. He'd have supported the suicide theory as long as he reasonably could, instead of turning it down flat at the first opportunity. When it looked like murder, he could at least have hinted at some affair of his wife's instead of defending her honor as he does. *Could* a murderer be so stupid?"

Perkins raised his neat eyebrows a trifle. "The answer, of course, Mr. Easterbrook, is that there are no limits either to the stupidity or to the duplicity of murderers. The casebooks prove that. But there are, as you point out, certain—er—psychological improbabilities about Lambert's alleged conduct, and we shall, of course, exploit them to the full. That's why it's so important that we should brief leading counsel—the best we can get. The question is how far can we rely on the jury to appreciate psychological subtleties which the prosecution will undoubtedly brush aside as fanciful? The jury will concentrate on the girl, Lucy. That's something that juries always understand—the other woman. In my experience, few juries can distinguish clearly between murder and domestic infidelity! This jury will start with a moral bias against Lambert. If he goes into the box—and it's virtually his only hope—prosecuting counsel will give him a very grueling time. I'm not at all sure how he'll shape under cross-examination."

"But if he sticks to the truth . . ." said Max.

Perkins shook his head. "It depends on *how* he sticks to the truth. I talked to him yesterday, as you did. His attitude to his wife—his late wife—would probably have impressed a jury favorably. Here was a man who, after twenty years of respectable domesticity, had suddenly lost his head over a pretty girl and wasn't very happy about it. That's all right—to err is human. But he evidently feels strongly about this girl. If he is provoked in the box, I tremble to think what he may say. If the girl is attacked and branded, as she will be, how will Lambert react? An unrepentant sinner can expect little sympathy—a defiant one even less. The very loyalty which led him to lie to the police about the girl may cause him to give the jury the one impression that will certainly hang him—that he cares about the girl to the exclusion of everything else."

"Surely he can be warned . . ."

"Certainly. But good advice is not always remembered when someone one loves is being pilloried in court. Still, perhaps I'm being pessimistic."

"In any case," said Max, "however conventional the jury is, it will need evidence more concrete than a love affair, surely. There isn't really much evidence that Lambert did it. There's merely a lack of evidence that anyone else did it."

"Precisely, Mr. Easterbrook. And that will be very important when a jury is trying to make up its mind whether there's a reasonable doubt or not. Apart from Lambert, the stage is completely bare. The jury faces no problem of elimination or choice. Lambert is the sole candidate. In these circumstances he is likely to be elected unopposed."

"Nevertheless," said Max, "*someone* must have done it. Perhaps a passing tramp . . ."

Mr. Perkins smiled indulgently. "That, Mr. Easterbrook, is the remark of a good friend, not of an ex-intelligence officer. In my experience, passing tramps are no more than the last resort of a desperate defense counsel. Of course, tramps do pass. Acts of brutal and senseless violence are committed every week by the lower criminal types—even in roads as solidly respectable as that in which Lambert's house is situated. His home would certainly not be immune from entry by someone bent on committing a felony—a burglar, for instance. But this was not a casual murder. Mrs. Lambert wasn't struck down by someone discovered in crime. Nothing was stolen; the place was in perfect order—and the murder was intended to look like suicide. No one would have gone to that trouble except a person who, but for the appearance of suicide, would at once have been open to suspicion." Perkins extended his hands. "In short, the husband."

Max said, "You talk as though you believe he did it. Do you?"

"I haven't the slightest idea, Mr. Easterbrook. On the evidence at the moment I should be inclined to say yes. From what I have seen of Lambert himself, I should be inclined to say no.

But then, one can so easily be mistaken about people. My duty, in any case, is simply to see that Lambert gets the best possible defense. You can be sure that I shall do that."

"I've no doubt about it," said Max. "All the same, your approach does strike me as a little—well, negative. It seems to me there are two ways of looking at the thing. We can say, 'There's no sign of anyone else having done it, therefore it must have been Lambert'—or we can say, 'Lambert didn't do it, therefore it must have been somebody else, and who was it?'"

"Well," said Mr. Perkins, tolerantly, "who *was* it?"

"I don't know, but I'm going to try to find out. I saw Lucy Grant last night."

The flood of Mr. Perkins' eloquence was checked. "The girl? I can't feel that was altogether wise."

"Perhaps not—I'm not a lawyer. All I know is that if we just sit on our heels, we shan't find out anything. Lucy made it very clear that she'd taken a profound dislike to Mrs. Lambert."

"But of course."

"That's what *I* said. Since then, I've been thinking. What do we actually know about Mrs. Lambert? Have *you* a clear picture of her? I haven't. Until I talked to the girl, all I knew was what I'd gathered from George Lambert himself. And what did it amount to? That she was quite pleasant but rather strait-laced woman, a bit humdrum to live with but of a contented disposition. On the whole a rather colorless, negative sort of woman —that's the impression George left on my mind. Well, it simply doesn't make sense. If George didn't do it—and I haven't any doubts about that—then his wife must have been very far from colorless to make someone want to murder her. Somewhere there must have been violent feelings, intense passions—love or hate —I don't know. But something more than we know, certainly. Something a bit more like Lucy's picture. Perhaps Lucy wasn't just prejudiced. What about a woman's intuition? Anyhow, I shan't rest until I've found out what Mrs. Lambert was really like—and then, perhaps, we'll be getting somewhere."

"At least, I hope you'll be careful," said Perkins. "The more this girl Lucy keeps in the background now, the better. And remember this, Easterbrook. Once you start stirring things up, you never know what you may find. You may discover a much better reason why George Lambert should have wanted to murder his wife than anything we know at present."

"I'm prepared to take that risk," said Max.

❧ THREE ❧

AS SOON as his interview with the lawyer was over, Max rang the Swan Park Mental Hospital again and made an appointment to see the medical superintendent on the following morning. By now, George's predicament was occupying his mind to the exclusion of everything else. He no longer felt like a man with nothing to do for a month. He had a lot to do, and he was beginning to be afraid there wouldn't be enough time to do it. He had to be systematic. He decided to spend the afternoon going out to Finchley and perhaps having a chat with some of the Lamberts' neighbors. After lunch he took the underground to north London and was soon walking up Adelaide Road.

He realized at once that the prospect of getting much information out of the neighbors was dim. This wasn't the sort of suburb where people kept a close eye on each other or spent hours chatting over the garden fence. The rather gloomy old houses were detached, well hidden by trees, and separated from one another by considerable areas of garden. It looked as though he would be wasting his time. However, now that he was here he might as well have a look at George's house.

He found it at the top of a rise, about two hundred yards from the main road. It was called Hillcrest. There was a gravel drive leading to the garage, and a gravel path to the front door and round to the back. The house was partly hidden from the road by tall evergreen shrubs. Max could imagine how easily anyone could have visited the house at half-past six on the night of the murder without attracting the slightest attention. The road was a very quiet one. Anyone could have parked a car at the bottom of the hill, out of the way, walked up in a few minutes, committed the murder, and slipped away unobserved.

He was just thinking that it might be worth while trying his luck next door when, peering between the shrubs, he thought he detected a movement at the back of the Lambert house. Odd! His curiosity aroused, he entered the drive and walked cautiously up to the wooden gate leading to the back. It opened at his push, and he went through. Yes, again that movement—something red, round the corner of the house. Beside the back door he found a plump old lady in a hairnet, shaking a rug. A striking print apron covered what, had she been sitting down, would have been an enormous lap. This must be Mrs. Biggs, who had been mentioned in the evidence.

"Good morning," said Max, pleasantly.

" 'Mornin', sir," said Mrs. Biggs. Her observant eyes took in the slow smile, the crisp brown hair, the straight tall figure. "There ain't no one at 'ome, I'm afraid."

"I know," said Max. "I'm a friend of Mr. Lambert's. I just happened to be passing, and I saw there was someone here, so I thought I'd drop in."

"You're very welcome, I'm sure. So yer knows Mr. Lambert, do yer? Yer knows all about this 'ere business, then?" She jerked her head toward the kitchen.

"Yes," said Max. "Dreadful tragedy, isn't it?"

" 'Orrible. Just 'orrible. Such a pleasant gentleman, too! 'Ow 'e could 'a' come to do what they say 'e did I *don't* know. I still can't 'ardly believe it. 'E couldn't 'a' bin in 'is right mind."

"Perhaps he didn't do it."

"I certainly 'opes not. But it do look black, I mus' say."

"Oh, he'll probably be back here in a week or two. I'm glad you're keeping the place nice for him."

"Well, I 'ad to do that, didn't I? I says ter meself, 'Mrs. Biggs,'

I says, 'you've been ter that 'ouse every Wednesday fer two years,' I says, 'an' yer can't stop goin' jus' becos they're in trouble,' I says. Empty 'ouses 'as ter be kep' clean same as full ones. Besides, I thinks, if 'e does come back 'e'll want to see the kitchen all freshened up. 'E won't want ter see it same as 'ow it was when she was lyin' there on the floor with 'er 'ead in the oven."

Mrs. Biggs gazed down at the red floor with morbid interest, and Max guessed that her presence in the house was not entirely the result of a sense of duty.

"Anyway," he said, "it all looks very nice and clean now. It's a credit to you. Do you think I might have a look round while I'm here?"

"Well," said Mrs. Biggs, "I s'pose there wouldn't be no 'arm in that, seein' as 'ow yer a friend of Mr. Lambert's. I didn't catch yer name."

"My name's Easterbrook. It'll be quite all right, I'm sure. I saw Mr. Lambert yesterday."

"Did yer now, Mr. East? An' 'ow is the pore man?"

"Not very cheerful, I'm afraid."

"Well, yer couldn't 'ardly expect 'im ter be, could yer? It ain't no laughin' matter, arter all. I s'pose you ain't seen anythink of 'is girl?"

"His girl? You mean . . . ?"

"'Is daughter—Jane. Awful for 'er, it'll be."

"Oh," said Max. "I'm hoping to see her tomorrow."

"Are yer now? I'm glad to 'ear that. Well, why don't yer step in an' 'ave a look round? You'll find everythink jus' so."

"I'm sure I will. I suppose the police have finished here?"

"I 'opes they 'ave. Lot o' dirty marks they left, that I do know. Didn't wipe their feet, anyone can see that. Like an 'erd o' buffloes, tramplin' about the place. An' leavin' their narsty powder around. Never mind, I've put it all ter rights now."

Max gazed round the kitchen, feeling a little lost. Whatever story this room might have told the police, it was silent now. Everything was spotless. The trail was cold.

He said, "It's almost *too* clean for a kitchen, Mrs. Biggs."

Mrs. Biggs pounced on the heresy. "Yer can't 'ave it *too* clean, Mr. East. Mind yer, I will say it don't look *used* the same as 'ow kitchens oughter. That was Mrs. Lamb, that was. 'I'm afraid I'm not a very good cook, Mrs. Biggs,' she used ter say, light-'earted like. 'You don't mind peelin' the pertaters, do yer, Mrs. Biggs,' she says. 'It'll be a nice change for you,' she saids, 'after all that cleanin',' she says. 'Oh no, yer don't,' I thinks ter meself. I tells 'er straight. 'Cleanin's my job,' I says, 'not peelin'.' Well, d'yer blame me, Mr. East?"

"Not at all, Mrs. Biggs. A most important distinction."

"Yus," she said, a shade doubtfully. "But Lor' bless yer, when I sees 'er choppin' them pertaters ter bits an' throwin' away 'arf o' them with the peel, I think ter meself, 'Oh, well, it takes all sorts ter make a world,' an' I does it for 'er. Sort of 'elpless she was—jus' not at 'ome in the kitchen." Mrs. Biggs's face took on a confidential look. "Between you an' me, Mr. East, she didn't try very 'ard, neither. Seemed ter take a pride in not bein' able ter do things in the 'ouse. 'After all,' she'd say, 'we can't expect ter be good at everythink, can we, Mrs. Biggs?' "

"Interesting," said Max. He opened the pantry door and looked in the dresser. "It *is* all a bit bare, isn't it?"

"That's it, Mr. East—bare's the word. I often says to 'er, 'What you want, Mrs. Thingummy, is some new things. Look at all these 'ere chipped cups,' I says, 'an' them burned saucepans. Now if it was me,' I says, 'I'd throw 'em all in the dus'bin an' finish with 'em.' Not she! 'The trouble is, Mrs. Biggs,' she says, 'it's such a bother buyin' new ones.' Same wi' the knives— 'andles comin' off through leavin' 'em in 'ot water. An' none o' them modern gadgets what makes work easy. Nor even a good sharp knife, believe it or not. ' 'Opeless,' I thinks, 'but what's the good o' talkin'? It's not *my* 'ouse,' I says ter meself, 'an' if things ain't jus' so it's 'er funeral, not mine.' "

"It was, too, wasn't it?" said Max, cheerfully. "But, Mrs. Biggs, if she didn't do much in the house, what *did* she do? Did she like gardening?"

"Gardening? Naow! *Mr.* Lamb, 'e did all the gardenin'. Always at it, 'e was—yer could see that by the way it was kep'. Used to 'ave the lawn a fair treat in the summer, 'e did, an' flowers everywhere. Active, 'e was, not like 'er. Yer'd never see 'er cuttin' the lawn—not likely. Get a deck chair, she would, an' sit out in the sun. Afternoon *or* mornin'—she 'adn't no shame that way. Stretch out, she would, with 'er long legs, like a great, big lazy cat. 'I think I'll go into the *garden* this mornin', Mrs. Biggs,' she'd say, pickin' up a magazine. Ten o'clock in the mornin', mind yer! 'An' why not, Mrs. Thingummy?' I says, 'umorin' 'er. But I thinks ter meself, 'You're a fine one, you are!' "

Max gazed at Mrs. Biggs, fascinated. "Didn't Mrs. Lambert ever go out?" he asked.

"Not if she could 'elp it. Sometimes she'd 'ave ter go out shoppin', o' course—then we 'ad a fine ole song and dance. ' 'Ave yer seen me basket, Mrs. Biggs? Do yer know where I put me bag, Mrs. Biggs?' I thinks ter meself, 'It's a wet nurse you wants, me gal.' In the end she goes saunterin' orf down the road, swingin' 'er bag like a kid, 'ummin' to 'erself. It looked funny, 'er bein' a big woman an' all. Back she comes an hour later, with 'er shoppin' done. 'I can't understand it, Mrs. Biggs,' she says, 'I seem to be short o' points this month'—just as though someone else 'ad spent 'em all for 'er! 'But I've got some lovely soup off points,' she says an' shows me 'er shoppin' basket all full up wi' tins. 'It's a good thing we all like soup,' she says. 'Soup!' I thinks, 'lot o' good that is fer a growin' girl.' But I keeps me own counsel. 'No good tellin' 'er,' I says ter meself. 'It's in at one ear an' out o' the other, like water off a duck's back. What she don't like she won't listen to.' "

"Did she talk a great deal?" Max asked.

"Well, she did an' she didn't. Sometimes she'd go on an' on, 'specially if she wanted somethin'. She and Jane was together a lot, an' she'd talk ter Jane all right—hours an' hours of it. But a book an' a nice cumfy chair was what Mrs. Lamb really liked. Twice a week she'd go traipsin' off to the libery. Best of all, though, she liked jus' sittin' still with a book open on 'er lap, dreamin'. Lor, 'ow she could sit an' dream!"

"It doesn't sound much of a life," said Max. "Didn't she ever have friends in? Company?"

"'Ardly ever. Now when I first come 'ere, just arter the war, they 'ad company once or twice. I remember 'er leanin' up against that there cupboard an' tellin' me about it next mornin' while I done the washin' up. But it didn't amount to anythink. Some'ow she never seemed to get goin' with 'er friends. It's months now since they 'ad anybody in." Mrs. Biggs picked up her rug. "Well, I mustn't stand 'ere all day talkin'—I'll never get through. You go on in, Mr. East, an' when yer done p'raps I'll make yer a cuppa tea, seein' as 'ow the milkman ain't stopped callin'. Waste not want not, that's what I says."

Max nodded absently and went into the sitting room. It was large and high and rather drafty. There was a cheap three-piece suite with worn upholstery standing on a faded Wilton carpet. The curtains were a shade too short for the windows. There was a modern coal grate, framed with a tiled tombstone surround which had one tile missing. On the settee were two library books —*The Fountain*, by Charles Morgan, and a novel by Elizabeth Bowen. Hilda's taste in literature had evidently not been commonplace. There was one small bookcase, but all the books were George's. Most of them were technical—books on architecture and town planning—and they appeared to have been well read. Against one wall was a piano, and opposite it a radio of an old-fashioned type. There was a solitary picture—a good reproduction of a Paul Nash landscape. There were also some family photographs, taken before the war—one of Jane, showing a dark-eyed, serious little girl of seven or eight, and a picture of a younger, happier-looking George.

It was on the photograph of Hilda that Max concentrated. She was much better looking than he had expected. At least, she had been in those days. She had a large, oval face, with a good forehead and regular features. The mouth was full and sensual. The eyes, Max decided, were easily her best feature. They were large and intelligent, and he wondered what color they'd been. Her eyebrows were strongly marked. Her lips had a faint smile—rather a secret smile, or was that reading too much into it? Her hair, straight as a ruler, hung down in an unattractive bob.

Max stood back and gazed at the picture. He'd been right about one thing, at least. This was the face of a woman of character, unusual and interesting. It might have been a handsome face if her coloring had been right. Not beautiful and not wholly pleasing with that self-satisfied smile. But certainly striking.

He passed on into the dining room. Here too the furniture might have come out of the stock of any mail-order house and looked as though it had done service since the Lambert wedding day. In those days, presumably, George had not had much money, but he must be getting a reasonable income now. It was odd that he should be so interested in architecture, in homes, and yet in his own home show so little taste and interest. Apart from the picture, these rooms were totally devoid of character and life.

A third room had a gas fire, an easy chair, a bookshelf with some more of George's books, and a bureau which was unlocked. On top of the bureau was an old photograph of Hilda, wearing a mortarboard and gown and looking very pleased with herself. Probably she had just graduated when the picture was taken. Max hesitated for a moment and then began to go quickly through the contents of the bureau. No doubt the police had already been through the place with a fine comb. It was unpleasant to pry, but half-measures wouldn't help George. He glanced through some old letters. Nothing of Hilda's—mostly business correspondence of George's. He opened a drawer and drew out a roll of stiff paper tied with green silk. Legal documents, perhaps. No—old certificates. Hilda's. Hilda's matriculation certificate— distinction in English. Hilda's intermediate certificate—pass. Hilda's bachelor of arts certificate—pass. H'm—not an outstanding academic career. But something. Nothing more of Hilda's. This, no doubt, was where George came when he wanted to be alone. There was one ash tray. Max wondered if George was sent in here when he wanted to smoke.

He climbed to the upper floor and went into the front bedroom. Bare, again—horribly bare. As impersonal as a hotel bedroom. More mail-order furniture. Ah, that looked like George's—a small silver cup. Tennis Championship, 1929. Max wondered if he still played. Again, not much of Hilda's. A piece of framed verse on the wall—that must be hers. "Give me the man that is not passion's slave. . . ." Adolescent. Stuck up and forgotten, no doubt. Odd thing to have in a bedroom!

Max went over to the mirror. There was a neat dressing-table set. He took the stoppers out of the little bottles and smelled them. Empty! Always had been empty! He opened the powder box. Empty!

He looked around, incredulously. Surely no woman could have used this room? No powder, no lipstick, no perfume, no cream, no nothing. The cave of an ancient Briton would have seemed a boudoir by comparison. At least there'd have been woad! He opened a wardrobe and shut it again. George's. He opened the taller one, took down a dress, then another. Undoubtedly a big woman. Outsize. The dresses were tasteless and drab. No long frocks. No doubt Hilda didn't dance. Max's eyes took in the big shoes, the sensible flat heels. Almost certainly she didn't dance. What the hell did she do? He opened a drawer. Hilda's. He took out a pair of old-fashioned bloomers—then flung them back with an exclamation of distaste. Hateful to do this. Far worse than interrogating prisoners. George wouldn't thank him. George would be mad if he knew.

He opened a drawer in the table beside the bed. Ah—Hilda's. An old notebook with some verse scribbled in pencil. Unfamiliar, obscure verse. Pages of it. Some of it was dated and initialed H.W.L. Early literary efforts by Hilda, not very good. Max delved further. A little sketchbook, with some pastel drawings and what looked like designs for textiles in water color. Also not very good. It looked as though Hilda had tried her hand at quite a number of things.

Max put the objects back carefully and explored the other rooms. Jane's room—also bare. A spare bedroom, blank as a wall. A junk room—nobody could possibly go through all that stuff. Even the police could hardly have done so. Max noticed an old tennis racket in a press and picked it up. A lovely racket—once! Now the strings were gone, the grip was moldering away. Evidently George no longer played tennis.

Max suddenly felt very depressed. How *could* George have lived in a place like this? It was worse than austere, it was barren. George had been the sort of chap who enjoyed the good things of life—the sort of chap one would imagine sinking into a deep armchair by a roaring fire with a glass of whiskey, a pipe, and a pair of slippers. Domestic bliss and comfort, after a day of honest toil. This tawdry lodging seemed utterly out of character. This must be Hilda's idea of home, and George had accepted it.

Max returned thoughtfully to the kitchen, where Mrs. Biggs had just made the tea.

"Not a very *cozy* house, is it?" he remarked.

"No," said Mrs. Biggs, stirring vigorously, "it ain't. Mind *you*, it ain't really the 'ouse what's so bad—it's what's in it. Lor' bless yer, I've got better stuff in me own 'ome. She jus' didn't *bother*, Mr. East, that's the long an' the short of it. Didn't care. I says to 'er, 'If this was my 'ouse,' I says, 'I'd get some new furniture now the war's over an' this 'ere utility's come off dockets,' I says. 'Yes, Mrs. Biggs,' she says, 'I suppose we ought to, but there's doctors' bills for Jane, an' housekeepin's so expensive,' she says, 'and we never seem to have any money to spare.' 'Bad management,' I thinks to meself, 'that's what it is. Too much sittin' about an' not enough gettin' on with things.' I remember once I was stayin' late doin' some spring cleanin', an' 'er 'usband come in. 'Oh, darlin',' she says, all sprightly as though she's got a wunnerful present for 'im, 'oh, darlin', I'm awfully sorry there isn't anything for supper!' Can yer beat it? But there, we shouldn't speak ill o' the dead. She was pleasant enough with it all, I will say that. Never a cross word nor a grumble did I ever 'ear from 'er lips. And 'oo ain't got shortcomin's, arter all?"

"There's one thing that struck me about her," said Max. "Didn't she ever use any powder or lipstick or anything?"

"Not a speck—she was funny that way. 'Course, she 'ad a nice 'igh color in 'er cheeks, and she'd go a lovely brown in the summer with all that sittin' out o' doors. But she could 'a' done with a bit o' lipstick to brighten 'er up a bit—*and* powder, come ter that. 'If I was you, Mrs. Thingummy,' I says, 'I'd take that shine orf me nose an' give me 'usband a treat.' Yus, I did. I talked plain to 'er—she didn't take no offense. Always ready ter talk about 'erself, she was. But she didn't take no advice if she didn't feel like it. She'd jus' smile. An' then 'er 'air, Mr. East! Any old 'ow it was, flappin' all round 'er ears, a proper mess. Just as though she didn't care *what* she looked like. Even Jane used ter go on at 'er Mum sometimes. 'Why don't you 'ave a perm, Mummy?' she used ter say, but she might 'a' bin talkin' to a post fer all the notice 'er Mum took. I couldn't 'ardly credit it when Mrs. Lamb suddenly says she's orf to 'ave 'er 'air done—much good it did 'er, pore woman."

"Perhaps she was going to meet a boy friend," Max suggested.

Mrs. Biggs gave him a withering look. "Mrs. Lamb? Naow—not she!"

"I don't see why not," said Max.

"Well, she didn't 'old with men."

"You mean she didn't like them?"

"She didn't 'old with other men beside 'er 'usband. Often talked ter me abaht that, she did. She'd read summat in the paper in the mornin'—*you* know, Mr. East—one o' them *juicy* cases—an' she'd talk abaht it fer hours. *She* wouldn't 'a' done nothin'—much too proper, she was."

"Well," Max persisted, "I'd have thought there'd be *some* special reason why she decided to have her hair done that day, if it was such an event for her. Didn't she give you any idea what it was?"

"No, she didn't," said Mrs. Biggs, emphatically.

"H'm. You may be right about a boy friend, Mrs. Biggs, but I bet she was going to see someone. I wonder who it was. You wouldn't know about letters or telephone calls, I suppose?"

"Not letters, Mr. East, but she did 'ave a telephone call that mornin', as I told the inspector. I can't say 'oo it was from, though."

"That's a pity," said Max. "It may have been very important."

"Well, sir, I couldn't listen, now, could I? I did just 'ear 'er say, 'All right, then,' as I went through the 'all, but that don't 'elp much, do it?"

Max was interested. "She said, 'All right, then,' did she? Well, there you are, Mrs. Biggs—she was making an appointment with someone."

Mrs. Biggs shook her head. "More likely it was the libery to say they'd got a book she wanted, an' she was tellin' 'em she'd go an' get it."

Max sighed. "Yes, I suppose it could have been something like that. Well, Mrs. Biggs, thank you for the tea and for your company."

"Yer very welcome, I'm sure," said the old lady, patting her hairnet. She dropped her voice. "Do you think they'll 'ang 'im?"

Max was about to say that he sincerely hoped not when the gate in the side passage banged sharply, and footsteps sounded on the concrete.

"Good afternoon, Mrs. Biggs," said a deep voice. "Can't keep away from it, eh?" It was a man in a soft hat and a mackintosh, fiftyish and a little gray. Suddenly he noticed Max in the kitchen. "Hullo," he said abruptly, "and who are you?"

Max came to the door. "For that matter, who are you?"

"Lor' bless yer, Mr. East," Mrs. Biggs broke in, "don't yer know the inspector? Took me fingerprints, 'e did. Narsty, dirty stuff."

Max joined the inspector outside. "I'm sorry," he said with a smile. "I really had no idea. You're Inspector Haines, are you?"

"I am."

"My name's Easterbrook. I'm a friend of Lambert's."

"Oh, you are." Haines looked him up and down, suspiciously. "What exactly are you doing here?"

"Nothing in particular. Just having a look round, you know."

"A look round what?"

"The scene of the crime."

"I see. Amateur detective, eh?"

"Not really. Just a friend."

Haines said, "Well, we'd better go inside for a minute or two. It'll be warmer." He led the way into the sitting room.

Max said, "I hope I haven't broken any rules, Inspector. If so, it was quite unintentional. I thought you'd finished with the place."

The inspector became less hostile. "No," he said, "I don't think you've broken any rules. I suppose Mrs. Biggs let you in?"

"Oh, yes—I didn't smash any windows, if that's what you mean. I didn't really expect to get in. I just thought I'd have a look at the house and perhaps have a word with the neighbors."

Haines smiled tolerantly. "You've never been in these parts before?"

"No."

"And yet you were a friend of Lambert's?"

Max laughed. "I've been abroad, Inspector."

"I see. Were you abroad at half-past six last Wednesday evening, by any chance?"

Max looked a little startled. "As a matter of fact, I was."

"Where, exactly?"

"Well, let me think. Wednesday. What a long time ago it seems! I suppose I was probably in the Vierlahreszeiten Bierhaus in Frankfurt, Germany. How's that for an alibi?"

Haines smiled. "It'll do for now. We have to be careful, you know."

"Don't apologize, Inspector. If you ask enough questions, perhaps you'll find the real murderer."

The inspector's face hardened. "Is that just a wisecrack, Mr. Easterbrook, or are you serious?"

"Quite serious. I don't believe you've got the right man."

The inspector said nothing.

"But I suppose," continued Max, "as long as the police can get someone hanged for a murder, they don't much mind who it is."

"That," said Haines, "is a most improper remark."

"I'm glad you're touchy on the point, Inspector. I'm not a detective, of course, but it does strike me that you've rather taken the path of least resistance. George Lambert is the obvious man, I agree, but isn't it possible you may have left a few stones unturned?"

"Such as?"

"Well, someone else may have had a reason for murdering Mrs. Lambert. A better reason."

"Who?"

"I don't know who," said Max. "That's your job—to find out."

Haines settled himself comfortably. "Mr. Easterbrook," he said, "the police force of this country has many qualities, but it is not psychic. We have fingerprint experts and ballistic experts and photographers and toxicologists and pathologists. If you can give me a footprint, or a hair, or a bloodstain, or a little dust, or a shred of clothing, or even a piece of chocolate that someone has bitten, you'll be surprised what we can find out. If you could produce a man—any man—and say, 'I think this man was at Mrs. Lambert's house on the night of the murder,' the chances are that we should soon know whether he was there are not. Modern science is a wonderful thing. But it may surprise you to learn that Scotland Yard employs no seers, no table rappers, no crystal gazers or mediums, and that we do not believe what the stars foretell. In short, Mr. Easterbrook, we cannot conjure a nonexistent suspect out of thin air."

"I appreciate that, Inspector. But perhaps you'd search a little harder if you hadn't already got a man under lock and key?"

"I dare say. That's only common sense. We're pretty sure we've got our man. But that doesn't mean we stop the investigation—provided there's anything to investigate. But what is there to investigate?"

"Wasn't there any trace at all to suggest that someone else was in the house that night?"

"It depends what you mean by 'trace.' There were, for instance, footprints on the gravel path—or rather, bits of footprints. Dozens of them—we took a lot of photographs. Plenty of people use a gravel path—the householder and his family, the char, the postman, the milkman, the window-cleaner, the laundryman, the casual visitor. We have no Prince Charming, Mr. Easterbrook, to go round among fifty million people looking for a foot that fits. Bring me a man—a suspect—and his shoe may fit. Otherwise, we're helpless. The same thing applies to other 'traces.' It's very likely, for instance, that if any other man had been in the house that night, he'd have taken away something on his clothes—a microscopic speck of fiber from Mrs. Lambert's dress or from the carpet—something which he'd never notice. If we had the coat that such a man was wearing, we could almost certainly identify such a speck, and the expert testimony might well hang him. But *is* there such a man? My answer is that we have no reason to believe in his existence. We can't spend the taxpayers' money chasing something that hasn't even got the substance of a shadow."

"But isn't there anything to give you a lead?" asked Max. "It seems to me you're concentrating on a man—admittedly he's a friend of mine—who's psychologically incapable of having committed this murder. Why don't you concentrate on his wife? She was a pretty peculiar woman—you can see that by just looking over the house."

"If you mean that it's rather a neglected house," said Haines, "—and that's hardly a ground for murder—I can only say that the husband was the person most affected."

"I don't mean only that," said Max. "If she was odd in one

way, she was probably odd in others. There are little things—oh, I know they're quite trivial and wouldn't cut any ice in a court of law, but they help to build up her personality. At the moment, she's quite unsubstantial. *I* don't know what she was like—*you* don't know. Do you realize what she did most of the time, Inspector? Just sat about! What went on in her mind during twenty years of sitting about? We just don't know. Why, she might have had a heart as black as a Borgia."

"Her husband didn't give me that impression," said Haines, mildly. "He would surely have known."

"I'm not at all certain of that."

"Why—would you consider him a stupid man?"

"Not at all—but he may have preferred to turn his attention to something else. His work, for instance, or his friends. He's a good mixer—he was one of the most popular chaps in our camp, and he seems to have got on well with his colleagues here. I may be wrong, but I don't think he's the sort to sit down and mope about his domestic background or dissect the character of an unsatisfactory wife. He'd switch his energies to other things."

"Such as his girl friend?"

"Yes, if you like. I think it's astonishing that he behaved himself for so long."

"No doubt you will be called as a witness for the defense," said the inspector, sardonically.

"All I'm saying," Max persisted, "is that he probably never got a picture of his wife clear in his mind, and that we've got to look somewhere else for information. Neighbors, relatives, friends—anywhere. I still say that's your job—and, frankly, I doubt if you're doing it."

The inspector said quietly, "Mr. Easterbrook, what do you do for a living?"

"Why do you ask?"

"I'm just interested."

"Well, as a matter of fact I work for the International Refugee Organization."

"Ah! And what exactly does your work consist of?"

"It's a sort of salvage job. Picking up bits of human wreckage. Tracing friends and relatives of people who got separated during the war. Trying to find places where people can settle in other countries."

Haines nodded. "It's not work I'm very familiar with," he said, "but I haven't the least doubt that you know what you're doing, and that you do it conscientiously and efficiently."

"Thank you, Inspector."

"And I should be grateful if you'd assume that I do my job equally conscientiously and equally efficiently." The inspector got up and moved toward the door. "Oh, by the way," he said, "In case you *are* thinking of talking to the neighbors I can probably save you a visit. On *this* side"—he pointed with his thumb —"they keep themselves to themselves. On *that* side there is a very deaf old lady and her aged companion. You can, of course, try the tradesmen, but I don't think you'll get much out of them. They all tell me Mrs. Lambert was quite a pleasant woman. Good day, Mr. Easterbrook."

❧ FOUR ❧

DR. CHALLONER, the medical superintendent of Swan Park Mental Hospital, sat back and eyed his visitor. "So you're a friend of George Lambert's," he said, and Max's sensitive ears caught a note of reproof in his voice. "An onerous position, Mr. Easterbrook."

"I find the burden supportable," said Max, slightly annoyed.

"Things look black for him."

"Yes, but in fact he's innocent."

"H'm," murmured Challoner, noncommittally. "Well, I must say it's a most regrettable affair from every point of view. A woman murdered, a daughter partly or wholly orphaned, the career of a good nurse ruined, the routine of a public institution upset. . . . Whoever is responsible has a great deal to answer for."

"A great deal," said Max.

"All this publicity . . . !" Challoner went on. "We've been overrun with reporters. Do you know one of them had the effrontery to try to penetrate the ward where Jane Lambert is a patient? Lamentable—really lamentable. It's a disgraceful thing that the popular press should take an interest in mental hospitals only when something sensational happens."

"Deplorable," said Max.

Challoner gave him a sharp look. "The whole thing's deplorable."

"Am I to be the whipping boy?" said Max.

The irritable expression faded from Challoner's face. "I'm sorry, Mr. Easterbrook. I'm afraid I've been wanting to get that off my chest for some days. Perhaps we'd better get down to business. I suppose you came here to talk about Jane?"

"Primarily, yes."

"Well," said Challoner, "I had a letter from Lambert this morning—he told me quite a lot about you and asked me to regard you as *in loco parentis* for the time being. That makes it much easier for me to talk to you. What exactly do you want to know?"

"I'd like to know just what is the matter with Jane."

The doctor sat back in his chair and began to fill his pipe. "I can tell you the label on the bottle," he said. "Jane's is a typical case of what we call manic-depressive insanity. . . . Do you know anything about mental illness, by the way?"

"It would be safer to assume that I don't."

Challoner relaxed. "You'd be surprised how many experts I talk to! Well, manic-depressive insanity is one of the commonest forms of mental illness—I suppose it accounts for about a fifth of all the cases in our mental hospitals. It often clears up in a fairly short time, though it's liable to recur."

"How do you recognize it?" asked Max.

"That doesn't usually present any difficulties. The characteristic outward sign is that the patient goes through alternating phases of depression and exaltation, often of a rather extreme nature. In the depressed phase the patient takes a despondent view of himself, thinks he's a useless creature, often imagines he's committed unmentionable crimes, and so on. In the exalted phase he's noisy and elated, has an exaggerated view of his own abilities, boasts of what he's going to do in the world, explains his own case to the doctor—that sort of thing."

Max nodded.

"Of course," Challoner went on, "we all of us have ups and downs of a similar kind—we all have an impulse of self-assertion and an impulse of submission, corresponding to exaltation and depression. But in the normal person these two impulses act as a constant check on each other, and neither is allowed to get out of hand. Then you have a balanced, integrated personality. But when, for any reason, the impulses aren't properly co-ordinated and harmonized—perhaps owing to faulty character development or to exceptionally strong causes lying in the individual history—then any breakdown under emotional strain may take the form of manic-depressive insanity with the typical emotional oscillations."

"And that's what's happened to Jane?"

"Yes. The phases were very marked at first—now they're a little less pronounced. She's making progress."

Max said, "I don't want to get too involved, Doctor, but I *am* intensely interested. Can you tell me what you do about treatment?"

"I can give you a general idea. In the first place we try to find out the causes of the emotional condition which has given rise to the neurosis. That involves careful and sympathetic questioning of everyone concerned. It means going back into the patient's life-history. If we're successful in tracing the immediate cause— or *think* we are—then we try to modify the symptoms by argument and discussion. There's no magic about it—we simply try to make the patient see things a different way. We try to promote a clearer insight."

"Doesn't it all take rather a long time?" asked Max.

"That's the trouble, of course. We're rather fortunate here— this is a hospital for voluntary patients, and the idea is to make it as attractive as possible, so in fact we're not overcrowded. But with the best will in the world, it's impossible to give each patient the time that is really needed."

"I suppose you tend to concentrate on the more hopeful cases?"

"That is so," Challoner agreed. "And I, personally, am inclined to give special attention to young patients. The complete cure of a girl like Jane Lambert, with all her life before her, is very rewarding."

"Isn't there a short cut?" asked Max. "I seem to have heard something about electrical treatment. They use it in Germany."

"Oh, it's used everywhere—it's a well-established treatment. Passing an electric current through the brain. It doesn't get at the root of the trouble, of course, but it certainly clears up the symptoms in many cases."

"Has Jane been given this treatment?"

"Yes, and it's had a marked therapeutic effect."

"I see. Then you think she'll get better?"

"I haven't a doubt of it. All being well, she should recover in a few weeks' time."

"I'm glad to hear that," said Max. "I suppose you haven't told her anything about this wretched business?"

"No—not yet."

"When she does know, I should think the shock will be enough to cause a relapse."

"That's open to doubt, Mr. Easterbrook. She'll have a very bad time of it, as anyone would. She seems fond of her father— if he's executed she'll suffer horribly. But her neurosis is caused by a specific emotional condition which this—this tragedy—may even relieve. That's by no means certain, but I think it's possible."

"Really? And what is this specific emotional condition—have you managed to find out?"

Challoner sighed. "That, of course, is the problem."

"Well, what is the *kind* of situation that brings about these neuroses? I'm sorry if I sound very much the layman."

"Don't apologize, Mr. Easterbrook. I have a lot to do, but if you want to help Jane I'm interested enough to tell you what I can. Let me give you an example. Suppose, for instance, a person has to choose between two lines of conduct which are incompatible. Suppose the person's moral self is emphatically on one side, but the motives on the other side are equally strong—as when a man of high principle falls in love with another man's wife. Then something obviously has to give way. The strong-minded man deals with the situation adequately, either by giving up the woman or, perhaps, by adjusting his principles and running off with her. But if, through some weakness in his make-up, a person cannot resolve a conflict of this sort, then nature steps in and obscures it by repressing one of the sentiments, by taking it out of consciousness. Then you get a complex and, perhaps, a psychosis. Precisely the same sort of thing might happen if a person developed a feeling of hatred for some other person whom, according to all his moral standards, he ought to love."

There was a little pause while Max digested this. Then he said, "Is what you're telling me now, Doctor, specifically related to Jane Lambert's case?"

Challoner hesitated. "It's difficult to say without more data. There has undoubtedly been a clash between the girl and her mother—not an open one, of course." He broke off. "You realize, Mr. Easterbrook, that I'm talking to you freely like this only because of the quite exceptional circumstances. Normally, it would be most improper. But the mother is dead, and the father . . ."

"The father soon may be," said Max.

"It's a possibility, shall we say. To resume, then—about this clash. You know how parents often cause distress and humiliation to their children by expecting them to show abilities and talents which they don't possess. It can be extremely bad for the children, especially if the pressure is very great—they're often turned out into the world completely lacking in self-confidence. Jane Lambert has undoubtedly suffered in this way."

"Why, what did her mother expect of her?"

"Mrs. Lambert was determined that her daughter should distinguish herself academically. In the short conversation I had with her, she made it clear that Jane was expected to take a degree and become a schoolteacher. Jane is a girl of at least average intelligence, and if she put her mind to it, she'd probably do quite well in the academic field, but it so happens that she doesn't want to."

"Has she said so?"

"It emerged quite plainly during my talk with Mrs. Lambert,"
said Challoner. "I don't know what pressures were brought to
bear by the mother, but they were definitely overdone. The girl
has lost all confidence about her school work, and she's terrified
of examinations. Mrs. Lambert herself admitted that."

"Then surely . . ."

Challoner went on. "I discussed with Mrs. Lambert various
alternatives for Jane—things like dressmaking or nursing or even
agriculture. Jane is a practical sort of girl, good with her hands—
you can tell that by the things she's made while she's been here.
We canvassed several possibilities, but none was thought suitable. Mrs. Lambert seemed to have the idea that work with the
hands was too menial for Jane. I'm afraid I completely failed to
modify her attitude. She just smiled in a peculiarly irritating way
and said, 'Perhaps when Jane's passed school certificate we can
think about it again.' I've rarely felt so angry. I gained the impression that, having set her mind on an academic career, she
wasn't going to be deflected by anything—even by insanity!"

"Mrs. Lambert had a sort of academic career herself," said
Max. "It didn't seem to get her very far."

"Perhaps she hoped her daughter would do better. That's
understandable, but at least she should have had the sense to see
that the time had come to abandon that particular ambition."

"What about Lambert himself? Surely he wasn't so unreasonable?"

"Oh, far from it. He'd known that Jane wasn't very happy
about her school work, but he hadn't realized that her fears had
been abnormal. He was most upset when I outlined what I con-
ceived to be the true position, and he promised he'd talk the
whole matter over with his wife. I don't know how far they'd got
—this business happened almost immediately afterwards."

Max was listening with close attention. "Do you think," he
asked, "that Jane's anxiety about school and examinations would
be enough to account for her condition?"

"By itself? I don't think so. Troubles of this kind occur frequently, but they very rarely reach the psychiatric clinic. There may very well have been an unresolved conflict—between Jane's desire to please her mother and her distaste for the scholastic life—but it would hardly be sufficiently intense or deep-seated to cause a bad psychosis. I feel there must have been something more." Challoner looked at Max reflectively. "What do you yourself know of Mrs. Lambert?"

"Not very much—yet."

The doctor smiled. "Isn't it a bit late to start?"

"There's a fair amount of source material," said Max. "One just has to dig. To be frank, Doctor, I'm hoping to dig up something that will throw light on why she was murdered."

"I see. Something that will exonerate Lambert?"

"Exactly."

"H'm—it sounds an ambitious project, but I should think there are many worse approaches to a murder problem. Have you —dug up anything yet?"

"A little, yes."

"I'd be most interested to hear your findings."

Max looked keenly at Challoner. "You're not pulling my leg, Doctor? I'm very serious about this."

"By no means. I'm serious about it, too. You think that Lambert's fate may turn on a correct analysis of his wife's personality. Jane's future may equally depend on that. Go ahead."

"Well, provisionally, I'd say she was a woman of exceptionally strong character, mentally alert, introspective, egotistical, and extremely obstinate. I'm not trying to give you a character sketch. These are a few of the qualities for which I have independent evidence."

"That's quite a start, anyhow," said Challoner. He was warming to Max. "I don't think I'd quarrel with any of it. Strength of personality, undoubtedly—to a most unusual degree. You could add, of course, that she was highly emotional."

"Oh? I understood her general demeanor was rather placid."

"Entirely superficial—and most misleading. Emotionally, she was as active as a volcano about to erupt. Indeed, when she visited us here, she did erupt."

"I didn't know that."

"Yes—over the child. As I told you, we discussed the educational problem and Jane's future, and then I explained to Mrs. Lambert that what Jane needed was to develop her own personality and stop being an extension of her mother's. I said that it was high time she was allowed to stand on her own feet, emotionally. I might just as well have saved my breath. Instead of talking to the girl sensibly and quietly when she saw her, Mrs. Lambert apparently gathered her up in the maternal arms, metaphorically speaking, and plunged both herself and Jane into an emotional bath. It seems to have been an exhibition of pure cannibalism—a mother emotionally devouring her helpless young. Naturally, Jane was much worse afterward, and I had no alternative but to tell Mrs. Lambert that it would be better if she didn't come again for a while."

"I had no idea she was so possessive," said Max.

"Oh, quite immoderately. This particular piece of self-indulgence at the child's expense fitted into the wider pattern. I soon discovered that she'd kept Jane very close to her all the child's life. She'd put obstacles in the way of her going anywhere alone or of spending holidays with other girls. She'd controlled every detail of her daily routine. She didn't attempt to hide the fact. When I suggested that, at seventeen, Jane needed to have a life of her own, Mrs. Lambert said, 'Well, of course, she isn't very strong.' That was quite untrue—physically she's as strong as a young horse. It was just an excuse. The truth is that when her mother was around, Jane as a personality became a complete cipher. It was most noticeable that when Jane was asked questions, her mother nearly always answered for her. 'Oh yes, Jane likes that, don't you, darling?' Or 'You wouldn't want to do that, would you, dear?' That sort of thing. Of course, it's a common fault with parents, but with Mrs. Lambert it was a vice."

Max was absorbing and storing every word. "I wonder what made Mrs. Lambert behave like that," he said. "If her attitude was exceptional, perhaps there were exceptionally strong compulsions?"

"There may well have been," Challoner agreed. "One can formulate theories. It's quite possible, for instance, that she found her own existence rather futile and that unconsciously she was trying to compensate for inadequacies in her own life by living again in Jane. That's the kindest explanation. But it seemed to me that there was something more than that—something conscious and, therefore, vicious. Almost an element of deliberate cruelty, as though she were taking it out of Jane for some reason or other. Perhaps she had an unsatisfactory sex life. Whatever the reasons, I felt that her attitude was entirely selfish. She didn't give the impression of being very *unhappy* about Jane, in spite of the tears and the excess of apparent affection. I think she felt deprived. The emotional scene with the child was probably a demonstration—reasserting her domination over a daughter she seemed in danger of losing."

"Do you think she knew she was in danger of losing her?"

"I think so, yes. I'd hinted that it might be better if Jane were to try to get a job away from home as soon as she was fully recovered. Mrs. Lambert obviously intended to prevent that if she could. She seemed to have no appreciation of the seriousness of Jane's breakdown or the risk of recurrence if the girl went back to the old conditions. She was the complete wishful thinker, turning her back on unpleasant facts. *Her* explanation of the whole affair was that Jane had been overworking and had got 'tired' and 'nervy,' and that after a short rest she'd be her old self again and would be able to go back home and resume her normal life exactly where she'd left it off. You said earlier, Mr. Easterbrook, that Mrs. Lambert was an obstinate woman. She certainly was, but she was obstinate in a peculiar way. She didn't simply state a point of view and stick to it. When she didn't agree with what I was saying, she'd just let my words flow over her head, and in the end she'd make some remark which showed quite plainly that she hadn't really taken in, let alone considered, a single word."

Max smiled. "That's almost exactly what Mrs. Biggs, the char-lady, said! 'In at one ear and out of the other, like water off a duck's back!'"

Challoner laughed. "Then she's a penetrating woman. It's absolutely true. Mrs. Lambert had her own fixed set of ideas about Jane's breakdown—naturally exonerating herself from any responsibility—and nothing affected them. Do you know, she rang me up on the morning after her visit and said didn't I think that Jane would be happier at home! When I answered with an emphatic no, and explained why, as patiently as I could, she said, 'Of course, Doctor, she doesn't *have* to stay, does she?' What a woman! I felt as though I'd like to shake some sense into her."

Max raised his eyebrows. "It's becoming more and more obvi-ous to me," he said, "that Mrs. Lambert was capable of arousing violent emotions—and in the most unexpected quarters."

Challoner looked a little sheepish. "I'm afraid that wasn't the psychiatrist speaking."

"I can understand how you felt. May I come back to Jane for a moment? What does *she* say about her mother?"

"She varies. She's been very ill, of course, and she hasn't been in a condition to give us much help so far. Sometimes she's ap-peared deeply devoted to her mother; at other times she's been quite indifferent. In her exalted phases she's been frankly critical. In those phases inhibitions are reduced to a minimum, and some of her deepest feelings may have broken out. But, up to now, she's been mainly very depressed, or so excited that it's been difficult to make much of what she's said. Now that she's so much improved, I'm hoping we shall learn a good deal more."

"It seems to me," said Max, "that you've formed a fairly definite view already—about the case as a whole, I mean. You haven't much doubt that the root of the trouble lies in Jane's past rela-tionship with her mother?"

"I'll put it this way, Mr. Easterbrook. I think a possible explanation—I stress the word *possible*—is that, in Jane's case, the normal and proper sentiments of filial love and duty may have clashed with an intense but unconscious resentment at having her life completely dominated under the cloak of maternal affection. If Jane really *hated* her mother, and felt at the same time that it was wicked to do so—all subconsciously—then that would be quite enough to account for the psychosis and the breakdown. But it's a tentative hypothesis—no more."

"At least I see now what you meant when you suggested that Jane might not necessarily be made worse by knowing about the tragedy."

"As far as her mother's death is concerned," said Challoner, slowly, "it might be the making of her."

"It's a dreadful condemnation of anyone, isn't it? Assuming that there's something in your hypothesis, what astonishes me is that all this seems to have happened in the Lambert household without George Lambert himself being aware of it. Don't *you* think that's surprising?"

Challoner considered. "No, I don't think so—not in the circumstances."

"But he's so fond of Jane."

"Affection doesn't necessarily make a man a psychologist. I wouldn't expect a fellow like Lambert to make a conscious and determined effort to get inside the minds of the people he lives with. He's not the type. As for affection, there hasn't been any obvious unkindness, remember—very much the reverse. His wife would appear to him a loving and devoted mother. It's true that Jane's school life left a good deal to be desired, but that happens very often with children. The fact is that husbands are usually content to let their wives deal with these problems, unless something goes badly wrong. When the wife was Mrs. Lambert, that's certainly what I'd expect."

Max nodded. "You think there's not much doubt that she wore the trousers?"

"Well, I wouldn't put it quite like that myself. I'm not familiar with their domestic situation, but my feeling is that Lambert is not a weak man—he's a peace-loving man. He didn't so much fight a losing battle as accept the fact that the home was his wife's province. If his wife had lived, I think it's quite possible that Lambert, having had his eyes opened, might have put his foot down about Jane and made his wife accept my advice. I'm certain he would have made an effort."

"Did you like him?"

Challoner puffed thoughtfully at his pipe. "I find it a little difficult," he said, "to dissociate my feelings about Lambert from his recent conduct—or what appears to have been his conduct. I know your point of view, but the fact remains that on present showing the evidence is very strongly against him. I can't feel any great liking for a man who killed his wife in cold blood because of a girl! But if you ask me what I thought about him when I first met him, I can only say that he seemed to me a good-natured, sensible, straightforward sort of chap, and I did like him. I wouldn't have expected him to murder anyone—not while he was in his right mind."

"You haven't any doubt that he *was* in his right mind?"

Challoner looked surprised. "Not the least. Have you?"

Max shrugged. "I just wondered whether Mrs. Lambert might have had an effect on him that we didn't know about. After all, if she could do so much harm to one person's mind . . ."

"No, no. I'd say he was completely sane and certainly responsible for his actions. People don't become unbalanced without showing some symptoms—he showed none whatever. I'm afraid there's no help for him in that direction."

Max got up. "Well, Doctor, I've taken a lot of your time." He hesitated. "Would it be possible for me to see Jane before I go? I know Lambert would like it."

"What are you thinking of saying to her?" asked Challoner, cautiously.

"I thought of listening, mainly. And I have a little present for her."

"Forgive my curiosity—what is the present?"

"Oh," said Max, "it's something I picked up on the way here. A box of perfume and powder and—I think—lipstick. After all, she *is* seventeen!"

Challoner smiled and rested a friendly hand on Max's shoulder as they walked to the door. "By their gifts ye shall know them. No scissors? All right, Mr. Easterbrook, you can see her. I think perhaps you'll do her good."

"Thank you, Doctor. And thank you very much indeed for talking so frankly."

"I hope it's been useful," said Challoner. "I can honestly say I wish you luck. Nothing would give me more pleasure than to know that Lambert was cleared." He opened the door. "You'll find Jane in the block just opposite. I'll ring through and tell them it's all right. Perhaps you'll have better luck with her than the inspector did."

"The inspector?"

"Yes, Inspector Haines. He's working on the Lambert case. He called and had a long talk with me last week. We covered some of the ground I've been over with you. I thought he was remarkably intelligent for a policeman. But he certainly struck a bad day with Jane—she just sat and stared in front of her and was quite monosyllabic. Between ourselves, I was rather relieved. . . . Is anything the matter, Mr. Easterbrook?"

"Nothing, Doctor," said Max. "I was only thinking how mistaken one can be. . . ."

❦ FIVE ❦

MAX WALKED thoughtfully along the path which led between smooth lawns to the block where Jane was living. Just inside the entrance of the modern, red brick building sat a fat and comfortable nurse with glasses. She got up to meet him. "You've come to see Jane Lambert, haven't you?" she said.

"If it's convenient . . ." said Max.

"Yes, of course. It's not really visiting day, but it's quite all right. Jane's in her room—number 17 on the first landing. You'll find her a little bit excited, but I think she'll be glad to see you."

Max thanked her and climbed the carpeted stairs. The block seemed surprisingly quiet—more like a rather select hotel than a mental hospital. A million years from the days of Bedlam!

He had no sooner given one gentle tap upon the door of number 17 than it was flung open by Jane. Max, who had been thinking of George's daughter as a child, at once made a rapid mental adjustment. She was very much the young woman—a bit large and lumpy but by no means unattractive. Her hair and eyes were dark, and her round face had George's good-natured expression.

"Do come in," she said eagerly. "It's lovely to see you!"—and she quickly closed the door behind them. "You're Mr. Easterbrook, aren't you? Nurse told me you were coming. Did you meet her, she's quite nice, but not as pretty as Lucy, and she wears spectacles. They knew I liked Lucy, I don't know why they let her go away. Won't you sit down; you're not in a hurry are you; the days are so long here."

Max glanced round the little bed-sitting room. It was comfortably furnished with a table and chair for writing, an easy chair for reading, and a thick rug. From the window there was a view out over the woods. "It all looks very cozy," he said. "Will it be all right if I sit on the bed?"

"Of course. I often do. The springs aren't very good. Nurse said you were a friend of Daddy's, but you look too young. I'm sixteen, how old are you?"

Max smiled. "I'm thirty-two."

"I think you're rather nice." She seemed in high spirits and came skipping and twirling over to the bed like a child of ten. "I adore curly brown hair. Your tie's crooked, though, let me put it straight. There, that's much better. What's that parcel you've got, is it for me?"

Max said, "How did you guess?" He watched Jane opening it with quick, nervous fingers, forcing the string from the ends of the parcel and tearing off the wrapper.

"Oh," she cried, "it's *lovely*. Thank you ever so much." She leaned forward and gave him a resounding kiss on the cheek. "It would be nicer in a little silver box, though—why didn't you get one of those?" She darted across to the mirror and rapidly made up her mouth. "How's that?" she asked in a moment.

Max regarded the unskillful smudge of red benevolently. "Fine."

"Do I look like a Scarlet Woman?"

He laughed. "M'm—no, I think you've some way to go yet."

She dabbed a little powder on her nose, threw the pad on to the dressing table, and flung herself into the easy chair. "How's Daddy? Why doesn't he come and see me? I'm tired of being in this place; it's full of old fogies. Daddy never told me he knew you, at least I don't think so. He hasn't been for days and days, but I got a letter from him yesterday; he says he's very busy."

"Yes, he is busy—he really can't get away. That's why he

thought it would be a good idea if I came instead. He sends you his love."

"Poor old Daddy, he's so nice really. I hope Mummy's feeding him better than she usually does, but I don't suppose she is; I don't know how he keeps alive."

"He looks very robust."

"He must have good lunches in town; what Mummy gives him wouldn't keep a sparrow alive; it's really too bad. She's absolutely hopeless, I don't know how he stands it. When I'm married, I shall give my husband three large meals a day, all perfectly cooked and always different. I can cook very well, you know, much better than most of the girls at school. I'm much cleverer than they think; I'm not really appreciated. Your tie's still crooked; I wonder why it goes like that. I don't think you tie it properly. I'd like to do some cooking here, but they won't let me."

"What *do* you do here?" asked Max. It was already clear to him that his contribution to the conversation was likely to be a small one. Jane flew from one topic to another so quickly that it was difficult to insert a wedge. "I expect they keep you pretty busy."

"Oh, yes, we have occupational therapy; the idea is to take our minds off ourselves. I've done a lot of knitting, but I can't do it up here; they're afraid of the needles. They watch us all the time; I suppose they have to, but it seems silly. I don't think they know much about us really. I've made a jumper, just like the one in *Fashion*." She darted to a drawer. "Look, here it is; don't you think it's marvelous; I'll put it on if you like and show you."

"Well, I—I shouldn't just now," said Max, in some alarm about where her evident lack of inhibition might take her. "It *is* nice, though—I like the pattern."

Jane pushed it back among her other clothes and shut the drawer with a bang. "I made it in no time at all, and everybody said it was very good. Dr. Challoner said *he* could do with a pull over. I think *Fashion* is a lovely paper, don't you? I could spend hours looking at it. I'm a natural dressmaker; I've got taste; some of the clothes in *Fashion* aren't really what I'd call good; they're just eccentric. I'm sure I could design better ones; I think p'raps I'll get a job on *Fashion*. Mummy wears terrible clothes; have you seen them? She hasn't any taste at all; she'd just as soon wear woolen stockings as nylons; I can't understand it. I feel quite ashamed to go out with her sometimes; she looks just anyhow; it's like being out with a washerwoman. That straight, straggly hair of hers, it's frightful. I've told her ever so many times to have something done to it. I'm sure Daddy would like it better; he likes women to look nice, but Mummy doesn't really mind what he thinks. I don't believe she even likes him very much; she's not at all nice to him; though, of course, he doesn't see it, he's such an old dear. He's much too kind, really; she's awfully patronizing though she hasn't got anything to patronize him about; he does his best after all. Once she said she thought he'd done quite well, considering he'd never been able to go to a university. I felt so furious I could have killed her; I'm sure he must have hated it."

She stopped suddenly, mainly to get her breath. Max would have liked her to go on now but feared she might get too excited. He said, "The doctor tells me you're getting better, Jane, and that he hopes you'll be able to leave before long."

Jane said, "I know; isn't it wonderful?" She sat astride the hard chair, facing the back of it, and rocked herself to and fro. "I'll like getting away; it's such a beastly bore here, at least the people are; there's only one other girl and she's not very intelligent. The books aren't too bad in the library, but I've read most of the good ones now. I like reading; I could read when I was five, but Mummy won't let me read interesting books; she took *Ann Veronica* away from me; she said I'd understand it better when I grew up. She treats me just like a child; I wish she could hear some of the things we talk about at school. Mummy's an awful prude; I don't know how she could ever bear to get married; it must be dreadful for Daddy. Of course, some of the books here are rather stuffy; in fact, I got so tired of them I started to write a story myself; it was much better than the printed ones; I quite enjoyed reading it."

"I'd like to see it," said Max.

"Oh, I didn't keep it; I knew I could do a better one. I've got a very good style of writing; I've modeled it on Robert Louis Stevenson. I think I'd rather like to be a novelist; I wrote and told Miss Jones so; she's the English mistress; she always used to say I couldn't spell, as though that matters. I think it would be lovely to see a row of books on the shelves and know that you'd written them all, don't you? Mummy wants me to be a teacher; she's mad on teaching, but I should hate it; I think it's a frowsy old job, and anyway, teachers never seem to get married, do they? Mummy says getting married isn't the only thing in the world; she wants me to have a career; what do you think, Mr. Easterbrook?"

"I think it's probably a good thing to get married when you want to," said Max, cautiously.

"Are you married?"

He smiled. "I'm not, as a matter of fact."

"I suppose nobody would have you; I'd have thought you could have got somebody. The trouble is I don't meet many boys. I'd like to; I think they're fun, but every time I want to do anything where there are boys about, Mummy always thinks up a good reason why it would be bad for me. I wanted to join a dramatic society; I'm really a good actress; in fact, I have thought of being a professional, or perhaps a ballet dancer; but Mummy said it would mean staying out late, and she'd have to come and fetch me, so I wasn't allowed to go. I'm sure it was because there were boys there; just as though I couldn't look after myself. I think she's very mean; it was just the same over the rambling club. I thought it would be such fun going off on Sundays, but I got fed up with trying to persuade her in the end. If I raised the subject, she'd say in that awful way of hers,

'Let's sit down, dear, and have a nice quiet talk about it,' and then there'd be a long argy-bargy; and of course Mummy would cry, she always does; she just loves a scene; she can go on for hours; so in the end I just gave up, but it would have been fun."

"Oh, well," said Max, "you'll soon be able to please yourself about these things."

"I know; that's what I wrote to Miss Hurst; she's the head-mistress. I said I thought I'd had too much discipline, and I was sure her school hadn't done me any good; as a matter of fact, her educational methods are terribly out of date. You'd think a person like that would try to keep up with the times, wouldn't you? I told her I was thinking of going into an art school."

"Have you done any painting?"

"Not very much; I haven't had time with all the other things; but when you think of all the dreadful pictures that actually get sold in shops, there's no reason why I shouldn't do better. Daddy bought Mummy a thing called 'Wood on the Downs'; it was quite nice, but there wasn't really much in it; Mummy didn't like it anyway. Of course, she'd never let me be an artist, I know that; she doesn't think artists are quite nice. She likes respectable things, but they're all so dull. I don't know what I'll do; p'raps I'll go into publishing; that might be rather interesting."

Max struggled to keep pace with her. "But do you know anything about publishing?"

"No, but Mummy does; I heard her ringing up some pub-lisher people. She was talking to somebody called Stephanie, but she told me to go and get on with my homework. I'm sure I'd like publishing; it must be wonderful to be able to throw all the rubbish into the wastepaper basket and every now and then pick out something really good and make it into a best seller. I think life's wonderful, don't you; there are so many things to do." She jumped up and threw open the little window. "I'll be so glad when spring comes; I'd like to walk miles and miles. Oh, look, there's Dr. Gregory; he's one of my doctors. I have ever so many; they're most interested in my case; I don't know why. I don't think there's much wrong with me now; I feel fine. He's not really much good, but he tries to be nice. Daddy likes him, anyway. I think Daddy's a lamb, but he does give way to Mummy too much; she's frightfully selfish, really; she doesn't care at all about his work or anything. Of course, she pretends to, but you can see she doesn't; she doesn't listen to him half the time, and I don't think she understands what he's talking about, often. If she wants something herself, it's quite different; she just keeps on about it until she gets her own way; she'll never take no for an answer. I always know when he's really fed up, because then he says, 'Why don't you get a book, dear?' I think he's a very patient man." She made little pirouette towards the bed. "Can you dance, Mr. Easterbrook?"

"A little," said Max, watching her. "I'm not much good, though—I always tread on my partner's toes."

"Yes," said Jane, "you have got big feet. I love dancing, but I'm not much good at it either. I can't ever get any practice. We do country dancing at school; it's all right but it's not exciting like ballroom dancing. I wanted to have proper dancing lessons, but Mummy said I was too young. She can't dance; she's got big feet, too. I think she's an old stick-in-the-mud; I don't see how she could ever have enjoyed herself. A thing's only worth doing to her if there's an exam at the end of it, like music. She let me learn music; I liked that. I play the piano very well; you must hear me some time; I love it."

"I should like to, Jane. Do you play here?"

"Yes, often; they think it's good for me, but they won't let me play when the old fogies want to sleep in the afternoon; they're very tiresome about that. I can play all the classics; I took lessons for a long time. I practiced ever such a lot; Mummy was always wanting me to practice; but when I had the exam, I didn't feel very well; so I didn't pass, and then Mummy stopped the lessons. She said there didn't seem much sense in spending a lot of money on music if I wasn't going to get anywhere, but I did miss the lessons. I wanted to ask Daddy about it; but Mummy said I mustn't worry him; he'd got quite enough to think about. She didn't like me telling Daddy things. Mummy doesn't like music; I think she's tone-deaf or something. Daddy does, and I do; we like listening to symphonies and things on the radio, but it's very difficult. Sometimes I listen by myself, but Mummy pretends I can't really like it; she comes in and says, 'I don't think we want this noise, do we, dear?' and switches it off; and if I say I do want it, she says hadn't I better get on with my homework. She's an awfully bossy person; I wish you could meet her. I don't think she likes people to be happy at all; if they are, she just can't help interfering. I wouldn't interfere with my children; I'd let them grow up just as they wanted to."

"You may change your mind when you've got some," said Max, feeling like a sententious old man.

Jane laughed and broke into a little snatch of song. "I'll have two boys and two girls, and we'll live in the country," she said. "Have you seen our house? I hate it, it's so dark and dreary; and there's no *fun*. Mummy's so dreadfully exasperating; you can't possibly understand if you haven't known her. It's the way she puts things, as though everything she suggests is for your benefit, like 'You get on with your Latin, dear, and I'll darn your stockings.' "

"That sounds rather kind of her," said Max. "I don't see why you should be annoyed."

"Oh, *you* wouldn't," said Jane, rudely, "but I like darning stockings; I do it ever so much better than Mummy; and I hate Latin, and she knows I hate it."

"Oh, well, I shouldn't worry about it," said Max, "I don't suppose you'll have to do any more Latin."

"Oh, yes I shall; I know I shall, if I go home. You can't argue with Mummy. I'd like to travel. I'd like to go to Italy. We always go to such dull places for our holidays and never meet anybody interesting."

"Didn't—doesn't your mother ever meet anybody interesting, Jane? Didn't people come to the house when you were there?"

Jane stretched out her long legs and kicked off her shoes. "Only tradesmen, not anybody nice. Mummy's awful; she just doesn't know anybody at all. I don't think people like her. I say, it's funny you should have come to see me; I don't know who you are really at all. How is it I've never seen you before?"

"I've been away—I've been in Germany."

"How horrid! I think you're silly to work there. What do you do all the time?"

"I look after refugees."

"You mean people out of the camps? I know all about the camps, and the gas chambers—Mummy used to tell me about them when the flying bombs were over and we slept in the air-raid shelter. She read about them in the papers and then told me. I used to dream about them; I don't think it was a very good thing to talk about at night, do you? Have you ever seen people beating each other?"

"No," said Max, horrified.

"Mummy used to talk a lot in the air-raid shelter because she was frightened; we were both frightened. She used to cry a lot, too. I think wars are very stupid; are you going back to Germany?"

"I expect so, in a week or two."

"P'raps somebody else will come and see me; somebody came the other day, but I can't remember now who it was; I know it was a man; he was very kind. There are a lot of things I can't remember; that's one of my troubles. I can't remember coming here, so I suppose I must have been ill; it's all a blank now, but. Dr. Challoner says it wasn't worth remembering anyway. I don't have to stay here, you know. I can go when I like; Mummy told me that. All I have to do is to give three days' notice, and then I can just walk out if I want to. Mummy didn't like it here; she said it felt like a prison. Sometimes I don't like it either; I hate being locked in at night; I think they don't trust me. They're quite beastly, sometimes, last week they stopped me dancing in the sitting room; they said I'd have to sit alone in my room if I didn't behave. So I gave in my notice, and it was fun; the doctor had to come here and argue about it; and I told him I wasn't going to be treated like that and I'd had enough of his horrid old hospital."

"But you're still here."

"Well, I thought about it, and I couldn't think of anywhere to go except home, and I didn't want to go home; so, in the end, I had to stay. I expect I was wrong to make a fuss; they said everything they did was for my own good; and anyhow I was very miserable the next day and didn't feel like going anywhere. I do get miserable sometimes; I don't know why; but I feel fine today, and it's been fun seeing you, even though you don't talk much. You'll come again, won't you?"

"I expect someone else will come if I can't," said Max. "And anyhow, you'll be out of here soon." He listened to her prattling on for a while. When finally even her torrent of words showed signs of abating, he made a move. "Well, goodbye, Jane," he said, "I'll tell your father that you're feeling cheerful. Be good, won't you, and do as the doctors say. They really do want to get you better—I expect they're as keen for you to leave here as you are to go."

"Yes, they are; they told me so. They want the bed. Dr. Challoner says when I've stopped getting excited, I can go into Jenkins Ward—that's the convalescent block. They have a wonderful time there; it's mixed, and they have regular dances and parties and all sorts of things. Must you really go?" She gravely shook hands. "Give my love to Daddy, and tell him to come soon; I'm sure his old work can't be all that important. Goodbye!" She swung for a moment on the door handle and then slammed the door with a tremendous crash.

Max walked slowly downstairs and into the entrance hall. There was an easy chair for visitors, and he sank into it. He felt quite limp. He touched his forehead and found it damp with sweat.

The fat nurse came bustling by. "Is everything all right, Mr. Easterbrook?"

Max smiled. "Quite all right, thank you, Nurse. I'm a bit exhausted, that's all."

The nurse was sympathetic. "You get used to them," she said.

"I suppose so. I wouldn't have your job, all the same. You were right—she *was* excited. I didn't have any difficulty in getting her to talk!"

"No, you wouldn't. Still, it's much worse when they just sit about looking like statues, and Jane *is* getting better. You should have seen her a week or two ago. She's been pretty bad, you know."

"I can see that. It isn't the most likable characteristics that come out in these exalted moods, is it?"

"No—it can be rather trying, but we've all got it in us to be like that, you know. You mustn't let it worry you. She's a very nice girl really."

"You like her, do you?"

"We all like her—she's got a sweet nature. You mustn't judge by today. When they're in this state, they say the first thing that comes into their heads. In a little while you won't know her."

Max got up. "You're very comforting, Nurse. I can see she's in good hands."

"Oh, we'll look after her. Goodbye, Mr. Easterbrook." She watched him walk down the path and then hurried off about her duties.

❦ SIX ❦

AFTER DINNER that evening Max took a taxi out to St. John's Wood to see Hilda's brother, Andrew White. He'd made a point of getting the address from George, but he felt no great enthusiasm for the interview. It was already clear to him that Hilda had been a singularly unpleasant woman, and in spite of George's kindly remarks he thought it more than probable that the brother would prove equally unlikable. However, it was obviously important to see him, for he and his wife would almost certainly know more about the dead woman than anyone else.

The taxi pulled up outside an attractive detached house, and the front door opened almost before Max had alighted. A tall man with thick chestnut hair came from a well-lit hall and held out a hand in greeting. He had a pleasantly deep voice, and Max's first impression of Andrew White was distinctly favorable.

"This is Mr. Easterbrook, Rose," said White, as he guided Max into a sitting room. A pretty, young-looking woman got up from the cushion where she had been sitting in front of a large log fire. She smiled at Max with natural friendliness and shook hands with him. Her husband went to the sideboard and began to pour out drinks.

"Do make yourself comfortable," said Mrs. White. "I'll go on sitting here, if you don't mind." She tucked herself up on the cushion again as Max sank into a soft chair. He took the glass of whiskey Andrew White held out to him. Looking at his host in the light, he realized that the brother bore very little resemblance to the Hilda of the photograph. The features were equally well marked, but the whole expression was different. Andrew had a cheerful, open face. His eyes were blue, and his hair, Max now saw, was almost red. He also had very different ideas about how to live, Max thought, as his glance took in the agreeable room with its thick wall-to-wall carpet, its deep chairs, and its soft lighting. What a contrast to the Lambert home, he reflected, with a stab of pity for George.

Mrs. White seemed to read his thoughts. "We saw George this morning," she said, handing Max a cigarette. "He told us about you, so we weren't surprised when you rang."

"How did you find him?" Max asked.

"Well, he's rather depressed, naturally, but he tries not to show it."

"He'll probably buck up," said Andrew, "now that they've briefed Everton."

"Oh," said Max, "they've managed to get Everton, have they? That's good news. I wrote to George today about Jane, but he won't get the letter till tomorrow. Do you know if he's heard from the nurse—Lucy?"

"Yes, he has," said Mrs. White. "I think she must be rather nice. She seems to be standing by him."

Max nodded. "She doesn't believe he did it."

"Of course he didn't do it," said Andrew. "The whole thing's preposterous. I've never heard anything so bloody silly in my life. I've known old George for twenty years, and he simply hadn't got it in him."

"Everyone I talk to seems to agree about that," said Max, ruefully, "but it won't help much unless the real murderer can be found." He sipped his whiskey and studied Andrew White's troubled countenance. "Your sister's death must have been a great shock to you."

"Yes and no," said Andrew. "I always thought she'd come to a sticky end."

Max stared at him in astonishment. "Really? Why?"

"She asked for it," said Andrew, grimly.

"Didn't you like your sister, Mr. White?"

"Like her? I loathed her," Andrew replied. "Dreadful woman!"

There was a moment's silence while Max readjusted his ideas. "Well," he said, "now we know where we are. Do you mind telling me why?"

"I've no objection at all," said Andrew. "But we've only got an hour or two, so I'll have to make it sketchy! By the way, Easterbrook, just what are you aiming at in this business? I know you're an old friend of George's, and that's enough for me. If you want to know about Hilda, I'll tell you all I can. But where's it going to get you?"

"I'm trying to get a line on someone who might have had a good reason for killing Mrs. Lambert. And I can't do that unless I know something about her."

"Good God!" exploded Andrew. "Everyone who knew her had a good reason for killing her. She was a menace."

"A menace—to whom?"

"To George, to Jane, to Rose and me, to everyone who had the misfortune to know her. I told the inspector so."

"The inspector? Oh, he's been here too, has he?"

"Some days ago. Sunday, wasn't it, Rose? You and he ought to amalgamate—you seem to be working on the same lines. But he's 'way ahead of you at the moment."

"I'm only a beginner," said Max. "How did he take it when you said Mrs. Lambert was a menace?"

A reminiscent grin flitted across Andrew's face. "He asked me where I was on the night of the murder."

"And where were you?"

"I was traveling up from Birmingham. The inspector's already contacted the man who saw me off on the 5:30."

"Everyone's got a good alibi except George, apparently," said Max. "Anyway, let's get down to business. What about Hilda?"

"Well," said Andrew, "she and I didn't hit it off—ever. I thought she was an unmitigated pain in the neck from the moment I began to think about her at all."

"And when was that?"

"Well, we were brought up together as kids, of course, but otherwise I didn't actually see much of her until just after she married George Lambert. I'd been abroad, you see. But I suppose I'd better start at the beginning. My old man, rest his soul, was devout. He had a lot of qualities, I dare say, but he was a narrow-minded, fanatical old bigot. He was a Methodist, God help him. Mother wasn't much better. It was an unbelievable household—teetotal, vegetarian, nonsmoking, Sabbatarian, and bloody dull." He caught his wife's eye. "So it was, darling—bloody dull. I couldn't stand it. We had a lot of rows, and when I was sixteen, I got a job with an oil company and went out to Burma. I stayed there till I was twenty-two, and then I got some lousy tropical disease and had to come home. Hilda had just got married—she was three years older than I. I liked George, but I just couldn't stand her. She seemed too much like the old man. Result of toeing the line all those years, I suppose."

"Did you see much of her after you got back?"

"A damn sight too much. She was a woman you couldn't shake off. I think she wanted to reform me. I drank beer and smoked and swore and liked pretty girls—eh, Rose? Hilda was always fascinated by anyone who had the guts to enjoy himself."

"You sound very caustic," said Max.

"My dear Easterbrook," said Andrew, "if you think I'm being excessively harsh, it's simply because you didn't know Hilda. She was incredible."

"In what way?"

Andrew threw out his hands. "Rose, where do we begin? Why was she incredible? You tell him."

Mrs. White was gazing with a furrowed brow into the fire. She said, "I hate talking about her."

"I'm sorry," said Max. "But if you could . . ."

There was a short silence. Then Mrs. White said, "I don't think it was any one thing. Not with me, anyhow. It was her whole attitude. She was the most infuriating woman I've ever known. All the more infuriating because you couldn't put your finger on the trouble. . . . She came to live with me for a while during the blitz. I took a house in Wales while Andy was away—a quiet spot near the sea—and Hilda practically invited herself along. She said that if she and Jane stayed in London they'd get bombed, and she implied that it would be my fault. I didn't like her, but I could scarcely refuse. So I said of course she could come, and I went to quite a lot of trouble to get things ready for her. Then I had a letter saying that, after all, she thought Wales was a bit far, and she'd made arrangements to stay with an old school friend in Somerset. I was a little annoyed, having made so many preparations, but, on the whole, I was rather relieved. Then it appeared that Hilda wasn't getting on too well with the old school friend—she had become extremely selfish, according to Hilda. After about two months I got another letter. It was just a scrappy note written on a piece of paper torn from an exercise book. I can't remember exactly what it said, but it was something like this: 'My dear Rose: We think perhaps after all we'll come and stay with you, dear. It will be nice for Jane by the seaside, and it must be very lonely for you with just the two children. So expect us on Thursday.' "

Andrew gave a short laugh. "The authentic touch," he said.

"It must have been very trying," said Max.

"Trying!" said Andrew. "Bloody cheek, I call it."

"I *was* cross," admitted Mrs. White. "But that was nothing to what happened afterward. From the moment she arrived, she took charge of things. It was done in such a subtle way, too— that was what was so maddening. If she'd been rude or domineering, I suppose I should have flared up, and we'd have had a first-class row. But she was always so amiable. Do you know what it reminded me of, Mr. Easterbrook? That game—

Grandmother's Footsteps. Did you ever play it when you were little?"

"Of course," said Max. "You stand with your back to people, and they try to walk up to you without being seen."

"That's it. You don't hear anything, but suddenly you turn round—and they're there. That's just how it was with Hilda. She hardly ever made a move that I could object to. She was always amiable and friendly and so *reasonable* that it nearly drove me mad. And yet I knew that, little by little, she was beginning to run the house and my life and the children and everything. Can you understand what it was like?"

"I'm trying to," said Max. "What *sort* of things did she do and say?"

"Well, now, let me think. She was bone-lazy, of course. She loved sitting about while other people did the work. She'd make suggestions that were designed for her own comfort, but she'd put them in such a way that they sounded generous. I can't remember half the things now, and anyway they'd sound petty to you. That was the trouble with Hilda—when you start thinking of the things that made you dislike her, they seem so insignificant. But this is the sort of thing. In the mornings, if it was a warm sunny day, she'd say, 'There isn't much washing up, dear. If you'd like to do it, I'll take the children down to the beach and look after them.' If I objected, she'd say, 'No, really, dear, I don't mind. I know they're rather a bother, but it's my turn, I'm sure.'"

"That's it," said Andrew. "That's just the technique. 'I'll put the kettle on, dear, and you can make a cup of tea.' The times I've heard her say things like that."

"But what happened?" asked Max, curiously. "Did you have quarrels?"

Mrs. White shifted uneasily on her cushion. "That's the odd thing—we didn't. I was simmering all the time, but it was impossible to row with her. Nobody could have done. She would never see that there was anything to row about. It's quite true, you know—it does take two to make a quarrel. She'd sit there, looking pleased with herself, and say, 'Well, of course, dear, if you feel like that, let's have a good talk about it and get it out of our systems'—just as though I needed psychoanalyzing. I can hear her now saying, 'Don't you think perhaps you're *exaggerating* things a little, dear?' after I'd made some protest. Always that maddening *reasonableness*. And as for persistence! Perhaps she'd have a plan that I didn't like—she was always full of plans. We'd talk about it all day long till I was absolutely sick of the subject, and I'd make it quite clear to her that I didn't like it, and I'd assume that that was the end of it. But not a bit of it. Next morning she'd take it for granted that everything was arranged. 'But I thought we'd *discussed* all that, dear,' she'd say—and then we'd start all over again. She was just like a rubber ball, wasn't she, Andrew?"

"Absolutely," said her husband. "You couldn't make any impression on her at all. I was away most of the time, of course, but I saw enough when I was on leave to get the form. Tenacity —you've no idea! You'd think she'd retired, defeated, and a couple of hours later she'd be advancing again with her forces regrouped and her morale unimpaired. Frontal attack, flank attack, steal in round the back, guerrilla tactics—she knew all the moves. She was a genius at getting her own way, and she planned her campaigns like a general. She'd never take a beating, would she, Rose? She had complete faith in her ability to do you down in the end. I watched it going on and I was fascinated. But Rose was beginning to crack up, and in the end I had to take strong measures."

"What did you do?" asked Max.

"I threw her out," said Andrew. "I almost literally threw her out. It was the devil of a business—it took a whole leave. She simply couldn't understand what the trouble was about, of course—or professed not to. We had some fearful scenes."

"She adored scenes," said Mrs. White. "They always left me limp as a rag, but Hilda flourished on them. She got terribly emotional. She said we were sending her and Jane back to be bombed, which was quite untrue—she didn't have to go back to London, and we had said we were quite ready to keep Jane. It was frightful. Hilda cried . . ."

"Blubbered!" said Andrew.

". . . and, in the end, she got hysterical. I would have been sorry for her, but I couldn't believe she was really feeling anything at all. It was just an act—she could turn emotion on and off like a tap to get her own way. I think she watched herself doing it all the time and admired her own skill."

"But she went?" asked Max.

"She went, yes," said Andrew, grimly. "But, by God, what a battle it was! She kept saying she was sure it would be all right if we just tried again, and I kept saying no. I'd had enough, and I dug my toes in. She wanted me to give her a *reason*, but as Rose says, it was a damned difficult thing to do. I told her quite plainly that I couldn't stand the sight of her, but she still didn't go. She had a hide like an elephant's. She said she thought I was 'unsporting' and that I was behaving like 'a bit of a rotter.' She often talked that schoolgirl stuff—I think protracted adolescence was part of her trouble. Anyhow, in the end, I told her that if she didn't go, I'd put her into the street with my own hands. So she went and got lodgings in the village."

"Yes," said Mrs. White. "And twenty-four hours later she came back and said she was sure we hadn't really meant it!"

Max looked from Mrs. White's flushed cheeks to Andrew's angry eyes. "Mrs. Lambert certainly had a way of stirring people up," he said. "Except, strangely enough, George."

"That wasn't because she was nicer to him," said Mrs. White. "I've heard her say some awful things. Disparaging things. She never criticized him directly, but she liked to make slighting remarks that she must have known would hurt."

"That's right," said Andrew. "She was always making cracks about his low income, for instance, when she knew damn well he was doing the best he could. The civil service isn't exactly a gold mine, after all. We'd be talking about holidays, perhaps, or buying a new car some day, and she'd say to me in his presence, 'Of course, Andrew dear, it would be different if George had your income, but then *you're* so clever, aren't you?' It wasn't as though she really cared about the money. I'll say that for her—she wasn't grasping. Material things didn't mean much to her—you could tell that by the house she lived in. She was just a born mischief-maker. Her whole attitude to George used to make me squirm. She knew she had things the way she wanted them, and yet, when they were with other people, she'd go all girlish and pretend he was the great he-man in the home. Once, I remember, when we were talking about marriage, she simpered at George and said, 'I promised to obey, didn't I, dear?' I could have kicked her."

"How was it George didn't feel like that, I wonder," said Max.

"George is different," said Andrew. "He's not like us—he's got a nice nature."

"I honestly don't think George cared enough about her for violent action," said Mrs. White, thoughtfully. "It was as though he'd written her off in his mind. He can't have had many illusions toward the end—I think he'd just accepted her for what she was and was making the best of it. Besides, I don't think George has got it in him to hate—not the mother of his child, anyway."

"Why do you think he married her?"

"Oh, that's easy," said Andrew. "Hilda just swept him along. She wasn't unattractive, you know. I was away when it happened, as I told you, but I could see, when I got back, that George really hadn't had much of a say in it. I doubt if she'd waited for him to say yes. She had a terrific personality. I don't suppose George had an inkling of what she was really like. He was probably intrigued, and you can bet your life she flattered him. But if you're thinking from all that that George lacked guts, you're reckoning without Hilda. There aren't many men who could have handled her even as well as George has."

"He could have left her, surely?" said Max.

"I doubt if he'd have wanted to. As Rose says, he'd come to terms with the situation in his own way. And then there was the kid. Anyway, Hilda would never have let him go, never. She'd have reveled in a big crisis. She'd have chased him and worried the life out of him."

"What do you think made her behave as she did?" Max asked.

"God knows," said Andrew, gloomily. "Upbringing had a lot to do with it, I think. If Hilda had kicked over the traces and left home, as I did, she'd probably have been quite different. I think she's been making other people pay for what she had to go through. But there's more to it than that, I'm sure. She had a streak of something pretty nasty, hadn't she, Rose? She could be more vicious in that sly, knowing way of hers than anyone I've ever met."

Mrs. White nodded agreement. "You probably think we're fearfully prejudiced, Mr. Easterbrook," she said, "but my husband really isn't exaggerating. Hilda did enjoy getting people into her power and causing them pain. She tried to do it to me. I remember once, when Andy was away in Egypt, she said to me, 'Of course, dear'—she always started her most outrageous remarks that way—'of course, dear, you've never *understood* Andrew very well, have you?' I wish I could describe her expression when she said that. She gave me a sort of sidelong glance—to see whether I was wriggling, I suppose. I said, 'Oh, we don't do so badly,' or something offhand like that. She was the last person in the world I would have discussed Andy with. And then she followed it up with, 'Of course, Andrew isn't really a one-woman man at all.' Just like that, with absolutely no excuse! She couldn't resist saying anything she thought would hurt. It was the same with big things and little things—there was always a jab. When I tried to suggest she should do her fair share of the household chores, she said, 'I know I'm not very good at housework, Rose, but then it's so easy for you—you're not the intellectual type.' " Mrs. White lit a cigarette with fingers that trembled slightly.

Andrew said, "Don't upset yourself, darling—it's past history. But you see, Easterbrook, how it all rankles. And it wasn't just us. Look at what's happened to Jane. If ever a child was driven crazy by its mother, Jane's that child. She's been through hell. Do you know, my sister once sat in that chair where you're sitting now and said, with a self-satisfied smile on her face, 'Of course, I think we're all a bit sadistic, don't you?' I may say she'd brought up the subject herself—it was the kind of thing she loved talking about. And she added, 'I know *I* am, I just can't help it sometimes.' She couldn't, either. Remember the 'tiger in the cupboard,' Rose?"

"What was that?" asked Max.

"Oh, something Hilda told us herself. Apparently, when Jane was small, Hilda used to go and tuck her up, and she would sometimes make a growling noise and say to the child, 'I think there's a tiger in the cupboard.' Can you beat it? 'Of course,' said Hilda, 'it was only teasing. I just wanted to see whether I could make her cry or not.' I told Hilda she ought to be locked up, but she just smiled in a superior way. Honestly, I could hardly keep my hands off her. And then there was that thing about the poison, Rose, when they were staying with us. Do you remember?"

"Jane had an influenza cold," explained Mrs. White. "Hilda took her up a cup of something hot at bedtime, but Jane refused to drink it, and I had to take it up instead. Jane was crying and she said, 'Mummy wants to poison me.' "

"Good Lord," said Max, "that's really horrifying."

"There was nothing in it, of course," said Andrew, quickly. "Just a child's imagination, but it did show there was something pretty wrong. Obviously, her mother had frightened her. . . . And then look at Jane's education. That child needs encouragement, but Hilda always contrived to make her feel inadequate. I've heard her say in front of my own children—*and* Jane, 'Of course, Jane doesn't get very good reports, do you, dear?' Jane would look down at her plate and mumble something, and then the wretched woman would say brightly to me, 'But then, we can't help it if she's not as clever as your children, can we?' Bah—it makes me sick to think of it."

"I'm rather surprised that you could bear to have her in the house," said Max.

"Surprised? My dear Easterbrook, I couldn't keep her away. I mean it. God knows, I'm not a weakling, but she was too much for me." Andrew's face was hard. "She simply didn't understand the word no. I tell you, man, there was only one effective way of dealing with her."

"What was that?"

"The way she's been dealt with! What's the good of mincing words? It's my profound conviction that whoever put Hilda's head in that gas oven has done the world an inestimable service, and if I can shake him by the hand before they hang him, I will!"

"Andrew!" said Mrs. White. Her face was pale.

Andrew mopped his forehead. "I'm sorry, darling, I oughtn't to have said that. It was going too far, I suppose." He looked at Max with some embarrassment. "Sorry, Easterbrook—let's have another drink."

There was a moment's painful silence while Andrew poured out three stiff tots of whiskey. Presently Max said quietly, "How much do you think George knew—I mean about all the things you've been telling me tonight?"

Andrew considered. "I should say not much. I don't know what Hilda said to him when they were alone, of course, but I can't believe he'd have stood for it all if he'd realized. I often wanted to have a heart-to-heart talk with him, but I never did. I didn't know it was all going to end in tragedy, and, after all, it's a pretty serious thing to come between a man and his wife—particularly when the wife's your sister."

"That's true, of course," agreed Max.

"The main question now," said Andrew, "is what we can do for George—if anything."

"There's only one thing we can do for George," said Max, "and that's to find the man who is really responsible. Can't you help? Weren't there *any* men in Hilda's life besides George?"

Andrew shook his head. "I'd swear there weren't. Not during the past twenty years, anyway, and nobody would keep a murder on ice all that time."

"They might," said Max. "I doubt if you yourself will be able to talk coolly about Hilda in twenty years' time."

"You've got something there," said Andrew, with a grin.

"What did Mrs. Lambert do with herself while you were away in Burma—six years, you said, didn't you? That's a long time, and they would be important years in a girl's life—from nineteen to twenty-five. Didn't she ever talk about them?"

"Did she, Rose? I can't remember. I know she dabbled in various things. Didn't she have a shot at teaching or something?"

"Yes, she did," said Mrs. White. "She took an external degree, and then she tried teaching, but she soon gave it up. After that she tried secretarial work, I think, but she kept getting the sack. I remember how she smiled when she told me. And then, I think, she took an art course."

"She wasn't much good at anything, actually," said Andrew. "I suppose that's why she gathered George up in such a hurry."

"Well," said Max, "we've just got to get a line on those six years." A thought occurred to him. "I suppose your parents aren't still alive?"

"No," said Andrew, "they died within six months of each other, soon after Hilda got married."

"There must be somebody who remembers her. Who was that school friend she stayed with during the war?"

"I've no idea," said Andrew. "Do you know, Rose?"

Mrs. White shook her head. "Her first name was Mary. I don't think I ever knew her surname."

Max sighed. "It's unbelievable that we shouldn't be able to

fill the gap. It looks as though I'll have to go and scout around. . . . You say Hilda was quite attractive. She must have had an affair or two during those six years. Can't you remember a single thing—a single person? Didn't anyone ever want to marry her?"

"They probably had too much sense," said Andrew. "Wait a minute, though. I believe there *was* somebody . . . Yes, I remember now. She told me when I came back. A fellow with an extraordinary name had proposed to her, and she joked about it. He was a lot older than she was. Now, what *was* his name— Rose, I must have told you. He was a local builder or something and a sidesman in the chapel. Fascinating discussions on Moody and Sankey they must have had!"

"I remember," said Mrs. White, suddenly. "It was Rumble. Hilda said she could never have borne being married to a man with a name like that."

"That's it," cried Andrew. "Rumble it was. Mr. Rumble, the builder. I dare say, Easterbrook, if you go to Laxted, in Surrey, you'll find him without any trouble—if he's still alive. These chaps don't usually move about much. And he could probably put you on to some other people."

"I'll go there tomorrow," said Max.

❧ SEVEN ❧

NEXT DAY Max hired a car and drove himself out into Surrey in search of Mr. Rumble. Running him to earth proved surprisingly easy. A large sign in front of a timber yard in the main street of the village read W. H. RUMBLE, BUILDER AND CONTRACTOR. Inquiries in the office revealed that Mr. Rumble had recently retired from active business and was living in a house he had built for himself near by on a slope of the downs.

Following the directions he'd been given, Max turned up a chalky road gouged out of the smooth bosom of the downland. For more than a mile he traveled between rows of staring, semi-detached villas. Finally he reached the entrance to the Rumble residence, which stood on its own beyond the villas in the shelter of a ring of trees. A pair of pretentious wrought-iron gates stood open, and Max drove straight in, parking his car beside a flashy limousine which was being polished by a uniformed chauffeur. The view from the drive was superb, but the formal garden, with its many crazy-paving paths leading from a sundial, was a work of geometry rather than of art. The house itself was an incredible hotch-potch of turrets, battlements, and gables. Mr. Rumble evidently had money, but it was less clear that he had taste.

In answer to Max's ring the door was opened by a fluttering, gray-haired little woman, whom he took to be the housekeeper.

"Is Mr. Rumble at home?" Max asked. "My name is Easterbrook. He isn't expecting me, I'm afraid."

"Will you come in, please," said the woman in a scared little voice. She disappeared into one of the rooms, and presently Rumble himself emerged.

"Good morning, Mr. Rumble," said Max. "I wonder if you could spare me a few minutes?"

"I expect so," said Mr. Rumble, running a keen business eye quickly up and down his visitor. "Come in—come in." He had a deep bass voice, famous for its reverberating amens and praise-the-Lords, and his manner was hearty. Max followed him into the sitting room, where a thin-faced, thin-lipped woman of forty or so was standing by the fire.

"This is my fiancée, Miss Coates," said Rumble, unexpectedly. He beamed affectionately at the woman. "We are to be married next week."

"In that case you must be very busy," said Max, a little uncomfortably.

"Not at all," boomed Mr. Rumble. He was an elderly man—well over sixty, Max judged—with a large head as hairless and shiny as a billiard ball, and close-shaven rubicund cheeks with slightly pendulous jowls. A gold watch chain hung across his ample waistcoat. He looked prosperous and smug. Max could imagine him moving with conscious piety from pew to pew in watchful pursuit of the collection plate.

"Anyhow," said Max, "I won't take up much of your time." He glanced doubtfully at Miss Coates. "I wonder if perhaps . . ."

"You can speak up," said Rumble, encouragingly. "My fiancée won't mind, will you, Mabel?" He gave her another intimate smile, and Max feared for a moment that he was going to chuck her under the chin. "Mabel was my confidential secretary for many years."

"It's rather a delicate matter," said Max. "I think if you don't mind . . ."

"Have it your own way," said Rumble. "We shan't be long, my dear—there are some chocolates on the piano. Come into the study, Mr. Easterbrook."

Max followed him into a large, gloomy room paneled in oak

and lined with hundreds of expensively bound books. A grand-father clock ticked sonorously in a corner. The room looked unused and smelled of new leather and furniture polish.

"Make yourself comfortable," said Rumble, heartily. "Now then, what can I do for you?"

"It's about a woman whom I believe you once knew as Hilda White," said Max, watching the builder's pale, shrewd eyes.

Rumble, who had relaxed in his chair and was gently patting his paunch, sat up straight as though he had been accused of breaking into the vestry. "Bless my soul!" he said. There could be no doubt about his astonishment. "Hilda White! My word, that takes me back a long time. What about her?"

"You remember her, then?"

"Indeed, yes. How is she?"

"She's dead, I'm afraid."

"Oh, dear me! Dead, eh? Well, well, I'm sorry to hear that." He seemed interested and slightly puzzled but not particularly upset. He gazed thoughtfully out of the window, and the work-ing of the rusty wheels of memory was almost as audible as the ticking of the clock. "Why, she couldn't have been more than forty," he said.

"She didn't die naturally," Max explained. "She was mur-dered."

Rumble stared as though he hadn't heard correctly. "*Mur-dered?*"

"I'm afraid so."

Rumble looked very solemn. "I can hardly believe it. Hilda White murdered! How *very* shocking. Who—how did it hap-pen?"

"The police think her husband did it. He's been arrested. I thought perhaps you might have seen a report in the papers."

Rumble slowly wagged his head, and his jowls quivered like jelly. "I don't read such things. I only see the *Telegraph* and the *Methodist Recorder*." He still looked a little bewildered. "How do *you* come into this? You're not the police, are you?"

"No," said Max. He watched carefully for some sign of

relief but saw nothing except curiosity. "I'm a friend of the husband. Hilda married a man named George Lambert."

"Lambert?—that's right, yes. I remember hearing that name."

"I'm trying," said Max, "to find out something about Hilda White's earlier years—before she married Lambert. I'm doing it in a purely personal capacity."

"What made you come to me?" asked Rumble.

"Hilda's brother, Andrew White, remembered you. He had an idea that you'd known her in connection with church affairs."

"That's quite true," said Rumble. "We were both active in the church. I was superintendent of the Sunday school, and Hilda taught one of the younger classes for some time. Oh, yes, she was a great help. She was also most valuable in the Band of Hope."

"I suppose you knew her pretty well," said Max, feeling his way.

"I think I may say we were good friends. We were brought together by our devotional work on many occasions."

"Was she an attractive girl?"

Rumble's eyes glowed reminiscently. "She was pleasant to look at, yes. She had—how shall I describe it—a dewy innocence."

Max smiled. "It must have been a pleasure to know her in those days." He looked questioningly at Mr. Rumble, hoping for spontaneous confidences. As none were forthcoming, he said, "Andrew White had an idea that you once thought of marrying Hilda. I don't want to appear prying . . ."

Rumble waved away Max's disclaimer. "I don't mind telling you at all. I *was* hopeful at one time that Hilda would consent to become Mrs. Rumble. I felt that it would be a suitable match. We had both lived all our lives in nonconformity. I could offer her a comfortable home and an assured future. Yes, I was hopeful."

"But it didn't come to anything?"

Mr. Rumble sighed. "Alas, I could offer her everything but youth." He stroked his smooth skull, reflectively. "There was, of course, a great difference in age. I pointed out to Hilda the attractions of a life of joint service, but her youth would not be denied. She refused me. I was disappointed, but I could understand her point of view. I accepted her decision without complaint. I dedicated myself to the church and tried to forget her."

"I take it you succeeded," said Max.

"Oh, yes, indeed. I married soon afterward. My dear wife died only last year."

"I see," said Max, gravely. There was a moment of tactful silence. "I suppose you saw a good deal of Hilda before she declined your proposal?"

"As I say, we were brought together. There were many happy moments provided by our common faith—the brief but pleasant exchanges after service, the little contacts in Sunday school, the long hours of the annual children's treat. I think I may say I neglected no opportunities. If stalls had to be arranged for a sale of work, or lemonade prepared for one of our social evenings, I was always to be found by her side. When I could not be with her, I worshiped from afar."

Max nodded sympathetically. "Many of these contacts were of a rather superficial nature, I suppose. Did you ever get to know her really well? Did you go out with her at all?"

Rumble looked a little surprised. "Naturally, we never went anywhere *alone*. I should have hesitated to suggest such a thing. Hilda's parents were God-fearing people—Christians of the old school—and Hilda herself was not a flighty girl—far from it. She was a serious-minded and home-loving girl. No, Mr. Easterbrook, I attempted no liberties. I spoke to Hilda only after I had received the blessing of her parents. When she decided that she was unable to match my affection with an equal affection of her own, our paths diverged."

"So, in fact, you never really learned much about her history or her activities outside the church? You don't know, for instance, where she went to school?"

"If I ever knew," said Rumble, "I've certainly forgotten."

"Or how she earned her living afterward?"

"Her living? I think she was once a teacher, but I have no idea where she taught. If you'd asked me these things twenty years ago, I might have known—today my recollections are very hazy. Let me see—I seem to remember hearing that she took up art."

"Yes?" said Max, encouragingly.

"She was always rather talented in that direction. She was most helpful in painting texts and posters for the Rechabites. I can see them now on the walls of the schoolroom—WINE IS A MOCKER, STRONG DRINK IS RAGING—beautifully done in old English characters." Rumble sighed. "She showed great promise, but between ourselves I think perhaps there was a worldly streak. I fear her work at the art school may have been of a less educational nature. Had she become Mrs. Rumble, I cannot help thinking she might have come to a less unhappy end."

"I suppose you don't know the name of the art school she attended?"

"I've no idea at all. I had already lost touch with her by then. I received from time to time fragmentary and possibly inaccurate reports of her activities—that was all. And, as I say, I have forgotten even what I once knew."

"Do you think there's anyone living round here who might remember more, Mr. Rumble?"

Rumble pursed his fleshy lips. "I very much doubt it. Hilda had no special friends that I can now recall. No doubt there *are* people, but—well, much water has flowed under the bridge since those days. Twenty years ago this place was little more than a hamlet—now it's a dormitory of London. I can't say the change has been altogether for the better—with a population ten times what it was, the congregation at our little bethel has steadily diminished. These are pagan days, Mr. Easterbrook."

"Surely the older members of the congregation are faithful," said Max. "Wouldn't they remember Hilda? There must be some of them about."

"A few, perhaps, but only a few. Some have died, and many have left the district. Most of the present residents are newcomers. Everywhere you'll see new houses. I myself must have built more than a thousand houses in this very neighborhood. I dare say you saw some of them as you came up—you can't miss them."

"Indeed you can't," said Max. "Well, if my chances of finding other people are slight, that makes your help all the more valuable. I suppose you don't happen to recall whether Hilda had any other suitors during the time you knew her? That's a thing you'd remember, isn't it?"

"It's so very long ago," said Rumble. "I believe I was the *first* man to propose to her. She had led a sheltered life, and I remember feeling I must be careful how I approached the subject in order not to embarrass her. After that—now let me think—I believe I did hear of someone . . ."

"Yes?" said Max, eagerly.

"I seem to remember hearing about some young man—there was talk of an engagement . . ."

"You don't mean Lambert?"

"No, no—before Lambert. Dear me, I'm afraid that's all I do remember. I'm sure I never heard his name. I have it in my mind that there was something not quite satisfactory about him. The minister mentioned it . . ."

"If you could only think of the name," said Max, earnestly. "It's of the greatest importance."

"I'm sorry. I'm quite certain I never knew it. Quite certain. I have a feeling he wasn't a local youth."

"Could I ask the minister? Is he still alive?"

"Oh no, he died a long time ago. Ten years ago, at least."

"What about the other officers of the church? Weren't any of them friends of the Whites? Mightn't they remember?"

Again Rumble shook his head. "Most of them are dead. I was by far the youngest. Let me see, I suppose the only one of the old trustees still alive is Mr. Bates—but he couldn't help you. He had a stroke last year and has practically lost his memory."

"What about Hilda's contemporaries?" Max persisted. "The other teachers in the Sunday school? Or the pupils?"

"All dispersed and scattered, Mr. Easterbrook, I'm sure. In any case, I don't recall a single name. Tell me, why is this young man so important? Surely it's not suggested that after all this time . . .?"

"It's just a shot in the dark," said Max. "There's not much else to go on."

"Isn't it, perhaps, more likely that the husband was responsible? You say the police think so. I have always found them a very sensible body of men."

"It's the obvious conclusion," said Max, "but I don't think it's the right one. That's why I've worried you with all these questions. I'm sorry to have taken up so much of your time." He got up—it was clear that Mr. Rumble had nothing more to tell. "Miss Coates will be getting restive," he said with a smile.

"*Dear* Mabel," said Rumble. "She is looking forward very much to becoming the mistress of Treetops. A most affectionate nature—she'll be a great comfort in my declining years. Well, goodbye, Mr. Easterbrook. I'm truly shocked at your news. Truly shocked. If there's anything more I can do . . ."

"If you happen to remember the name of the man," said Max, "or of anyone who might know about him, I'd be grateful if you would get in touch with me at the Lavenham Hotel. Goodbye."

Max drove to the bottom of the hill, parked the car by the roadside, and sat pensively at the wheel, wondering what to do next.

Nothing useful had emerged from his talk with Rumble except the possible existence of another boy friend, and that wasn't very helpful unless he could get hold of the name. It was conceivable that if there'd been an official engagement, the local papers of twenty years ago might have announced the fact, but the task of wading through innumerable files of old newspapers would be stupendous. And even if Max discovered the name of the man, that didn't mean he'd find the man himself. He might have been killed in the war; he might be living in

Manchester; he might have emigrated to New Zealand. It might mean months of inquiry. There just wasn't time.

That was the trouble—time. Max hadn't a doubt that, if he went on with his questioning, he would find something in the end. All round this quiet suburb, whatever Rumble might say, there must still be tenuous threads leading back to Hilda and her life here as a girl. In villages everyone gossiped—there *must* be people who still remembered. Little by little, no doubt, it would be possible to reconstruct her life at school, her early jobs, her personal relationships. But how slow and uncertain it would be! And even when the early period was covered, there would still be the whole of her married life to investigate.

Max felt his spirits droop as he contemplated the field of research. Hit-and-miss inquiries by one man couldn't possibly cover the ground in time. This wasn't a job for a single individual at all—it was a job for a vast machine such as the police alone possessed. If only the inspector could be persuaded to undertake it! At least there could be no harm in trying to see him again— he might be interested to hear about Rumble, anyway. A talk with Haines, Max decided, could hardly be less productive than sporadic questions in Surrey. Resolutely he headed the car for London.

Inspector Haines tapped the dottle from his pipe and swung his chair round toward the door as Max entered. His expression was sardonic.

"Well, Mr. Easterbrook, this *is* a pleasure," he said.

Max looked at him suspiciously. "I hope you mean that."

"Indeed I do. I need a little relaxation. How's the crystal ball?"

Max said, "May I sit down?"

"Of course." The inspector carefully blew through the stem of his pipe. "Well, what's on your mind?"

"Inspector, I think I owe you an apology."

Haines leaned back and regarded him with interest. "I see. So you've called to tell me that you think our policemen are wonderful. That's most gratifying."

"I've called to tell you that I did less than justice to you personally, Inspector, and I'm sorry. Mind you, I think you might just as well have told me that you'd already begun to make inquiries about Mrs. Lambert."

"Oh, you do? What *is* your rank in the police force, Mr. Easterbrook—it's just slipped my memory for the moment."

Max laughed. "All right, Inspector, I know I've asked for it."

"Oh, I don't blame you," said Haines. "If I had a friend in jail charged with murder, I should probably do just the same as you did. And if you were a policeman, you would do the same as I did. Anyway, I take it from your apology—which I provisionally accept—that you've been over some of the ground I covered."

"A good deal of it, yes."

"And what are your conclusions?"

"My main conclusion is that there's still a lot more ground to cover."

Haines smiled benevolently. "Ah, so that's it. Well, we shall be happy to place a posse of uniformed officers at your personal disposal whenever you say the word."

"I wish to God you wouldn't treat me as though I were a comic turn, Inspector. It may all seem quite amusing to you, but I'm hanged if it does to me."

"You have a knack of provoking me," said Haines. "However, if you've anything constructive to say, I'll try to give it my serious attention."

"When you and I last talked, Inspector," said Max, earnestly, "we had some reason to believe that Mrs. Lambert was a mild and pleasant woman and that no one except Lambert had a motive for murdering her. We know now that we were mistaken."

Haines didn't say anything.

"In fact," Max went on, "she was a pretty dreadful woman,

and any number of people might have wanted to murder her."

"Who, for instance?"

"Almost everyone she came in contact with. People seem to have been unanimous in disliking her—Jane, Challoner, Lucy the nurse, Mrs. Lambert's brother, his wife . . ."

Haines said, "It's not a very imposing list, do you think? Jane couldn't have done it—she was safely in the hospital. I take it you're not accusing the medical superintendent? If the nurse did it, it could only have been in collusion with Lambert, and anyway, she has an alibi. White was on the train from Birmingham. His wife, it appears, spent the relevant part of the evening with a friend. Now where's your list?"

"I'm not suggesting that any one of these people *did* it," said Max. "All I'm saying is that if they could have felt as strongly as they obviously did, other people might have felt the same way. Isn't that so?"

"*What* other people?" asked the patient Haines.

"I don't know what people," said Max, irritably. "They need looking for, and only the police can do it. They exist all right. I'm sure they do."

"I see," said Haines. "You provide a haystack, you hope there's a needle, and Scotland Yard does the searching. Very pretty!"

"It isn't as bad as that. There *are* other people in the picture besides those you know about. If you probed enough, you'd find them. For instance, George Lambert wasn't the only man in Hilda Lambert's life. I saw an old friend of hers this morning—a builder named Rumble who once wanted to marry her."

"You get about, don't you?" said the inspector, pleasantly. "*When* did he want to marry her?"

"About twenty years ago."

"You should have been an archeologist," said Haines.

"It's easy to jeer" said Max, "but how do *you* know this chap Rumble didn't kill Mrs. Lambert?"

"Why should he?"

Max shrugged. "He's a wealthy old boy with a religious bent.

Perhaps—well, perhaps she was trying to blackmail him. Stranger things have happened."

"You're not serious?"

"Not about that, perhaps—I haven't any evidence, if that's what you mean. I'm merely trying to convince you that there may well be other 'possibles' besides Lambert and that they ought to be investigated. You could at least ask the fellow where he was on the night of the murder."

The inspector took a pencil and made a note. "All right, I will," he said. "Where does he live?"

"At Laxted, in Surrey." Encouraged, Max went on. "My point is that one thing leads to another and that inquiry is worth while. Rumble isn't the only man who was keen on Hilda. He told me this morning that she had another boy friend before she married Lambert."

"Oh, and who is this new suspect?"

Max shifted in his chair. "I don't know. It should be possible to find out, but how can I do it singlehanded? I spent the whole of this morning simply going out to see Rumble. In two or three weeks Lambert will be tried. There just isn't time for one person to make all the necessary inquiries."

"There isn't time for the Yard to make them, either. Why don't you employ private detectives if you're so anxious to dig up the past?"

"There still wouldn't be time. It's a tremendous undertaking."

"Now there I agree with you," said Haines. "That's precisely the trouble. I can see what's in your mind, Mr. Easterbrook. You want the pages of Mrs. Lambert's past life turned over and examined, leaf by leaf, from the time she was about nineteen until the day she was killed. You want that examination to go on until a genuine suspect pops out of the pages."

"Exactly," said Max.

"Well, I tell you flatly that it can't be done. We're detectives, not historians. It would take us months to do the job thoroughly. You know, we've been over all this already. I told you the last time I saw you that we have to draw the line somewhere. It was obviously necessary that I should make certain inquiries about Mrs. Lambert, and I did so. But that's as far as I can go unless I have a very much better reason for continuing than I've got at present. You want this probe because you've already ruled out Lambert on the strength of a personal liking for him. You can't expect us to do the same."

"I'm not asking you to rule him out," said Max. "All I'm asking is that you should make quite sure there's no alternative."

"In the circumstances," said Haines, "you're asking for the moon. If there were the slightest reason to believe that Mrs. Lambert's death *could* be traced back to something in her life that we don't know about, it would be our duty to search—and we'd do it. But there isn't the vestige of one. This alternative suspect of yours exists only in your imagination—there's not the tiniest scrap of evidence to suggest that there ever was such a person. We can't take valuable men off vital jobs and put them to work chasing shadows. Come, Mr. Easterbrook, be sensible. You're letting your feelings run away with you."

"Couldn't you at least advertise for people who knew Hilda Lambert?"

"And hope that the murderer would communicate with us?"

"No, hope that someone would communicate with you who could put you on the track."

"We've no grounds for such a step. We can't throw away public money like that. Why don't *you* advertise? This is a job for the defense, not for the police. We'd do it if we thought George Lambert was innocent, as I told you before, but we don't think he is."

Max was silent.

"My advice to you, Mr. Easterbrook," Haines went on kindly, "is to give Lambert such personal comfort as you can and to leave the rest to the defense counsel and the due process of the law. It's no good being obstinate. Surely, you must see for yourself that all the things you've found out about Mrs. Lambert in the past few days enormously strengthen the case against Lambert?"

"I don't agree at all," said Max, stubbornly.

"No? You said yourself that she was—what was your expression—a pretty dreadful woman. If she was—and I'm not denying it— who would know that better than her husband? Who would feel it as strongly as her husband. I can imagine that the provocation was considerable. I think it's as plain as daylight that, after living with her for twenty years, Lambert just couldn't stand the sight of her any longer. He had this nurse, Lucy, in the background, and he deliberately got rid of a wife he disliked and freed himself to marry the girl."

"Well, I suppose there's no point in arguing about it any more," said Max, wearily. "The case is strong—I grant you that. But in my view it rests on a psychological impossibility—a total misreading of Lambert's character. It presupposes that he consciously hated his wife, and I don't believe he did. He doesn't act that way."

"For a man used to handling men," said Haines, "you're remarkably credulous."

"It isn't credulous to trust one's judgment," said Max. "You've piled up a tremendous weight of circumstantial evidence and you're trying to pretend that all the pieces fit, but you must know that one of the pieces doesn't fit, and you're just hammering it into place. I think you're making a fearful mistake. You're going to destroy an innocent man and ruin God knows how many lives —all because you're so damned complacent about the evidence you've got that you won't take the trouble to look further. All right, I'll have to get along as well as I can on my own. I'll find out all there is to know about that woman if it takes me a year!"

"Well spoken, Mr. Easterbrook," said Haines coolly. "You're a headstrong young man, but I still wish you luck. You can be quite certain that as soon as there's anything concrete to investigate, we'll investigate it. If we get a lead, we'll follow it. But I mean a lead—not a cloud of dust that rose a quarter of a century ago! Good day, Mr. Easterbrook."

"Good *day*," growled Max.

❦ EIGHT ❦

ONCE AGAIN Max sat waiting in a visitors' room at the prison. This time he was impatient, not nervous. His fingers drummed a restless tattoo on the table as he reflected on what the inspector had said about George. Once and for all, this matter of the relationship between George and Hilda must be cleared up. It was vital.

There was nothing despondent about George's greeting when he came into the little room, but Max saw at once that the strain was beginning to tell on him. There were unaccustomed patches of white beneath his cheekbones, and a general tension that spoke of strong emotions held in check with difficulty. Max felt the old indignation surge up inside him.

George sat down. "What news, Max?" he asked, with almost pathetic eagerness. "Anything?" He searched his friend's face.

"We've made a little progress, I think," said Max, with more cheerfulness than the facts warranted. "I gather you've heard from Lucy?"

George nodded. "It was darned decent of you to see her, Max. She sent me a sweet note—I've been living on it ever since. She —she says she'll be waiting when they let me out. . . . I hope to God I can keep the appointment. Tell me honestly, do you think there's any hope?"

"Of course there is, old chap. Bags of it." Max grinned, encouragingly. "A damn sight more than there was in the ditch

that night outside Braunwald! Cheer up, it'll be all right." He
gripped George's arm reassuringly. "Did you get my letter about
Jane?"

"No—it hasn't come yet. Did you manage to see her?"

"Yes, I had half an hour with her. She's fine and she sends her
love."

· "Did she ask why I hadn't visited her?"

"Yes, but I told you'd been very busy. You needn't worry
about that—she's not feeling upset over it. Nothing stays in her
mind for long just at the moment."

"But she is improving?"

"Yes, she's making steady progress, and the doctor says she
should be out very soon. She was excited and very talkative, but
I'm told that's only a phase." Max hesitated. "Did you ever see
her like that on any of your visits?"

"No—whenever I saw her she was rather depressed and
quiet."

"That's a pity, perhaps. She never talked to you about her
mother?"

"No," said George, surprised. "Why, what's she been saying?"

"I'll tell you later. I hear they've briefed Everton."

"Yes, he's been here twice already. He's most impressive."

"A good dock-side manner?" asked Max, with a smile.

"I should think so. He's a fine-looking chap. He cheered me
up a lot, as a matter of fact. He seemed much more human than
Perkins."

"Do you know what line he's taking? What did you talk
about?"

"He asked me to tell him all the facts in my own words, as
simply as I could," said George. "When I'd finished, he said if I
could tell the story like that in court, he thought it should have
a good effect on the jury."

"Did he ask about your relations with Hilda?"

"Yes, he went into that quite a bit. He's anxious I should make it plain that there wasn't—well, that there wasn't any real trouble between Hilda and me."

Max regarded him thoughtfully. "I hope you can say it with conviction."

George was silent.

"You know, George, I wish you'd tell me about you and Hilda, right from the beginning. I realize you didn't feel like talking about her the other day, but it's terribly important you should. Why are you being so cagey? Is it chivalry or something, because if so, I think it's misplaced."

George's face clouded. "Of course it isn't chivalry," he said slowly. "It's just that—well, damn it all, a fellow doesn't always want to discuss his personal relationships, especially when the other person isn't there to put up a defense."

"Oh," said Max, "it's like that, is it? And why should Hilda have needed to defend herself? I wasn't aware that you had anything against her."

"Now don't go jumping to conclusions. I didn't say anything of the sort. I just . . ." His voice trailed off, and he stared miserably into space. "What exactly do you want to know, Max?"

"Well, how did you meet her, for instance? What was she like? How did you feel about her?"

George's face creased in thought. "I met her at the local tennis club," he said, after a pause. "I was twenty-two, and she was a bit older. She was rather striking to look at, and interesting, and somehow different from the general run of girls. She seemed to like me a good deal, and that in itself is pleasant, you know. I hadn't had much to do with women. We began to go out together, and very soon we got engaged. Hilda was keen to get married, and I hadn't anything against the idea, and in next to no time the thing was done."

"You don't make it sound exactly an impassioned affair," said Max. "Weren't you in love with her?"

George looked a bit sheepish. "I must have thought I was at the time, I suppose."

"How did it work out, anyway?"

"Oh, it wasn't too bad," said George, with no great conviction. "We got on pretty well, considering."

"Considering what?" asked Max, exasperated. "For God's sake, George, come clean! Did you enjoy her company? Did you like to hear her talk? Did she make you laugh? Did you go places together? Did you have common interests? Was she affectionate? Did she make a comfortable home for you?"

George looked glum. "I'm afraid the answer to most of those things, Max, is no. But I don't suppose it was altogether Hilda's fault. If the marriage was a mistake, it was as much a mistake for her as for me."

"How do you mean, a mistake for her?" asked Max. "The marriage was of her making, wasn't it? It sounds to me as though she wanted a husband, and any husband would do."

"You may be right," admitted George. "In fact, that would explain a good deal. You see, before our marriage she'd appeared to be keen on many of the things I liked—pictures and music and walking—even architecture. But after we were married, she showed no interest in these things at all. Or in anything else much, for that matter. She became quite wrapped up in herself, and she always seemed tired. At least, she was if I ever suggested doing anything or going anywhere. It was the same when friends came. She didn't bother to dress herself up for them or even make proper preparations. And somehow she always managed to put their backs up. They stopped coming after a while."

"How did you feel about it all?"

"I was a bit worried at first," said George. He seemed to be getting over his reticence. "I thought she might not be feeling well, and I wanted her to see a doctor. Then it dawned on me that she just wasn't interested. She wouldn't take any trouble over the home and our life together, because it didn't matter to her at all. It upset me when I realized that, and for a time I was pretty miserable. Then Jane was born, and, of course, that altered the whole situation. Whatever I'd felt about things, I'd just got to make the best of them now. And I must say that Hilda took an interest in the child. In fact, she concentrated on her to the exclusion of everything else. I didn't mind that; I thought it was a good thing. I had my work and my own friends. At least it was a peaceful existence," he added with a wry smile.

"It sounds perfectly bloody to me," said Max. "Didn't you ever want to break it up?"

"It did cross my mind once or twice before Jane was born," said George, "but not after. It wasn't the kid's fault if her mother and I didn't exactly hit it off. It might have been different if there'd ever been any rows, but there weren't. Jane always seemed fairly happy, until recently anyway, and I didn't want to do anything to make her feel unhappy. She always turned to her mother, and Hilda seemed devoted to her. At the same time Jane and I were good friends. I couldn't have broken that up. I couldn't have let Jane be tossed about between separated, squabbling parents. It was much better to put up with things. . . . Then there was Hilda herself. She wasn't the sort of woman who could go off and get a job and live an independent life. I felt a responsibility for her. For better or worse I'd brought the family into being, such as it was, and I'd got to keep it going. Perhaps I'm old-fashioned—perhaps I took the path of least resistance. But I know that I'd do the same again."

Max looked at his friend with something like awe. It was a damned shame that loyalty should have led an affectionate chap like George into such sterile paths, but the quality had to be respected.

"How did Hilda behave to you, personally?" he asked curiously.

George flushed. "Oh, she was a bit aggravating sometimes, but it was just her way."

"Well, I think you've had a raw deal," said Max, feelingly. "And you've behaved a lot more considerately than I would have done. I'm glad you've told me all this, George—you've no idea what a relief it is to know just what you really felt about Hilda.

All the same, you've been making a great mistake. You didn't really know Hilda at all."

"Oh, come, Max . . . !"

Max shook his head. "How can you possibly know what a thousand volts feels like when you've insulated yourself against it? That's what you did, you know. It's perfectly obvious that Hilda had practically no impact on you at all—but she had a hell of an impact on other people."

George looked puzzled. "What sort of impact? Why, she hardly knew anyone."

Max leaned across the table. "Look, George, I've got to talk very plainly. When I was here before, the few words you said about Hilda left me with the impression that she was a rather mild, harmless sort of woman, and that worried me. It worried me a lot. If she'd really been like that, I just couldn't see why anyone should have wanted to kill her, and someone *had* to have done, if only for your sake. So I couldn't accept the picture, and I set to work making my own inquiries about her—from people who hadn't built up a defense mechanism the way you had." He paused. "George, all the evidence I've got supports the view that your wife was an absolute pest. I'm sorry to have to say it, but that's the truth. Far from being mild and harmless, she was a selfish, venomous, dangerous woman who aroused feelings of the strongest dislike in almost everyone she met."

George was staggered by the sudden passion in Max's voice. "Surely you're exaggerating!" he said.

"I'm not, George. I'll even go further. I think Hilda was the perfect murderee—a woman specially designed by nature for a violent end . . . ! Look, it'll take a little time, but I'll simply have to tell you some of the things I've found out."

During the next ten minutes, Max gave a summary of the conversations he had had, skillfully piecing together the fragments of evidence, emphasizing the salient points, painting a picture that he hoped would convince. George sat quite motionless, listening with contracted brows, weighing Max's words.

Once or twice he seemed on the verge of argument or protest, but Max swept on, piling fact on fact. As the story unfolded, a look of dawning realization spread slowly across George's face; and when Max began to talk of Jane, and of Hilda's relationship with Jane, he buried his head in his hands and groaned.

Max wiped the perspiration from his forehead. He hadn't enjoyed that at all.

Presently George looked up, gray-faced. "You're right, Max," he said quietly. "I've been blind and stupid, but I can see it now. She *was* like that. It's true, absolutely true."

"You could hardly have known all these things," said Max. "Don't reproach yourself. The business with the Whites happened while you were away, and Jane wasn't encouraged to confide in you. . . . I wouldn't have told you all this if it could have been avoided. You had to know, George, because the police know. The inspector has been making the same sort of inquiries as I have. If you try to give the impression in court that you got on tolerably well with Hilda, they'll say you're deliberately concealing your true attitude. They'll say you hated her, and by the time a few people have been put on the stand to talk about Hilda, the jury will have no difficulty in understanding why. *I* know you didn't, but *they'll* never believe you."

"Still," said George, "I can only tell them what I felt."

"It mustn't come to that. We've got to find the murderer—there's absolutely no other way. Now, look, George, let's be systematic about this. I want all the information you can give me. We'll divide Hilda's life into three parts—before she met you; from the time she married you up to the time that Jane was taken to the hospital; and the few weeks since Jane left home. In one of those periods something *must* have happened that was the cause of an unknown person killing her. That's our axiom. Now what about the first period? She must have talked to you about her life before she met you. Can you remember anything at all about it that struck you as unusual? Can you recall anything significant?"

George, still a little shaken, made an effort to cast his mind back across the gulf of twenty years. "Actually," he said, "she led a very uneventful life. She lived at home until she married, and. her people kept a close eye on her. There were no opportunities at all for starting any dramatic train of events, I shouldn't have thought."

"Let's assume there were," said Max. "I want some contacts. What about the schools she attended, and the one she taught at?"

"I don't remember their names," said George, "but they were all near her home. I should think the local education people would be able to help there."

"Perhaps so. What about school friends? There was a Mary somebody."

"That's right—Mary Easton. Hilda wrote to me about her when I was abroad—told me she was going to stay with her. She lived at a place called Long Combe."

"I may look her up," said Max. "No one else you know of?"

George shook his head. "No one she talked to me about."

"Can you tell me anything about her jobs? The Whites had an idea she did some secretarial work at one time. Did she ever talk about that?"

George pondered. "I believe she was at an office in Redhill for a while, but I'm blessed if I remember where."

"What about the art school she went to? Where was that, do you know?"

"It was in London—she may have mentioned the actual name, but if so I've forgotten it. She never talked about it much—I don't think it was a very successful experiment."

"I must try to get a line on the place," said Max. "It sounds a more promising field of inquiry than the Band of Hope, at any rate. . . . Now, then, George, what about her early love affairs. I'm sure she chattered to you about her old flames."

George smiled. "I don't seem to remember they amounted to

much. Let me see, there *was* one fellow who wanted to marry her—now what was his name?"

"You mean Mr. Rumble?"

George looked a little surprised. "Rumble, that's right. But he cut no ice—Hilda used to laugh about him."

"You don't think that he could have cropped up in her life again after she married you?"

"Hardly. I think I'd have known. Anyway, Rumble was a most respectable old boy—a pillar of the church, and all that."

"I've met him," said Max. "He's a smooth hypocrite with too much money and a taste for women twenty years his junior. *I* wouldn't rule him out. Was there anyone else besides Rumble?"

"Not that I know of," said George.

"Think carefully. I'm told there was a chap she was keen on just before she married you."

"Oh?" George looked startled. "That's certainly news to me. She never mentioned him."

"You're sure?"

"Quite sure. After all, that's the sort of thing one would remember."

Max agreed. "It's interesting," he said, thoughtfully, "that she should have told you about the old buffer. she didn't take seriously, but not about the young man she did. Rumble thought she was actually engaged to the fellow."

"Really? Well, she certainly kept it dark. There was never a hint of him. Anyway, whoever he was, he's probably forgotten all about her by now."

"He'd be somebody to follow up," said Max. "One contact may lead to another—we've so little to go on, we simply can't afford to neglect anyone. Well, what about the second period—the years of your marriage?"

"All I can say about that," said George slowly, "is that if Hilda had any sort of secret life, she was remarkably skillful in the way she conducted it. Obviously I don't know half as much as I thought I did, but the fact remains that, except during the war, there were precious few nights that I didn't spend under the same roof as Hilda, and as I told you, Jane was always with her."

"Didn't Jane ever visit relatives or friends?"

"Not often and never without her mother. They were practically inseparable."

Max sniffed. "The ivy on the wall." He looked at George reflectively. "You know, I find it hard to believe that Hilda had no opportunities at all in twenty years—it's a long time. She had the days to herself, if not the nights. Was there never the slightest indication of anything under the surface—no embarrassing moments over letters or telephone calls. No suggestion of anything at all?"

"Nothing like that at all," said George, emphatically.

Max sighed. "Well, what about the last period? What did Hilda do with herself after Jane was taken to the hospital?"

"As far as I know," said George, "she carried on much as usual."

"Didn't she get out and see people? She must have felt at a loose end. It was a good opportunity."

"She never said that she'd been anywhere or seen anyone. She might have done, of course, but it all comes back to the same old thing—she hardly knew anyone. Her contacts never lasted."

Max dug in his memory for some buried detail. "Jane mentioned some woman—what was her name, now? Stephanie. Who was she?"

"Stephanie?" George looked blank. "I've no idea. I never heard of her."

"Jane said something about Hilda having talked to a Stephanie who was something to do with publishing. Quite recently, I gathered."

"Jane may have imagined it. I certainly don't know anything about it."

"Oh, well, that's something else to inquire into." Max got up. "There's plenty to be going on with, anyway. I'd better get to work."

"I'm afraid I haven't been a lot of help to you," said George.

"Not a great deal, perhaps," Max admitted, "but now you've begun to delve, you may recall something that'll really be useful. Concentrate on it, there's a good chap. You'll be surprised what you can remember."

"I'll try," said George. "It'll help to pass the time."

Max gripped his hand. "And don't worry," he said. "You'll keep that appointment."

❧ NINE ❧

STEPHANIE FRANKS leaned back in her swivel chair and stared out into the quiet square. Once a fashionable residential area, its tall, narrow houses now lent dignity to a few of the more select London publishers, lawyers, and learned societies. A restful outlook, certainly, but she wasn't sure that at twenty-six she needed so much rest.

Her gaze returned to the room, caught the reflection of her pale blond hair in the big mirror over the fireplace—"like a barley field with the sun on it," Alec had said. Trust a painter to get his details right.

With difficulty she gave her mind to the peevish gnatlike voice at her side. "But *why* this extraordinary delay?" it was saying. "Can't you make the printers understand the importance of this work?"

Stephanie turned limpid eyes on the bent figure seated by her desk. Sheer habit, she reflected, for he was certainly no longer susceptible to feminine charm.

"I know it must all seem dreadfully slow, Professor," she said, "but there are so many bottlenecks. The binders are worse than the printers now. However, things may be better by the time your book reaches that stage." She glanced down at the pile of galley proofs in front of her. "There's just one other thing before you go. Would you mind looking at this paragraph I've marked? It seemed to me there was some ambiguity." Blandly she watched

124

the professor as he put on his spectacles and read through the paragraph, muttering the words to himself and pulling at his wispy gray beard. "Perfectly clear," he announced presently. "A model of lucidity."

"If you're satisfied, of course . . ." murmured Stephanie, reaching for the galley.

"All it requires is intelligent reading," said the professor, testily. He mumbled through the passage again. "However, if you think the slow-witted will be unable to distinguish between women and camels without the help of a comma, I've no objection."

"Thank you, Professor," said Stephanie, sweetly. "And I'll write to those people about the quotations. Goodbye. I'll let you know when publication date is fixed."

The door had hardly closed behind the professor when it burst open again, and a young man came in with the dust jacket of a novel in his hand. " 'Morning, Stephanie," he said, cheerfully, eying the slender ankles just visible beneath the desk. He caught her lingering smile. "And what are you looking so amused about?"

"Only old Hubbard," said Stephanie, extracting a cigarette from a small silver case and flicking on a lighter with practiced fingers. "I always thought men of science were impervious to the passage of time, but he's in a terrible hurry. He takes seven years to write a book and wants it published in a matter of days. What have you got there, Mike?"

"It's the cover for the new Ballington thriller. Like it?"

Stephanie surveyed it through a cloud of smoke. "M'm. Lush, isn't it? Yes, I like it."

"Good—I thought you would." Mike glanced round the scantily furnished room. "What does it feel like to have an office of your own?"

"It's wonderful," said Stephanie. "I'm thrilled to bits. I'm wondering if I can squeeze a carpet out of Amos. You won't know this room when I've put up some pictures and had some more shelves made."

Mike strolled over to the window and looked out at the bare trees. "Not a bad view," he said.

"I think it'll be rather pleasant in summer," said Stephanie.

Mike hung about. "We miss you out there."

"You can always come and call on me," said Stephanie, graciously.

"That's not the same. Well, I suppose I'd better be going." He still hovered. "You wouldn't have lunch with me, would you?"

"I'm sorry, Mike."

"Is it that chap again?"

Stephanie gave a tolerant little laugh. "Why don't you find yourself a vivacious brunette, Mike? Someone about eighteen. I'm old enough to be your mother."

"What, at twenty-six?"

Stephanie picked up the galley. "Run along, Mike, there's a good boy. I've got work to do."

Mike went out gloomily and Amos Frame came in. The head. of the firm was self-consciously handsome, with shining silver hair. "Hello, Stephanie," he said with easy friendliness, clearing a small space on the corner of her desk so that he could sit down. "Well, did you manage to read the Beetons' book?"

Stephanie nodded. "I read it last night. I like it better than the last one, but it needs pruning."

"I know," said Frame. "They think up first-rate plots and then ruin them with padding. Beeton *will* have his purple passages."

"I thought his wife was going to be ruthless," said Stephanie. "Wasn't that the idea of the collaboration?"

Amos Frame laughed. "He puts extra bits in, now, for her to cut out, so they're back where they were. Still, I think they'll produce a winner one day if they don't squabble too much. By the way, did you see John Shaw?"

"Yes, he brought the translations along. They're quite pleasant."

"Are the songs very Russian?"

"Oh, very. He's called the collection *Suliko*—'Suliko' is the title of a charming little thing about a man who's searching everywhere for his sweetheart's grave!"

The publisher chuckled. "Just right for our spring list, eh?" He shook his head thoughtfully. "I don't believe there's any market for that stuff now, but I'd like to have a look at it." He got up. "Doing anything for lunch, Stephanie? Johnson's meeting me at the Savoy Grill at one—perhaps you'd care to join us?"

"I'm sorry—I have a date," said Stephanie, demurely.

"Pity. You're looking very smart today. New suit?"

"It's the one you admired yesterday," said Stephanie.

"Oh," said Frame, calmly. "Then it must be the blouse." He gazed thoughtfully around. "How do you like the room?"

"Very nice, thank you. I'm going to have a patent lock put on it."

Frame grinned. "All right, I'll leave you to your galleys." He stopped at the door and stood for a moment, looking back at her. "Executive at work! Most decorative!"

Stephanie made a little face as the door closed and took up her pencil. In a few moments she was completely immersed in the text. Her eyes moved rapidly from line to line, and her face wore a look of deep concentration.

Then the telephone rang. A frown crossed Stephanie's forehead, and she lifted the receiver with her pencil still poised in the other hand. "Yes?" she said.

"Is that Miss Stephanie Franks?" asked a man's voice.

"Yes, this is Stephanie Franks speaking. Who is that?"

"You don't know me," came the voice, "but please don't ring off—it's very important. Are you the Stephanie who knew Mrs. Hilda Lambert?"

Stephanie's face lost its abstracted air, and her voice took on an edge. "Hilda Lambert?" she said. "Why, who *are* you? Why do you want to know?"

"My name's Easterbrook. It's rather a long story, and I'm afraid I can't explain on the phone." The voice, normally an attractive one, Stephanie judged, sounded rather agitated. "You *are* the right Stephanie, I suppose?"

"Well," said Stephanie, dubiously, "I knew Hilda Lambert slightly, if that's what you mean."

"Thank God for that!" There was a sigh of relief over the wire. "Listen," Max went on urgently, "I wonder if you'd do me a great favor? Can I see you for a few minutes? There's something I want to ask you."

"If it's about Mrs. Lambert," said Stephanie, "I don't think I want to talk about her. And in any case, I knew her only very superficially."

"But it's a matter of life and death. Honestly. Can I call at your office? Or would you lunch or dine or something?"

Stephanie considered. It always went against the grain for her to say no to anything new, in case it should turn out to be interesting. Her curiosity was aroused, and the voice really was an extremely pleasant one. She said, with the right amount of condescension, "I'll meet you for a drink this evening, if that will do."

There was an explosion of gratitude. "Thanks enormously. Where shall it be? Anywhere you say."

Stephanie thought. "Do you know the King's Head on Chelsea Embankment? Let's say there at six-thirty, shall we?"

"Fine," said Max. "How shall I recognize you, by the way?"

"Well, I'm fair, and I shall be wearing a camel's-hair coat." Sudden temptation overcame her. "I have a slight stoop, and I wear pince-nez."

"I don't mind if you have horns and a tail," said Max. "I *can* rely on you, can't I?"

"After that," said Stephanie, "nothing would keep me away."

At twenty minutes to seven that evening Stephanie pushed open the door of the saloon bar at the King's Head and surveyed the throng of people drinking there. In the far corner a tall, hatless man in a tweed overcoat stood holding a tankard and watching the door. His eyes met Stephanie's, noted the shoulder-length fair hair, swept over the loose camel's-hair coat. He gave a tentative smile and put down his tankard.

Stephanie walked across to him. "Are you my mysterious caller?" she asked. "I'm Stephanie Franks."

"Yes, I'm Max Easterbrook," said the man. "It was wonderful of you to come. What would you like to drink?"

"May I have a Martini, please?—dry." As Max turned to the counter, Stephanie gave him a careful inspection. The high cheekbones, the rather ascetic face, the sweep of brown hair, and the slim figure added up, she thought, to something very presentable.

Max picked up the drinks. "Shall we sit down?"

"Yes, over by the fire. It's my favorite seat."

"You sound as though you're a regular."

"It's my local. I live quite near." They sat down on the horse-hair bench.

"Well, cheers!" said Max, smiling across at her. "Tell me, where are the pince-nez?"

"I only wear them at work," said Stephanie.

"No marks of pince-nez," said Max.

"I wear them very infrequently."

"I see. No stoop, either."

"I'm trying to cure it."

Max laughed. For the first time since his arrival in London he was beginning to feel cheerful. He had always rather liked sophisticated women, and this girl certainly betrayed no immaturity or awkwardness. His glance took in the sleek perfection of her hair style, with the silver-blond hair falling almost straight to the shoulders before curling slightly under; the discreetly tinted fingernails; the expensive casualness of her clothes. Elegance and poise!—and yet, as the large gray eyes sparkled with amusement, Max thought he could detect the *gamine* behind the careful façade.

"It was a great stroke of luck finding you," he said.

"Was it so very difficult?"

"Difficult! All I knew was your first name. Do you know how many publishers there are in London?"

"Dozens, of course."

"In the work of reference I consulted," said Max, "there were four hundred and twenty-one names, and just under a hundred were 'possibles.' When I spoke to you, I had already telephoned forty-eight of them."

"You poor man," said Stephanie. "No wonder you sounded relieved. It must have been awkward, asking at all those places for someone whose name you didn't know."

"You have the gift of understatement," said Max. "I never want to speak to another switchboard girl in my life. I said to one of them, 'Can you tell me if you have a woman called Stephanie in your office?' She said, 'Stephanie who?' I said, 'I don't mind—any Stephanie will do,' and she said, 'Wolf!' and hung up."

"I don't believe a word of it," said Stephanie, laughing.

"It's quite true," Max assured her. "And I *did* make forty-eight calls. Thank goodness you have an unusual name. I was most relieved when *your* girl said, 'You must mean our Miss Franks.'"

"Hundreds of years ago," said Stephanie, "some forebear of mine married a Hungarian princess, and the name's been in the family on and off ever since. At least, that's my story. Now tell me, what do you want to know?"

"Let me get some more drinks first," said Max. "The same again?"

"Please."

The bar was filling up. Max collected a Martini and a pint of beer and rejoined Stephanie on the bench. The mild hubbub was like a curtain of privacy around them.

"Now," he said, "Hilda Lambert. You know what's happened to her, do you?"

"You mean that she's been murdered? Yes, I read it in the paper. How do *you* come into the picture?"

"I know her husband," said Max.

"The murderer?"

"The police think he is. I don't."

Stephanie's extremely articulate eyebrows shot up. "Don't say you're being a Sherlock Holmes!"

"A very inferior one, I'm afraid. I haven't got very far. What I'm trying to do is to talk to all the people who knew Hilda Lambert in the hope that somewhere I shall find a clue to the real murderer."

"That sounds rather sinister," said Stephanie. "May I ask if I'm the first?"

Max gave a hollow laugh. "You're about the thirty-first," he said. "I've been at it a week. I've already talked to everyone I could think of who was associated with her. Husband, relations, acquaintances. . . . During the past three days I've visited her old school and discussed her with two mistresses. I've seen the headmaster at a school where she used to work, and I've made a trip to Somerset to interview an old friend."

Stephanie regarded him with respect. "You're really taking it seriously, aren't you? Have you made any progress?"

"Not much, I'm afraid. I've learned a good deal about Hilda, of course, but nothing that seems to bear materially on the case. I rang you as a last resort."

Stephanie wondered if his face always had those rather attractive hollows under the cheekbones or if he'd worried himself thin. She said, "It must be disheartening when you don't get results."

"It is," said Max. "And very tiring. Imagine—for nearly a week I've been nothing but an amiable stooge prompting people to unburden themselves by timely interjections of 'Really!' 'You don't say!' and 'Well, I never!' "

A smile hovered round Stephanie's mouth.

"I wouldn't mind so much," said Max, "but I'm afraid my friend is going to be hanged."

The smile faded.

"It must be frightful for you," said Stephanie. "If I can help by telling you anything about that detestable woman, I'll be glad to."

Max put down his tankard abruptly. "Now that's interesting," he said. "So you feel that way, too? There seems to be complete unanimity on the subject."

"I'm not surprised," said Stephanie. "She was quite insufferable." She began to search in her handbag for a cigarette.

"Allow me," said Max, holding out his case. He lit the cigarette for her. "How did you come to meet her?"

"It was at an art exhibition about five weeks ago. A friend of mine, Alec Forbes, was giving a one-man show in the West End, and I went along with him one lunchtime. Hilda Lambert was there. Apparently she'd known Alec years and years ago, and when she saw the announcement in the paper, she'd decided to come into town to see his pictures. . . . Why are you staring?"

"I'm sorry," said Max. "What, exactly, happened?"

"It was most embarrassing," said Stephanie, looking cross. "I was standing with Alec in front of one of the pictures and making admiring noises in the hope that somebody would buy it, when a large, gushing woman came sailing across to us, pushed past me, and said, 'Hello, Alec, don't you remember me?' Alec looked at her for a moment, without recognizing her, and then he said, 'Christ Almighty, it's Hilda White!' "

Max grinned. "In tones of affection?"

"Far from it. It wasn't very polite, of course, but he was so surprised. He introduced us—I remember Hilda reminded him rather archly that her name was now Lambert—and then for the next fifteen minutes she absolutely monopolized him. She ruined my lunchtime."

Max made a sympathetic sound. "I take it that Forbes is a boy friend of yours?"

"What makes you think I go in for quantity?" asked Stephanie.

"I beg your pardon," said Max, with a disarming smile. "It was clumsily put. May I say 'your boy friend?'"

"If you must use that horrible phrase," conceded Stephanie. "We go around together."

Max said, "You're sure you don't mind my asking these questions?"

"I'll tell you when you overstep the mark."

"Fair enough. Well, what did Forbes say about Hilda afterward?"

"It was really rather funny," said Stephanie, not without complacency. "He was very fed up. I could tell from Hilda's behavior that there'd been something between them once, but she looked such a frump with her frightful hair and shapeless clothes and no make-up that he hated admitting it. Am I being bitchy? I suppose I am. I said I didn't mind how many affairs he'd had in the past, but that I couldn't help being appalled by his taste. Then he began to tell me how good-looking she'd been twenty years ago—when I was six, if you please!—and we had a flaming row. Poor old Alec!" She smiled reminiscently. "It was all my fault, of course."

"Did he tell you how he met her in the first place?" asked Max.

"No. I meant to ask him, but I didn't in the end. It seemed too cruel. It *must* be rather humiliating when your past turns up after twenty years looking like the char. He did tell me that he'd known her for only a very short time and that it hadn't amounted to much."

"I think they must have met at an art school," said Max, thoughtfully. "So that's really all about you and Hilda?"

Stephanie gave him a wry glance. "Oh, not by any means. I wish it had been. By the way, did *you* know her?"

"I never met her," said Max. "But I feel as though I've lived with her all my life."

"You don't look as though you have!" said Stephanie. "I only asked because if you never met her, I don't see how you can possibly understand what she was like."

"No?" Max smiled quizzically. "All right, let me guess what happened next. She invited you and Alex to visit her!"

Stephanie laughed. "You get five for trying. It was almost as bad as that. Naturally, I thought I'd seen the last of her, but to my astonishment she phoned me at the office the next day and suggested going out to tea, of all things. I was stupid to have told her where I worked, of course, but she asked me a direct question and I didn't have time to think. She was frightfully inquisitive."

"Like me," said Max.

"Yes," said Stephanie, "like you—but in a different way. Anyhow, when she rang, I was as unresponsive as I could be without being positively rude. It was awfully difficult—she was so persistent. She said she thought it would be nice if we could get to know each other." Stephanie gave a little shudder. "There was something about her that made my skin crawl."

"Please go on," said Max. He caught what he felt was a reproving glance and smiled sheepishly. "I'm sorry," he said. "That was the stooge speaking."

"Well, keep him quiet," said Stephanie. "Where was I? Oh, yes—anyway, I told her I couldn't come for tea, and I thought I'd managed to shake her off. But about a week later she rang me at my flat—the number's in the book—and asked if she could come along for half an hour. Apparently, her daughter had been taken to the hospital, and she had time to spare—so she said. She kept telling me how much she wanted to see me, and her voice was so full of—oh, I don't know—innuendo and *meaning*—that I thought whatever it was she had on her mind, the sooner I saw her and got it over the better. So she came along, and it was absolutely dreadful." Stephanie reached for a cigarette. "Do you think I deserve another drink?"

"We both do," said Max. "Don't let anyone pinch my place."

When he'd brought the drinks, Stephanie went on. "Everything about her irritated me from the moment she came in. There was something horribly *jaunty* about her. She seemed to assume that I was grateful to her for coming. She flopped into the best chair as a matter of right, as though she'd known me for years, and looked at me with a sort of lofty complacency that made me prickle. I don't know how it happened, but I was on the defensive right from the beginning. I offered her a drink, but she said she never touched alcohol, and she watched me drink mine as though I were indulging in some fascinating new vice." Stephanie wriggled.

"What had she come for?" asked the stooge. "To talk about Alec?"

"Of course, but she didn't at first. She knew that I knew she was going to talk about Alec. She knew I felt horribly uncomfortable, and she enjoyed it. She admired the flat and said she'd always thought it must be 'jolly' to be a bachelor girl—ugh!— and she said she liked the way I did my hair and how lucky I was to have a natural wave—as though *she* knew—and then she looked me up and down, as though I were a gown on a mannequin, and said in a patronizing tone that I was probably just the sort of wife that Alec needed. Damned nerve! She was jumping to conclusions anyway. I ought to have thrown her out there and then."

"Why didn't you?"

"I don't know," said Stephanie, slowly. "I just don't know. I've been surprised at myself ever since. If you'd met her, you'd understand. I couldn't come to grips with her. I suppose she saw by the look on my face that I was going to explode, and before I could get a word out, she said, 'How pretty you are, dear,' in such an ingratiating manner that it was impossible to work up a healthy quarrel. I had to stand up while she talked— I simply couldn't sit still. I felt like rushing out of the flat and leaving her to it. Presently she worked her way back to Alec. She said of course, I was much younger than Alec, but she supposed it was a good thing that girls should marry experienced men—Alec hadn't been experienced when *she* knew him! I couldn't stand it. I told her that I wouldn't talk about Alec and that, anyway, I'd got to go out to dinner. She looked at me earnestly and said she did hope I wasn't jealous—jealous! of her!—because, after all, she and Alec were such old friends. She couldn't have been more beastly if she'd still been Alec's mistress. Then she began to say nasty things about him in the nicest sort of way. She said he was a very good painter, wasn't he, and she'd always thought it such a pity that he drank so much and led such an unsteady life, especially with women, but then of course artists were like that. . . . And then, do you know what I did? I had a glass of gin and orange in my hand, and I threw the contents right at her."

"No!" said Max, incredulously. "What on earth happened then?"

Stephanie said ruefully, "It wasn't funny at all. She looked at me as a child might look if you suddenly smacked it for nothing, and then she burst into tears. I felt so humiliated, and I had to clear up the mess, and she got more and more emotional. I've never felt so miserable and degraded in my life. She said that the last thing she'd wanted to do was to upset my happiness, and that she oughtn't to have gone to Alec's show. She said that she'd always vowed that she wouldn't see Alec again until they were both fifty and beyond temptation! She thought she'd better go and see Alec and explain that she hadn't meant to butt in. Somehow that was typical of the whole visit. Everything that woman *said* sounded well meaning, and yet everything she *did* made things worse." Stephanie looked across at Max with troubled eyes, and she flushed. "I'm talking too much. It must be the Martinis."

"Don't worry," said Max. "You'd be surprised how familiar all this is. I suppose you told Alec all about it?"

"Yes, I had to. She'd upset me so much that I couldn't keep it to myself. Alec was furious about her, of course, and I was so angry that I'm afraid I took it out on him. You know how beastly women can be. Alec has a frightful temper when he's roused, and I'm no angel. We said some dreadful things to each other. It was horrible—and we'd always got on so well until Hilda made her appearance."

"And was that the end of the matter?"

"Well, not quite," said Stephanie. "She rang me again— twice—and wanted to see me. She promised that if we could meet again, she wouldn't say anything to upset me. She kept saying she was feeling lonely with her child in the hospital."

Max nodded thoughtfully. "Yes, that must have left a vacuum. With Jane out of the way, you got the full force of her attention."

"I suppose so. Anyway, she begged and wheedled so much that I think I might have weakened, but when I told Alec he got mad again and said I was a fool and that Hilda would pester me into a breakdown if I went on seeing her. I knew that was sensible, so the second time she rang I said flatly that I didn't want to see her again, ever. She said wouldn't I see her just *once* more, and I put her off by saying I'd think about it. A few days afterward I read in the paper that her husband had murdered her—and I must say I hardly blamed him."

"But he didn't," said Max.

Stephanie looked at him sharply. "Oh, no," she said, "I forgot. You must be very fond of him to go to all this trouble."

"George has been to a good bit of trouble on my account in his time," said Max. "I'd do anything to help him out of the mess he's in. And it's not just that, either. I've spent a large part of my life—professionally, I mean—trying to understand people, and I think I understand both George and Hilda. It may be vanity, but I don't want to be proved wrong." He smiled. "Besides, there's a policeman—an inspector—who has rather put me in my place. I'd love to see him bite the dust."

"You ought to be able to write us a good thriller when it's all over," said Stephanie. "Well, I hope you're satisfied with the way you've turned me inside out? I shall probably hate the thought of you tomorrow. It must be that understanding, sympathetic, interested manner of yours."

Max grinned. "Oh, that's only the stooge. I'm hard as nails."

Stephanie appraised him carefully. "Yes, I think you might be. What are you going to do next?"

"I suppose I ought to have a word with your Alec," said Max, "and see if he can give me a lead."

"Oh!" said Stephanie. She bit her lip. "Damn, what a fool I was to talk to you."

"I'll try not to stir things up too much," said Max.

Stephanie's left eyebrow went up. "*You're* rather complacent, too, aren't you? It might do you good to talk to Alec. You won't find him as easy to deal with as I've been. He'll probably tell you to go to hell."

"I can but try," said Max, modestly. "Where can I find him?"

"He has a studio in South Heath Close, Hampstead, and he's usually working there in the mornings. I warn you he'll be livid when he knows I've been talking to you."

"We'll see," said Max. "Tell me, how does he rank as an artist? I seem to know his name."

"He could be first-class," said Stephanie, with a slight shrug. "He is, actually, but he's a bit erratic. 'Wild,' as that wretched woman would have said."

"I wonder just how much of a sedative you are?" said Max, with a smile.

Stephanie gathered up her bag and gloves. "I have a feeling, Mr. Easterbrook, that you're finally about to overstep the mark." She looked at her watch. "Heavens, it's a quarter to eight."

"Yes, the time's flown," said Max. "I trust you won't be late for dinner?"

"I shall be too late to cook my sausages."

"Oh, come! You mean you haven't a date?"

"With my sausages, yes."

"Then please, *please* dine with me. We can get a cab and be at the Café Royal in ten minutes."

Stephanie hesitated. "I'd like to. I'm ravenous."

"Let's go, then," said Max. "It'll be the first civilized thing I've done since I got back to England."

"On one condition," said Stephanie, "not another word about Hilda!"

"Good God, no," cried Max. "I want to enjoy my dinner. We'll forget all our troubles and confine our conversation to mutual admiration, shall we?"

Stephanie laughed. "That suits me," she said.

❧ TEN ❧

ALEC FORBES stood at the window of his studio in Hampstead and glowered out at the dank November fog. What an unspeakable climate! Some Japanese painter, he recalled, had come to England especially to study the colors in the native fog. Well, he could have them. For his part, Alec would welcome nothing so much as the opportunity to escape from the winter grayness.

Gloomily he turned away and resumed his slow pacing up and down the spacious studio. At one end, under the big window, the paraphernalia of the artist was scattered untidily round an easel. The other end was comfortably furnished as a sitting room. A wooden staircase led up to a gallery which ran right round the walls, widening at one end to accommodate a tiny bedroom and bathroom. Alec had always liked the place, which perfectly suited his needs, but today he hated everything about it. If only, he thought again, he could get away to some place where there was color and warmth and peace of mind. Madeira would be pleasant. Or the Greek islands. Or anywhere with sea and guaranteed sunshine. And Stephanie, of course.

He paused for a moment to watch the milkman. A gray wraith, the clatter of a bottle on the step, a cheerful whistle. How the devil could anyone want to whistle on a day like this?

Alec filled his heavy, curved pipe and continued his restless walk. Ten paces up to the beautiful model of a windjammer in full sail; ten paces back to the Laocoön in green stone. A power-

ful piece of work—too powerful. Tortured writhing! A fine
piece, but not comfortable to have about.

Past the easel with its unfinished canvas, past the scatter of
brushes and paints and rags, past the model throne with its
purple draping, past the stack of unframed pictures, past the
too-ambitious portrait of Stephanie. . . .

He stopped in front of it. Not a masterpiece by any means,
but what pleasure it had given him—given both of them—in
those carefree summer days. The coloring wasn't right, but he'd
caught the expression. Caught it perfectly—the gaiety, the
slight impudence. God, those days seemed a million years away!

He sank heavily into one of the easy chairs, the picture of
dejection. It was going to be a hell of a day again. He couldn't
go on like this—his nerves wouldn't stand it. If only the fog
would clear, he would walk across the Heath to the Spaniards,
little though he liked walking. But it didn't look like clearing.
There was the whiskey in the cupboard, thank goodness, but
he'd made some fool promise to Stephanie about laying off the
whiskey. Well, she should be here with him. Why the hell did
she want to go on working in an office day after day? Like a
typist. Why didn't she marry him and live with him. . . ?

He sat glooming for a while, then went to the telephone and
rang her up. He heard, resentfully, the sounds of someone
talking to her as she lifted the receiver. As usual, she seemed
perfectly in harmony with the world. "Hello, darling," she said.
"Nice of you to ring. How are you?"

"I'm lousy," said Alec. He could almost see the smile fading
and felt a tinge of malicious pleasure. "I'm lousy and lonely.
Why don't we go to Cannes?"

"To where?"

"To the Riviera, to Madeira, anywhere you like."

"Sorry," said Stephanie. "Can't today—I've got some stuff to
send off to the printers."

"Stop fooling, Stephanie—I'm serious. Let's get married and
go away."

"Why the terrific hurry, suddenly?" asked Stephanie, with a laugh.

"It's not sudden," said Alec. "I'm tired of asking you. You know damned well you'll marry me in the end, so why all this coyness?"

"Shush! Office hours, office ears!"

"To hell with that—let them listen. Think of it, Stephanie—blue water, white sand, ruffles of foam around the rocks, swimming all day, picnicking just when we feel like it. Wouldn't you like that? Come on, leave the office. Let them all stew."

"Don't be silly, Alec. You know I can't leave my job just like that. There are things I'm responsible for, and *I* take them seriously even if you don't. Besides, you know we'd be quarreling even before we'd decided where to go. Let's meet for dinner tonight and go on somewhere to dance. How's that for a substitute?"

"Rotten. This place has got on my nerves. I tell you, I must have sunshine. I must get away."

"Well, darling, it's only another day before the weekend, and we'll drive out somewhere—if you've got any petrol."

"That's no good—I must get out of England."

"If you feel as restless as all that, why *don't* you? Take a holiday. I won't run away."

There was a smothered curse at the other end of the line. "You know I can't go alone. Stephanie, please give in your notice, and let me fix up for us to get married."

"I'm not going to discuss this over the phone," said Stephanie, firmly. "What are you doing this morning?"

"Not a thing. I can't work—it's hopeless."

"Why don't you come in for lunch?"

"Because I'm sick of filthy streets and bad restaurants. And I'm sick of the studio, too. I *must* get away. I can't stand the smell of dead leaves. Stephanie, I don't believe you give a damn about me."

"You know that's not true."

"It is. If you did, you wouldn't put the job first and me afterward. Well, I suppose I'll have to get drunk."

"Oh Alec, don't do that," pleaded Stephanie. "You know you'll feel like hell afterward." She suddenly remembered Max. "And anyway, I think someone's going to call on you this morning."

"Who for heaven's sake?"

"You'll see. Alec, I *must* ring off. There's somebody waiting to see me. I'll meet you at six-thirty at the usual place—all right?"

"I suppose so," said Alec, wretchedly. He threw the telephone receiver back onto its rest and sat scowling. What was all the mystery about? He didn't want any callers—none at all. He walked to a cupboard built into the wall, took out a full bottle of whiskey and a glass, and poured himself two fingers, which he drank neat.

Blast Stephanie, he thought. Why couldn't he ever quite bring her to say yes. It was that damned streak of the big business executive—it made her too independent. And yet, he supposed, that was partly why she was so attractive. She'd miss him if he went off to France and stayed there—and serve her right! He *could* go. He went to the bureau and took his passport from a drawer. Yes, it still had a year to run. He tried to visualize himself packing, catching a plane, drinking coffee in a boulevard restaurant—alone. He flung the passport back and slammed the drawer. Not without Stephanie. It wouldn't be any good without her. Even London, with Stephanie, was better than any other place without.

He sat with his head in his hands, gazing into space. What a fool he'd been to talk to her like that on the telephone! She'd be thinking him an inconsiderate swine—and so he was. He was always trying to pick a quarrel with her these days, always grumbling, always demanding. Well, it was her fault for putting on this governess act with him. Still, suppose she got fed up with him—suppose she began to dislike him! He couldn't bear that—he *couldn't* lose Stephanie. . . .

A sharp click at the front gate made him jump. He went to the window and saw the gray figure of a man hesitating in the path. Alec impatiently flung open one of the double doors that led into the garden. "This way!" he shouted.

Max emerged from the fog, peering. "Are you Alec Forbes?" he asked.

"I am," said Alec, standing in the doorway. He gave Max an unfriendly stare. "What do you want?"

"I should be glad if you could spare me a few minutes," said Max, mildly. "May I come in?"

Alec made way ungraciously and slammed the door behind them with his foot. "Well," he said, aggressively, "what is it?"

Max looked at the artist for a moment without replying. A big chap—he must weigh nearly sixteen stone. He'd make two of Max. Impressive, with that saturnine face. Black hair, black eyebrows, black looks! Good features, though, and sensitive. Better reserve judgment.

"My name's Easterbrook," he said and hesitated. Alec's expression was uncompromisingly hostile. Still, there was no point in beating about the bush. "I wanted to talk to you about Hilda Lambert."

For ten seconds Alec stood absolutely motionless, staring. He might have been one of his own plaster figures. Then he said, "Oh!" in an unexpectedly matter-of-fact tone, and the tension eased. "In that case, we'd better sit down."

"Thank you," said Max, much relieved. He sank into a chair. "I'm a friend of Hilda Lambert's husband," he said, wondering how many more times he'd have to use those words.

"Yes?" said Alec and went on staring. Max took out a cigarette and lit it with deliberation. This wasn't going to be at all easy. "I think you knew her," he said, attempting a friendly smile.

"I did, yes." Alec's expression was still wooden and unhelpful.

"Perhaps I'd better explain," said Max. "I'm not just being a busybody. You know about the murder, of course. My interest in the matter is on behalf of my friend George Lambert. I don't believe he killed his wife, and I'm trying to find out who did.

I can only hope to succeed if I know something about *her*. I'm talking to people who knew her. You're one of the people."

"Very lucid," said Alec. For the first time his dark eyes switched from Max's face, and he seemed to reflect for a moment. Then he said, "I don't know that I can help you, but I will if I can."

"That's very good of you," said Max. Perhaps things weren't going to be so difficult after all.

"If I seemed unfriendly," continued Alec, "it was because I couldn't see how you knew about me and Hilda. But I suppose my fiancée told you?"

"Hilda Lambert's daughter spoke about her mother knowing a Miss Franks. I got in touch with Miss Franks yesterday, and she told me how she happened to meet Hilda." Max smiled. "It was quite simple."

"What exactly did Stephanie tell you?"

"Well, she told me how the two of you ran into Hilda at your exhibition."

"Yes."

"And she told me, of course, that you and Hilda had been old friends. She talked mainly about her own attitude to Hilda. I gathered there had been some unpleasantness."

Alec frowned. "Why the devil can't women hold their tongues? It was a purely private matter."

"You must blame me," said Max. "I'm afraid I pressed her."

"Well, I resent your interference."

"I can see your point of view," said Max. "But I had to do it."

Alec still looked annoyed. "It was a trivial episode," he said, "but one which I'd prefer to forget, all the same. How would *you* like to have your personal affairs discussed with a stranger?"

"I shouldn't," said Max. "I assure you I wouldn't dream of this intrusion if a man's life weren't at stake."

Alec's irritation seemed to evaporate. "From what I've read," he said, "the evidence is pretty thin. I wouldn't have thought he was in any danger."

"No? You're the first person I've met who takes that view.

I wish I could agree with you. I think there's a distinct possibility that he'll be hanged."

"They can't hang a man if there's a doubt," said Alec.

"That's just the point. If we can't find an alternative suspect, I don't think there'll be a doubt—not in the minds of the jury."

Alec knocked out his pipe noisily and began to fill it again. "Well, *you've* studied the case—you ought to know. Anyhow, what do you want me to tell you?"

"Tell me this," said Max. "If you believed George Lambert innocent and wanted to find the real murderer, where would *you* start? From what you knew of Hilda, is there anything that suggests itself?"

Alec drew steadily on his pipe for a few seconds. "That's a tall order, isn't it? I wouldn't know where to begin."

"You can't think of anything in her early life that might have started a train of action ending in murder?"

"Well, marriage itself has been known to do that," said Alec, with a grin.

Max seized his opportunity. "You were engaged to her yourself, weren't you?"

"Engaged? Good heavens, no—it wasn't as serious as that. It was only a mild affair. You know how it is at twenty—trial and error. I happened to meet her at an art school, and we went around together for a while. It was very innocent—there was absolutely nothing to it."

Max raised his eyebrows. "I imagined it went deeper than that. Miss Franks had the impression . . ."

"She doesn't know anything about it," said Alec, his face dark with anger again. "Women always jump to conclusions. I tell you there was nothing in it at all."

"So you really didn't know her very well?" pursued Max.

"Quite superficially. It was a passing affair—adolescent stuff."

"I thought Hilda was twenty-three or twenty-four."

"Well, you know what I mean."

"I'm not quite sure that I do," said Max. "Adolescent stuff is usually pretty fierce."

Alec glared. "Well, this wasn't," he said shortly.

"What brought you together?" asked Max. "Art?"

Alec smiled, and Max saw how attractive his face could be. "No, not art," he said. "She hadn't a clue."

"What, then? Was she very good-looking?"

Alec shrugged. "She wasn't a glamour girl, but she had something."

"An interesting woman?"

"Unusual, I'd say. She wore bizarre clothes, and she was rather striking to look at."

"She seems to have been quite a personality," commented Max.

"Oh, she was a personality, all right," said Alec, with some bitterness. "Her ideas were as odd as her clothes. Bloody silly ideas."

"Not a woman you'd feel neutral about, evidently," said Max.

Alec was on the defensive again. "I wouldn't say that."

"Did you never even think of marrying her?"

"I might have toyed with the idea in a casual sort of way," said Alec, loftily. "I can hardly remember now."

"What about *her*—did she want to marry you?"

"No, as a matter of fact, she didn't," said Alec. "She thought I wasn't steady, and she was damned right!"

"At least she wasn't indifferent," said Max. "Anyhow, don't women usually find that sort of thing attractive?"

"I don't know about that," said Alec. "Their parents don't."

"Oh—you knew her parents?"

Alec threw Max a sharp glance. "I met them once or twice—family supper parties, you know."

"Not as a prospective son-in-law?"

"Hell, no. They didn't take to me, and the feeling was mutual. Look—can't we skip all this? I'm sure it's not getting you anywhere."

"Perhaps not," agreed Max. "I'm disappointed you didn't know her better. What happened in the end—did you have a row or something?"

"A row? What was there to row about? No, we just drifted apart."

"It seems to have been a most colorless episode," said Max.

"That's just what I've been telling you. Placid, platonic, and brief."

"H'm," murmured Max, doubtfully, looking at Alec's arrogant face. "Did you keep in touch at all afterward?"

Alec shook his head. "No, I lost sight of her completely. I never saw or heard a word about her again until we met a month ago at my show. That's why it was such a surprise running into her. Like seeing a ghost."

"The ghost of your past, eh? I gather from Miss Franks that Hilda was extremely pleased to meet you again."

Alec frowned. "Hilda was always romantic."

"Do you think she might have been nursing a secret passion all those years?"

Alec gave a self-conscious laugh. "I shouldn't think so for a moment."

"Anyway," said Max, "there isn't much doubt that you were well rid of her. She seems to have become an extremely unpleasant woman, as you yourself discovered."

"I don't know that I'd go as far as that," said Alec, guardedly. "She was pleasant enough in the old days, and I don't suppose she'd changed a great deal."

Max looked at him in astonishment. "What about all this trouble she gave after your meeting? I've only had an outline from Miss Franks, but it sounded pretty frightful."

"I don't think too much should be made of that," said Alec. "Women always scrap. She and Stephanie got across each other, and Stephanie blew up. Quite natural in the circumstances."

"Six of one and half a dozen of the other, in fact," said Max, hardly able to believe his ears.

Alec stirred uncomfortably. "I wouldn't put it quite like that, but I do think Stephanie lost her head a bit."

"I thought it was you who got extremely angry," said Max.

Again, Alec's eyes flickered with annoyance. "I was a bit fed up, perhaps. I hate getting involved in female squabbles. But I certainly didn't lose any sleep over it."

"I doubt if Miss Franks could say the same."

"Oh, she exaggerated the whole thing. There wasn't any real malice in Hilda. She was genuinely glad to see me again after such a long time, and it was unfortunate that she had such a tactless way with her, that's all. It was exasperating, perhaps, but nothing to make a song about."

"Well," said Max, "you're certainly giving me a new angle. Did you see Hilda at all after that first reunion?"

"Why should I want to do that?" asked Alec, looking blank.

Max shrugged. "It does happen. Renewing acquaintance with the past."

Alec gave a rather forced laugh. "Not me. I kept as far away from her as possible. I don't suppose for a moment that she had any designs, but I wasn't taking any chances. She'd turned into a bit of a hag, you know. Not that I was interested, one way or the other. After that passing incident of our meeting, I hardly gave her another thought."

Max sat silent for a moment. "What I find extraordinary," he said after a pause, "is that you don't feel more strongly about Hilda. The almost unanimous view is that she was poison. That's certainly what Miss Franks thinks. You, on the other hand, seem to be very tolerant."

"I simply don't see anything to be intolerant about," said Alec. "There was nothing in Hilda that I could get worked up about."

"She upset your fiancée," Max persisted. "I should have thought she was treading on your toes quite a bit."

Alec scowled. "What exactly are you getting at, Easterbrook?

Are you hinting that *I* might have had a reason for wanting her out of the way? Because that's what it sounds like."

"You have a sensitive ear," said Max. "As a matter of fact, I suppose you might be considered to have had a reason. She was being a damned nuisance to you, whatever you may say. But then, she was a nuisance to everybody." He smiled. "And I'm quite sure you've got a good alibi—everyone has."

"You've a hell of a nerve," said Alec. "I don't know why I don't throw you out."

"Now you mention it," said Max, "one of the things that has surprised me most about this interview is that you haven't already done so."

Alec's grin was touched with embarrassment. "I keep telling myself you mean well," he said. "All the same, it's going a bit far when you accuse me of bumping off a woman because my girl friend didn't get on with her very well. When *was* this murder, anyway?"

"A week ago yesterday—Wednesday."

Alec pondered. "Well, now, let me think. Wednesday. Oh, yes, I spent all the afternoon with a chap named Bradshaw—a commercial artist. He's got a studio near Sloane Square. His wife gave me tea, and I left there about six. I drove back here, had a wash, and just after half-past six I went along to the Bush and Kettle to play darts. I always play there on Wednesdays." He smiled. "How's that?"

"You have an excellent memory," said Max. "Didn't I say you'd have an alibi?"

"You can check up if you're suspicious."

"I'm no more suspicious of you than of half a dozen other people who couldn't have done it," said Max. "I'm sorry about all this, Forbes. Believe me, I'm not prying for pleasure. I loathe the whole business."

"I understand," said Alec. "I'd be the same if I had a friend in jug. I'm sure he'll be acquitted, though. I think you're wasting your time. Look, what about a drink?"

"I ought to be getting along," said Max. "It's a bit early for me, anyhow."

"Nonsense, my dear fellow. It's never too early for Scotch."

"A small one, then." Max took the glass, feeling slightly ill at ease. He gazed around the studio. "You have an attractive place here," he said politely.

"Not bad," said Alec, now quite affable. "I more or less inherited it from an uncle of mine. He painted and made money. I'm afraid I just paint."

"I understand you've quite a reputation," said Max. "I'm sorry I don't know more about the subject." He drained his glass. "Well, I must be off."

"What's your next move?" asked Alec, curiously.

"Do you know," said Max, "I haven't the slightest idea." He gave Alec a friendly nod as the artist held the door open, and walked out into the fog.

Alec stood with his hand on the doorknob for a moment. His sociable smile faded and his face darkened. He strode across to the telephone and furiously dialed Stephanie's number.

"Will you hold on, please?" said the switchboard girl. "Miss Franks is engaged."

Alec smothered a curse. "I'll ring again," he said. He never had the patience to hold on. He poured himself another whiskey, drank it, and walked twice up and down the room, nursing his frustrated anger. Then he tried the number again.

"I'm sorry, Miss Franks is still engaged," said the girl.

Alec flung down the receiver, seized his overcoat, and banged out of the studio.

Max walked slowly through the fog, frowning. It was quite true, as he had told Alec, that he really didn't know what he was going to do next. It had been a most puzzling interview. The artist's manner had been frank and friendly on the whole, yet Max was not convinced of his sincerity. That odd attitude toward Hilda—why had it been so different from Stephanie's?

A telephone box loomed out of the fog, and, on an impulse, he went in and dialed Stephanie's number. As he waited for the connection, he became conscious of an agreeable excitement.

"Yes?" said Stephanie's voice.

"It's Max Easterbrook. Remember me?"

"Oh, hello," said Stephanie, pleased. "Are you still in one piece?"

Max chuckled. "Everything went off very smoothly," he said. "I thought you'd like to know. Alec even gave me a drink."

"It's that technique of yours," said Stephanie. "Wasn't he furious with me?"

"He was a bit peeved at first, but it passed off. I didn't get much help from him, though."

"I didn't think you would," said Stephenie. "What are you going to do now?"

"I should like to take you out to lunch," said Max, promptly.

"I'm sorry—I've just fixed up."

"Oh," he said, disappointed. "Well, couldn't we meet for a few minutes afterward? Where are you lunching?"

"At the Falstaff in Fleet Street." She hesitated. "It doesn't seem very sensible."

"But it would be very nice," said Max. "Won't you? Please!"

"Well, only for a few minutes."

"Of course," said Max. "I'm entirely in your hands."

Stephanie smiled. "About half-past two, then. Goodbye."

She replaced the receiver, thoughtfully, and turned with less than her customary attentiveness to the manuscript she was reading. This Max Easterbrook was a persistent man, in a quiet and cheerful way. Persuasive—not demanding, like Alec. She hadn't really meant to see him again, but there was something very likable about him. Alec would be outrageously jealous, of course, if he knew. But after all, she *had* urged him to come into town for lunch. If he chose to be difficult . . . Stephanie shrugged and concentrated on her manuscript.

For half an hour she worked in silence. Then, just before lunchtime, the telephone rang again. It was Alec, in a foul temper. As soon as he heard Stephanie, he exploded. "What the devil did you have to talk to that fellow for?" he demanded in a thick voice.

"But I thought . . ." began Stephanie.

"You've no right to babble about my private affairs," shouted Alec.

"I didn't babble," she said, resentfully. "I told him very little about you. He's trying to get his friend out of a jam—I couldn't refuse to talk."

"You might have thought of me," said Alec. "I've had a hell of a time with him. Damned embarrassing. I just didn't know where I was."

"I don't understand," said Stephanie, baffled. "He phoned me half an hour ago and said how well you'd got on."

"I see. First you set him on to me, and then he reports back to you!"

"Don't be a fool, Alec," said Stephanie. "It wasn't like that at all. He'd have come and talked to you, anyway. What on earth's got into you?"

"Nothing's got into me. But I don't like having my affairs pried into."

"You're making a ridiculous fuss about nothing."

"You call it nothing?" cried Alec. "Why, you've put all sorts of ideas into the fellow's head. I wouldn't be surprised if he thinks I killed Hilda."

"Alec, you're a lunatic!"

"And you're a gossiping little bitch!"

"For heaven's sake, pull yourself together. I'm going to ring off."

"I shall clear out for good," yelled Alec.

"Do," said Stephanie, now in a flaming rage. "And as far as I'm concerned you certainly needn't bother to come back." She hung up.

Max, on a stool at the Falstaff bar, glanced at his watch for the third or fourth time. Then he caught the sheen of silver-blond hair as Stephanie approached and stood up with a smile. But Stephanie had no answering smile for him. "I'm sorry I can't stop after all," she said, "I'm late." She walked past him toward the door.

Max stared after her for a second or two, then caught her up. "What's the matter?" he asked with concern.

Stephanie pushed open the door, her face expressionless, and went out into the street. She stood on the curb and looked up and down for a taxi.

"You might at least tell me what I've done," said Max, ruefully. "Or will a blanket apology cover everything?"

The ghost of a smile flitted across Stephanie's face, but she continued her futile signaling. "Don't sound so innocent," she said.

"Upon my honor," said Max, "I haven't the very slightest idea what you're talking about."

Stephanie regarded him over her shoulder. "What was the point of ringing up to tell me that you and Alec got on so famously?"

Max was astonished. "It was quite true," he said, "we did."

Stephanie gave him a withering glance.

A taxi drew up. "We don't want you," said Max abstractedly to the driver.

"Yes, we do," cried Stephanie.

"No, we don't," repeated Max, firmly. He laid a detaining hand on her arm and drew her away. "Stephanie, I must know what all this is about. I swear you're making a mistake."

The taximan cast up his eyes, then drove on. Stephanie said, "It may interest you to know that Alec rang me just before lunch almost speechless with rage. He's furious with both of us and especially with me. He blamed me for everything, including getting him suspected of murder! And you say you got on well with him!"

"But, Stephanie . . ." Max was bewildered and distressed. "I'm amazed. I'd no idea he was feeling like that. He certainly didn't show it. I told you he was a little annoyed at first, but he was quite amiable afterward, and we parted on the best of terms. He seemed most cheerful."

"Then why was he so angry when he rang?" Stephanie demanded.

"I haven't the slightest idea," said Max. "Perhaps he'd just stubbed his toe."

"Don't be silly," said Stephanie. She caught a glimpse of his troubled face and the dark smudges of tiredness under his eyes. "Still, perhaps it wasn't your fault," she said, relenting a little.

Max took her arm.

"I really must go now. . . ."

"You can't go until I'm quite forgiven," he said. "Let's stroll down to the river for a moment."

"It's too cold for walking by the river."

"Nonsense—it'll help you to cool off."

Stephanie laughed and allowed him to steer her toward the Embankment. This was an odd thing to be doing, she reflected, at three o'clock on a winter afternoon when she ought to be working.

They crossed the Embankment and leaned over the parapet. The tide was almost full, and several tugs were coming up on the last of the flood. The sun, a dusky red ball, was half hidden by the mists that hung over the river.

Max and Stephanie watched the peaceful scene in silence, close together and very much aware of each other.

"Calm after storm," he said.

Stephanie smiled, her equanimity quite restored. "I'm sorry I was cross," she said.

Max looked down at her, and suddenly he felt very lonely.

"I suppose you're extremely fond of Alec," he said, diffidently.

Stephanie considered. "Ye-es, I suppose I am."

Max plunged recklessly on. "And are you going to marry him?"

Stephanie laughed. "That *is* the idea," she said. "At least, it's

Alec's idea. He gets extremely annoyed with me because I won't take the final step. And I really don't know why I don't. . . ."

"From what you've told me, I should imagine he's a difficult sort of man," Max ventured.

"He is, rather," she admitted. "Perhaps that's one of the reasons why I go around with him. None of the women I know could cope with Alec, and it flatters me to think I can. But he's a great dear, really. You don't know him, of course. He's very witty —quite the most entertaining man I know. And he really can paint."

"H'm." Max frowned down on the water, not impressed by the catalogue of Alec's virtues. Uppermost in his mind, now, was the thought of the artist's exceedingly odd behavior toward Stephanie and himself—for which he could find no reasonable explanation—and a sense of foreboding on Stephanie's account.

❦ ELEVEN ❦

BUSINESS IN the saloon bar of the Bush and Kettle was very slack when Max pushed open the door on the following morning. The only customers, half an hour after opening time, were two men engrossed in conversation by the fire. Joe Smith, the barman, was leaning against the counter in his shirt sleeves, scanning a paper. He looked up as Max entered and gave him a friendly nod as though glad to see another face.

"A pint of mild and bitter, please," said Max. He glanced up at the well-used dartboard, inspected the men by the fire, and then turned his attention to the barman. "Wretched day again," he said.

"Shocking," said Joe. "I dare say it'll clear later."

Max nodded. "Bad for custom, eh?"

"Never seen the place so empty at this hour," said Joe. "Folks won't come out in the fog, and you can't blame them."

"You certainly can't," said Max. "It was pretty bad here yesterday. I nearly got lost."

"You can get lost round here easy," said Joe. "Stranger, eh?"

"Yes. It took me a good half hour to find the man I was looking for. Mr. Forbes, the artist—you probably know him."

The barman laughed. "Know him! I'll say we know him. He's often in here."

"So he told me," said Max. "Care for a drink?"

"Well, that's very friendly of you," said Joe. "I'll have a Guinness if you don't mind."

The two other occupants of the bar got up and left with a nod and a "Good day."

Max said, "I gather Forbes is quite a darts player."

"One of our best," said Joe, with enthusiasm.

"Does he play often?"

"Oh, he usually has a throw when he's in," said Joe. "Wednesday's really his night, though. Every Wednesday him and a pal of his have a proper set-to. Worth watching, believe me."

"That accounts for it," said Max. "I was trying to get him on the telephone a week Wednesday—between six and seven in the evening. I couldn't get an answer. I suppose he was here."

"He must have been on his way," said the barman, wiping the counter. "He usually gets in about a quarter of seven."

"Not before?"

Joe stopped wiping and looked up curiously. "What *is* this— a ruddy quiz?"

Max leaned across the counter. "It's worth a couple of pounds to me," he said quietly, "to know exactly what time Mr. Forbes came in here a week Wednesday. Are you interested?"

The barman eyed the notes and gave a little shrug. "No harm in telling you that, not if I can remember. Now let's think—a week Wednesday. Why, of course, that was his bad night. It took him eight throws to get a double—I've never known it happen before. Sykes wiped the floor with him—Sykes is the chap he plays with. He was in great form, Sykes was—went 'round the clock' without a miss while he was waiting." Joe gave an admiring shake of the head as he recollected Mr. Sykes's virtuosity.

"Did you say while he was *waiting*?"

"That's right," said the barman. "Mr. Forbes was late that night—I remember now. I reckon it was ten past seven when he came in. Between ten and a quarter. Said something about trouble with his car."

Max looked hard at Joe. "If I were to swear to you," he said, "that Mr. Forbes was drinking in this bar at twenty minutes to seven that night, what would you say?"

Joe looked startled. "I'd say you was balmy. It was seven-ten. Anybody could tell you that. You ask Sykes if you don't believe me."

"Thank you," said Max and handed over the notes.

He walked slowly toward the studio. Unpleasant though the prospect was, it was clear that he'd have to see Alec again. He had already come to that conclusion after a sleepless night. The contradictions in the artist's attitude had to be cleared up. And in view of what he'd learned at the Bush and Kettle, a talk was now all the more necessary.

He mustn't, he told himself, start jumping to conclusions. There wasn't a scrap of solid evidence against Alec. It was true that the fellow had definitely tried to give the impression that he'd arrived at the Bush and Kettle at about six-thirty, but he'd probably be able to account for the time in some other way. It would be necessary to proceed very cautiously.

As Max pushed open the front gate of the studio, his pulse quickened. Alec wouldn't enjoy being questioned again. Now there probably *would* be a row. Max consoled himself with the thought that nothing was so revealing of character as a row.

This time there was no sign of the artist as he approached the door. It was nearly half-past eleven—surely he was up! Max rapped sharply and waited. There was no sound at all from inside. Perhaps he'd finished that bottle of whiskey and was sleeping it off. Perhaps he'd gone out to get another one. Perhaps—no, surely he wouldn't have cleared off! More likely gone up to town to lunch with Stephanie and make up their quarrel.

When a second loud knock brought no response, Max tried the studio door. Rather to his surprise it was unlocked. He put his head inside and called in a loud voice, "Are you there, Forbes?" There was still no answer. He hesitated on the threshold. Should he wait or go? Time was precious—he didn't want to waste a morning hanging about, and yet he didn't want to have to come out to Hampstead again. He would wait for a little while, anyway. Alec might be back at any moment. He would hardly have left the place unlocked if he'd gone off for the day.

For a few minutes Max sat on the arm of one of the chairs, thinking things over. It certainly looked as though Alec *could* have done it. There'd have been plenty of time for him to drive back from Finchley between half-past six, when Hilda was killed, and ten past seven, when he reached the Bush and Kettle. It couldn't be more than fifteen minutes' drive. If he'd done it, of course, his peculiar attitude during their talk would be explained.

Even if he had, though, how would it be possible to prove it? Mere unsupported suspicion of Alec wouldn't save George. There would have to be some concrete evidence. The inspector, of course, had seemed to think that once he had the suspect he'd be able to find the evidence. Before long it might be necessary to have another talk with the inspector—but not yet.

Max wished that Alec would come. It wouldn't be a pleasant meeting, and the sooner it was over the better. He got up and began to walk slowly round the studio, examining the pictures. Alec knew his stuff, there was no doubt about that. Even to an untrained eye his use of color was arresting. And that portrait of Stephanie—definitely clever. It didn't do her justice, of course— but then, nothing could.

He stopped by the easel and gazed at the unfinished canvas. The paint on it was dry and hard. So was the paint on the palette lying by. It didn't look as though Alec had been doing much work recently.

A door banged upstairs, and Max jumped. Surely Alec wasn't there after all! It might be as well to look, anyway. He climbed the wooden staircase and put his head into the tiny bedroom. Empty. The bathroom too. It must have been the bathroom door that had banged. He returned to the studio, slightly on edge. For the first time it occurred to him that waiting for a possible murderer on his own territory was not the most enjoyable of pastimes.

For some time he prowled around, aimlessly. He took a book of Da Vinci's drawings from a shelf and skimmed through them. He switched on the radio but turned it off again before it had warmed up. He picked up a sketchbook from the table and idly turned its pages. It looked as though this was where Alec tried out his ideas. Most of the drawings were mere fragments. A tree branch, part of a boat, a rock and some birds, a torso. Little anatomical studies—an arm, a thigh, another torso, crisscrossed with geometrical lines. Very technical. A man's head. Ah, this was familiar—Stephanie again. And again. Wonderful how a few lines could make a recognizable face.

Max turned a page. This looked like doodling—two sets of noughts and crosses, a spider's web, a parallelogram with the corners blocked in, a series of whorls and patterns. More heads . . . But what was this? Max stared down at the book with fascinated eyes. Slowly his mind absorbed the meaning of what he saw.

Christ!

So Alec *had* done it! Surely that was the only possible conclusion? Or was it? Could there be another explanation? It needed thinking about—but he couldn't think here. If Alec were to come back now, anything might happen. The main thing was to get the evidence away—get it out of Alec's reach.

Max slipped the sketchbook under his coat and walked swiftly to the door. No sign of Alec. He went out, softly closing the door behind him. His heart was hammering; his thoughts were in a whirl. Good old George!—there was hope for him after all. Hope for George and Lucy and Jane. A blessed thought. But it was going to be tough for Stephanie, if the sketches meant what they seemed to mean.

At the thought of Stephanie he came to a full stop. She'd hate him forever if anything happened to Alec because of him. All the same, he'd got to go through with this. After a moment's reflection he decided to show the book to Stephanie and tell her what he proposed to do. She should see the sketches herself.

Then, if there *was* some other explanation, it would be up to her to suggest it.

At six o'clock that evening he was pacing up and down outside Stephanie's Chelsea flat, waiting anxiously for her arrival. All traces of elation had vanished, and he felt horribly depressed, almost scared. Telling Stephanie was going to be dreadful—far worse than conveying the news of a sudden death.

A taxi crept out of the evening gloom and trickled to the curb opposite the turquoise front door. "Hello," said Stephanie, alighting and paying the driver before Max could reach her. "What's the trouble now?" She gave him a quick smile as she put her key in the lock. "You sounded quite worked up over the phone. Come in and tell me all about it—though what Alec will say if he arrives and finds us having a cozy chat together, I hate to think."

"I'm afraid it's not going to be a cozy chat," said Max, following her in.

At the tone of his voice, Stephanie turned. "What on earth's the matter?" she said. "Have you seen a ghost?"

"It's been rather a day," said Max.

"Well, have a drink," said Stephanie, going to a side table. "You look as though you could do with one."

"I won't have one now, Stephanie, if you don't mind," said Max. "I've got something I want you to look at."

He produced the sketchbook, and Stephanie stared at it. "Isn't that Alec's?" she said.

"Yes," said Max. He flicked over the pages quickly. "This is what I wanted to show you." He pointed to the small drawing of a head. "Do you recognize her?"

"Why, it's Hilda," said Stephanie, looking at the sketch. "It's not bad, either."

"And this one?" said Max, turning the page.

Stephanie bent closer. Her hair brushed his hand, and he was conscious of its faint perfume. "That's Hilda, too," she said. "I wonder when he did them." She turned back to the first one. "He's got that awful smile of hers perfectly."

Max said slowly, "You're quite sure they're meant to be Hilda?"

"But of course. They're unmistakable."

"That's what I thought," he said. "But I had to make certain."

"For goodness' sake," cried Stephanie, "stop looking so ridiculously solemn and tell me what all this is about."

Max took a deep breath. "All right," he said. "It's a simple point. When do you think Alec saw Hilda with her hair done like that?"

Stephanie examined the sketchbook again, frowning. "I don't know. . . ." she said. "Of course, Hilda's hair was straight, wasn't it?" She looked at him sharply. "What *are* you driving at?"

"Hilda had her hair waved on the day she was killed," said Max. "And that seems to have been the only time in her life that she ever had it done."

Stephanie looked at him, incredulously. "You're not suggesting . . . ?"

"I'm suggesting that the only time Alec could have seen Hilda with her hair like that was on the day she was killed. I'm suggesting, Stephanie, that he killed her. For your sake, I hope to God I'm wrong. But somehow I don't think I am."

Stephanie stared at him as though he'd lost his senses. "You *can't* be serious," she said.

"I've never been more serious in my life. What other explanation can there be?"

"Why, the whole thing's fantastic." She reached for a cigarette with fingers that trembled. "I don't know how you dare. Of all the flimsy evidence! Alec would never do a thing like that. Never!"

"It's natural that you should say so. . . ."

"Oh, for God's sake, stop being so damned understanding," she flared. She paced angrily up and down. "It's quite obvious what happened—he must have run into her some time during the day. After she'd been to the hairdresser's."

Max shook his head. "I'm afraid not. The charwoman mentioned to me that Hilda had been to the hairdresser's on the very afternoon that she was killed. Alec, according to his own story, spent the whole afternoon with a fellow named Bradshaw. Until six o'clock. You probably know the man, don't you?"

"Yes, of course," said Stephanie, biting her lip. "I remember now, Alec told me. Well, then . . ." She stopped, nonplussed.

"Well, then, what?"

"Oh, don't bully me. You're intolerable." She flung herself into a chair, away from him. "It's quite absurd. She probably wore her hair like that when he knew her in the old days."

"I don't think so. I've seen a picture of her when she was twenty. Her hair was straight then."

"But it's so ridiculous. After all, Alec's an artist. He draws the way other people think. He's always got a pencil in his hand. He was probably thinking how awful Hilda looked and wondering if she'd look any better with her hair waved—and those sketches just came."

"I wonder if he'll explain it like that himself," said Max, thoughtfully. "Of course, I never saw Hilda, and I don't know how accurate the likeness is. But she was photographed after she was dead. The hair in these drawings doesn't look to me like a casual invention. I rather fancy that it'll prove to be precisely similar in the police photographs."

"And what if it does?" cried Stephanie. "It'll be pure coincidence. Good heavens, you don't suppose he'd have left that book lying about if he'd killed her?"

"Why not? He probably doodled these heads almost without knowing he was doing it and promptly forgot all about them. Anyway, I don't suppose for a moment he'd realize the significance of the hair. Nobody's suggesting that he's been a skillful, calculating murderer, planning everything in detail from the beginning. He's been a clumsy novice. Why, he hasn't even got a decent alibi!"

"How do you know?"

"He told me he was playing darts at the Bush and Kettle soon after half-past six. But he wasn't."

"Then he must have been somewhere else quite innocent. He probably forgot. Is it likely that if he'd killed Hilda he'd have told you something you could prove to be untrue? He'd have had a good story ready."

"Not if he was a bungler," said Max, doggedly. "He told me because he was suddenly faced with the necessity of telling me something, and it was the best thing he could think up on the spur of the moment."

"You're twisting everything," cried Stephanie, an angry glint in her eyes. "What a fool I was ever to talk to you—what a fool! I wish he'd thrown you out."

"If he had," said Max, "I'd almost have believed in him. Instead, he put on a phony act. I practically accused him of being a liar and a murderer, and he was still quite friendly. If he'd had a clear conscience, he'd never have let me talk as I did. He may be a good painter, but he's a rotten actor. He overdid it. *You* know what he really thought. He made that clear when he rang you up."

"He was upset yesterday," said Stephanie. "We'd had a bit of a row earlier—I don't suppose he knew what he was saying. He gets frightfully depressed sometimes."

Max's face softened as he looked at her. "You're doing your best for him, but it's not good enough. He knew what he was saying. He deliberately put on an act. He lied—consciously and clumsily. Unless, of course," he added, "*you* did." He held Stephanie's gaze.

"What do you mean?"

"He told me, not once but several times, that he'd never disliked Hilda and that her behavior to you hadn't upset him in the least. He deliberately gave me to understand that the row was as much your fault as hers. Do you think that was a true account of the way he felt?"

"He was annoyed with me," said Stephanie. "He wanted us

to get married straight away, and I wouldn't. That's probably why he took Hilda's side."

"I don't believe that," said Max. "I think he denied having any grudge against Hilda because he wanted to conceal that he had a motive for killing her."

"It wasn't much of a motive," said Stephanie, scornfully. "A man can dislike a woman without wanting to kill her."

"It depends how much he dislikes her. There may have been something between Alec and Hilda that we don't know about."

"I suppose you hope there was," flashed Stephanie. "You've made up your mind about Alec, and you're determined to find something to prove that you're right. You've disliked him from the beginning, and you're letting your prejudices run away with you."

"That's not true," said Max. His face was pale and drawn. "And it's not fair. I'm not a policeman, out for his blood. My only interest is to help George Lambert. I *know* he didn't kill his wife."

"And you don't care who is accused as long as your friend gets off," cried Stephanie. The look on Max's face checked her, and she came over and sat beside him. "Max," she pleaded, taking his hand, "do stop all this nonsense. I'm sorry I said what I did. I do understand that it's George you're thinking of. But you're wrong about Alec, honestly you are. I know Alec as well as you know George. He's impulsive and temperamental and difficult, but he could never have plotted a dreadful thing like that and done it and kept it to himself. He can't hide things—he's like a child. I would have known. He'd have been miserable."

"*Wasn't* he miserable?" said Max. "Haven't you quarreled all the time since Hilda's death? Didn't you say that he hadn't been himself lately? When did he last do any work? Stephanie, you *must* face the facts."

Stephanie got up, her eyes hard again. "I'll never believe he did it," she said. "Never. I *know* you're wrong."

Max sighed. "Well, it'll be for the police to decide. God knows, I don't want to hurt you."

Stephanie swung round. "The police? You mean you're going to tell the police these crazy ideas of yours?"

"They'll have to know sometime."

"If I'd only realized what you were!" said Stephanie. "Anyway, you've no real evidence. The police won't listen to you."

"There's the sketchbook," said Max.

Stephanie whipped the book from the table. "Suppose there isn't?" she cried and began to twist and tear it with frantic fingers.

Max sprang from the settee and grasped her arms. "Stephanie, stop it," he ordered. He held her wrists. "You can't do any good."

The book fell from Stephanie's hands, and she suddenly went limp in his arms. Max had an almost irresistible impulse to kiss her, but she wrenched herself away from him and sank into a chair. She put her head on her arms and began to cry. Max, watching her with deep emotion, could think of nothing to say. He turned miserably toward the door. "I suppose I'd better go," he said. "I'm sorry if I hurt you, but I had to have the book."

Stephanie raised her head, seeming not to mind the tearstains on her cheeks. "Why did you come here at all? Why didn't you go straight to the police?"

"I wanted to talk to you," said Max. "I couldn't just go off— behind your back."

She was silent for a moment. Then she said, "Are you really going to tell them?"

"What else can I do?" He looked at her with a worried frown. "The only thing is that when they're told, the matter will be out of our hands. I almost think I'd like to talk to Alec once more first."

"Oh, yes, please do," cried Stephanie. "I'm sure he'll be able to explain. There *must* be some mistake. I'll come too."

Max was shocked. "No, Stephanie. You don't want to be in on this. It'll be terribly embarrassing—and it may be worse than that."

"Of course I shall come," said Stephanie. "What do you think I am? We'll go together."

Max looked very unhappy. "Why make things worse for yourself, Stephanie? You know Alec. There may be a fearful row. Anything can happen. You'll hate it."

"Let's go," said Stephanie, impatiently.

"Very well, if you insist. But there's just one thing. I'm going to do the talking. Somehow I'm going to get the truth. If you make things difficult for me, I shall have to ring the police. Is that clear?"

"I understand," said Stephanie.

Max tucked the sketchbook under his arm. "I think we'll drop this in at my hotel on the way," he said. "For safety."

❦ TWELVE ❦

ALEC SAT hunched over the electric fire in the studio, chewing over his predicament in a mood very near to despair.

How much worse the aftermath of murder was, he reflected, than the sudden resolve to do it or even than the deed itself. In those brief, fatal seconds, he'd thought only of deliverance. Perhaps it would have been different if he'd been quite sober. The alcohol had blunted his moral sense, his common sense. A quick temptation and a deadly execution. Violence, excitement, and fear had blinded him to consequences.

And now here he was, less than two weeks afterward, a man destroyed. Sleepless, nerves all to pieces, hating himself and hagridden by conscience. Images that wouldn't be shut out!—vivid pictures in the mind! Hilda on the floor where he had put her, sprawling, somehow obscene, going into her last poisoned sleep! Life into death—and by his hand! How *could* he have done it?

He'd never been meant for a murderer. It had been madness—madness! His conscience wasn't sufficiently calloused. He'd done an evil thing. He could never have altered his feelings for Hilda—even now, now that she was in her grave, he loathed the memory of her. But hatred, however provoked, couldn't justify what he'd done. A blow in anger, yes—but not *that*. The thought of it would haunt him for ever and ever. He groaned. No peace of mind, ever again. "Not poppy nor mandragora . . ." He'd see that sprawling body on those red tiles in the faces of friends, in

the waves that he painted, in his tankard of beer, in the very
sky. Always he'd carry it with him—the picture and the nagging
voice of guilt.

He felt lonely beyond human imagining. He was going to lose
Stephanie—he knew that now. He was going to lose her because,
though he wanted her so desperately, all his feelings for her
were curdled. All that there had been between them was spoiled.
She'd forgive him for words spoken hastily—she always did that
—but he'd say the same things again, and worse things, and go
on saying them, because his own thoughts scourged him and
drove him to bitterness and anger and hate. Never again could
there be serenity between them.

Soon she'd begin to suspect, if she didn't already. Easterbrook
would see to that. Easterbrook suspected, and he'd have talked to
her. She wouldn't want to believe—she'd try not to, but she'd
have to. Watching her would be agony. Seeing the confidence
turning to doubt, and the doubt to leaping horror in her eyes.
Watching love die, seeing her recoil. It would be unendurable.
And yet, somehow, he yearned to tell her—he *needed* to tell her.
If only for a brief moment he could have her pity—if only he
could cushion his head in her lap and hear her voice speaking
to him gently! She would never do that now. He'd forfeited the
right.

Another picture arose in Alec's mind. This chap Lambert!
Already nearly a fortnight in prison; soon to be tried for something he hadn't done; soon, perhaps, to be condemned. That was
something the imagination couldn't stand. What must Lambert
be feeling? For every anguished thought of his, for every spasm
of fear, for every moment of black despair in the long night of
the cell, Alec's was the guilt. It was true that he had always intended to give himself up if things went wrong at the trial. The
extra burden of a man's life, needlessly taken, was unthinkable.
But the waiting! The thought of this man, innocent, bewildered,
racked with uncertainty! There was his daughter, too—and the
woman, the nurse. God alone knew how many people were suf-
fering because of his silence. And when would it end? There

would be weeks still, perhaps, before the trial; and then what? A further wait till the appeal was heard, if Lambert was found guilty. Why wait? To wait was to die a thousand deaths. Far better to get it over.

To get it over? It was all very well to think that, but the resolute act was a different matter. Life was good—it wasn't an easy thing to walk into a police station and offer it up. At least, it *had* been good. Very good. Full of the freshness of spring, the unending joy of creation, the loving promise of Stephanie. But all the goodness had been cast away in five passionate, reckless minutes. If there was only a husk of life left now, why treasure it? Why not destroy it quickly and blot out the misery? Surely that would be better than the weeks of jail, the formality of a trial which could have only one end, the waiting and the waiting, the uncomforted execution? To die was not so bad, but to wait to die . . . that must be avoided at all costs.

Alec thought of death, and suddenly the love of living surged up in him. Could he not rebuild—escape and rebuild? If he could start life afresh somewhere else, perhaps in time memory would fade, and conscience cease to gnaw. Particularly if he left things right for Lambert. How could he do that? He couldn't just walk into his lawyer's office and confess to murder and expect to walk out again still free. But he could write out a confession, perhaps, and get two people to witness the signature, not the document, and leave it sealed with the lawyer to be sent to the police if Lambert were found guilty. Or, otherwise, to be destroyed. Surely that would do the trick. At the worst, it would allow him a week or two to reach some place of comparative safety. He could take a plane to Marseilles and cross to Algiers. He could lose himself in Africa. There'd be new scenes, new faces to help him forget. He was a strong man in the prime of life—he could always scrape a living. There'd be new things to paint, new colors to see. They'd never find him. He could change his name and grow a beard. In time he might even go across to South America. It would be an adventure.

An adventure? Yes, but a worth-while adventure? Wherever

he went he'd have fear at his side and regrets. A sordid disintegration, more likely! How long would it take him to drink himself to death? He'd be lonely—he'd always hated loneliness. He could find some woman, of course . . . *Some woman*, after Stephanie! His soul revolted. If Stephanie was lost, then he was lost. To remember her would be an intolerable agony. To remember her and all the might-have-beens. In time he might forget, but why go to all the trouble to forget? Was life worth preserving at such a price?

Alec stared into the fire. He knew he must do something quickly—he must make some decision, or the decision might be taken out of his hands. At least he would write out his statement. That was the first step—to get it all down. To get Lambert off his mind. He'd do it this evening—but first he'd pop down to the pub. He must see people—he'd go crazy if he didn't see someone, talk to someone. He'd have a couple of drinks and then come back and write.

He got the car out of the garage. He felt a little better now—the prospect of some action, *any* action, was comforting. He was just going to drive away when a taxi appeared and drew up in front of him. It must be Stephanie! She was the last person he wanted to see now. There was nothing he could say. She had probably come to make it up, in her generous way. . . . The irony of it! But he mustn't let her know anything, he mustn't give himself away. He must keep control of the situation till he'd made his own decision.

God, there were two of them! That fellow Easterbrook! Why on earth had they come together? What could they want? Anger seized him, choking him. No, *no*—he must keep his temper. It would be difficult, but he *must*. If he lost control, he was capable of saying anything. Of ruining everything. If he wasn't careful he would end up in a cell after all.

He slammed the car door and joined them by the gate. The very sight of Stephanie set his heart beating out of time. He must try to be normal, casual. He said, "Hello, Stephanie!" rather breathlessly. Thank God it was dark so that she couldn't see his face. He turned to Max. "Hello, Easterbrook, this is a surprise."

Stephanie put a hand on his arm, and he felt the urgent pressure of her fingers. "Alec, we want to talk to you." The agitation in her voice was unmistakable. "Let's go inside."

Alec sensed the crisis that he feared. He must be natural, but what was natural in a crisis? "I was just off to the local," he said. "Let's all go—we can talk there."

Max said quietly, "Can we talk about Hilda Lambert at the Bush and Kettle?"

Alec felt a leap of fear. So it *was* that! God, if he'd left it too late! "For Pete's sake," he protested, "do we have to go over all that again? I'm sick of talking about her."

Stephanie said, "*Please*, Alec," in a troubled, insistent voice. "We must. It's terribly important."

"It's not important to me," said Alec, irritably, his good resolutions scattered. He shook off her detaining hand. "Why can't you leave me alone?"

Stephanie's heart sank. "We can't talk out here," she said in a low voice. "Let's go in. There's something that's got to be cleared up."

"Cleared up? I don't know what you're talking about." Alec felt resentment rising and choking him, so that speech came thickly. Why did she have to make everything more difficult for him? What the devil had she teamed up with that fellow for? He mastered his anger with an effort. If they wanted to talk, he couldn't get out of it. "All right, you'd better come in," he said and led the way back to the studio. "You're becoming inseparable, aren't you? Perhaps you'd like to sit together on the settee?"

Stephanie looked at him, reproachfully, and Max said sharply, "Don't be a damned fool, Forbes. I assure you there's not going to be anything funny about this at all."

Alec gave a mirthless laugh. "What a portentous fellow you are, Easterbrook! Is it any good offering either of you a drink?"

"Not for me, thanks," said Max, and Stephanie shook her head.

Alec shrugged. "Just as you like. I will, if you don't mind. I've been on the wagon for the past half hour!"

Stephanie watched him anxiously as he poured the whiskey, and saw with relief that it was only a small one.

"Now," said Alec, "What's the deputation about?" He settled his bulk in an easy chair and began to fill his pipe.

"It's about a sketchbook" said Max. "Your sketchbook."

Alec's thick eyebrows shot up. His glance traveled to the table by the easel and back to Max. "What about it?"

"I may as well tell you," said Max, quietly, "that I called here this morning. You were out, but your door was unlocked, so I came in and waited."

"It was like your bloody cheek," growled Alec.

"While I was waiting," Max went on, "I took a walk round the studio, and I happened to pick up one of your sketchbooks. There were two drawings of Hilda Lambert in it."

Max paused and watched for a reaction. Alec, frowning, searched his memory but failed to recall anything significant. "You're a nosey, prying busybody," he said, "but it's quite possible. What of it?" He felt Stephanie's eyes upon him but avoided looking at her.

"In both the drawings," said Max, "you'd given Hilda Lambert tightly waved hair. When did *you* see her with waved hair?"

Alec stared at him. "What the devil are you talking about? Where are they?"

"You've probably forgotten them, Alec," Stephanie said. "Two little pencil drawings, just doodling really." She was very tense.

Alec looked from one to the other. "You may find this game very fascinating," he said, "but I still don't get the point."

"Let me make it clear," said Max. "Hilda Lambert always wore her hair straight. She had it waved for the first time on the afternoon of the day she was murdered. Your sketches show her with her hair waved. I'm asking you how you knew."

There was a moment's silence, broken only by the drip of water from the eaves. Stephanie was leaning forward, eagerly, as though to clutch the answer that she wanted to hear. Max sat immobile.

Alec fought down his panic. "Are you accusing me of murder?"

"Yes," said Max.

From Stephanie came a sharp exhalation of breath. "Alec," she cried, "there *is* some explanation, isn't there? There must be!"

"Shut up," said Alec, savagely. He turned on Max. "It's a dangerous thing to make a charge like that, Easterbrook, as you'll find—especially before a witness. Where *is* the book—let's have a look." He half rose.

"You needn't bother," said Max. "It's in a safe place."

"What the devil do you mean?"

"It's evidence. I took it away."

Alec's face flushed darkly, and the veins on his forehead stood out. He looked as though he were going to spring from his chair. "Listen, Easterbrook," he said menacingly, "if you don't produce that book right away, I'll break your bloody neck."

"Then you'll have two murders on your conscience," said Max. It was just as well, he reflected, that there *was* a witness.

Alec rose slowly from his chair, his face distorted with anger. "By God," he said, "if you think you can steal my property and get away with it, you're wrong. Unless you undertake to have that book here within the hour, I'll ring the police and charge you here and now with theft. Do you hear?" He strode to the telephone and lifted the receiver. "Well?"

"Go ahead," said Max. "The number's 999." He caught Stephanie's agonized look and had to turn away. Poor Stephanie! How she was willing Alec to ring that number!

Alec stood motionless by the phone, his finger on the dial. "It won't be very nice in a cell," he said. "I'm giving you a last chance."

Stephanie couldn't bear it any longer. "Oh, Alec, ring them, *please* ring them."

"Go on, ring them," said Max, tensely.

Alec, watching Max, began to dial. Suddenly he flung down the receiver. "This is ridiculous," he said.

Stephanie gave a little cry.

"Well, so it is," said Alec. He came slowly back to the fire and resumed his seat. "I don't suppose you intended to pinch the thing, Easterbrook," he said, lamely. "Anyway, I'm sure we can settle it without the police." He applied a match to his pipe and puffed furiously. "Now, then," he said, crossing his legs and leaning back as though nothing had happened, "what's all this rigmarole about hair?"

Stephanie began to fumble for a cigarette, and Max gave her a light. She was pale and frightened.

Max turned to Alec again. "All I want to know," he said, "is when you saw Hilda Lambert with her hair waved."

Stephanie couldn't keep silent. "For heaven's sake, Alec, do say something. When *did* you? It couldn't have been in the after . . ."

"Stephanie!" Max glared at her. "I thought you were going to leave this to me?"

"You're trying to trap him," said Stephanie. "It's not fair. . . ."

"I've asked a plain question," said Max. "All we need is the truth." He looked at Alec. "Well?"

"I can't see what all the fuss is about," said Alec. "A couple of sketches!" His voice was contemptuous. "How do I know why I drew them in one way rather than another? I don't even remember the damn things. I'm always drawing."

"Did you see Hilda on the day she was killed?" asked Max.

"I don't think I could have done," said Alec, cautiously, looking at Stephanie. "I was with the Bradshaws all the afternoon. You remember, Stephanie, I told you."

"Yes," said Max, "we all remember now."

"As a matter of fact," said Alec, slowly, "I don't think I *ever* saw her with waved hair."

"Not even when she was young?" asked Stephanie.

Alec shook his head. "No. Her hair was always straight. But what of it? I tell you, Easterbrook, you're making a mountain out of a molehill. As I say, I don't even remember doing the drawings, but if the hair's wavy I'm not surprised. Put it down to artistic license. I might just as easily have drawn her with snaky locks or a toupee."

Stephanie stirred impatiently. "Alec, it's much more serious than you think. The police have a photograph of her—if your drawings are like the photograph, it'll be terribly damning. Alec, look at me—tell me—you *didn't* do it, did you. You must tell me you didn't. Oh, God, I can't bear it. Say you didn't see her that evening. Say you didn't go near the house."

Alec suddenly felt tired of the struggle. He couldn't bear to look at her. He wanted to fall at her feet and tell her everything —he wanted to say, "Yes, I did do it, Stephanie, I did, I *did*," and feel her soothing hand. A great pit of desire had opened up in front of him, and he wanted to throw himself down and be engulfed. With a fearful effort, he struggled back out of danger, tearing his gaze from hers. "I didn't do it," he said, hoarsely.

Max sighed. "What *were* you doing that evening, Forbes— around half-past six?"

"I told you," said Alec, quickly. "I was on my way to the Bush and Kettle. I can't remember exactly what time I got there, but it was soon after half-past six."

"It was at ten past seven," said Max. "You were late for your darts game. I've made inquiries."

Uncontrollable anger gripped Alec. "You bloody little snooper!" he shouted. What a damned idiot he'd been not to get out while the going was good!

"Where were you between six-thirty and ten past seven," asked Max, remorselessly.

The spasm of rage had passed. "You can't expect me to re-member exactly what I was doing the whole time," said Alec. "What I told you was roughly true—I came back from the Bradshaws, had a wash, and went straight off to the pub. I thought I got there soon after it opened, but I may have been a bit later."

"You were a lot later," said Max. "There are forty minutes of crucial unaccounted time. There are also some excuses to explain away. For instance, where did you have trouble with your car?"

"Eh?" The look of panic flitted again across Alec's face. "Oh, that? Yes, I'd forgotten."

"You'd forgotten because it never happened."

"Of course it happened. It was on the way down to the pub. The engine suddenly stopped. It took me about twenty minutes to get it right again."

"What went wrong?" asked Max.

Alec shrugged. "How do I know—I'm not a mechanic. Perhaps it was a choke in the carburetor. I know I kept using the starter, and, after a while, the thing cleared itself."

"Whereabouts did this happen?"

"I told you—between here and the pub."

"Where *exactly*? You must know to within fifty yards or so where the car stopped. It's only half a mile to the pub anyway."

"Alec always drives there," said Stephanie, quickly. She turned to him with an appealing face. "Please, Alec, say where it was. Someone may remember having seen you. Oh, you're making things so difficult."

Alec scowled. "You didn't *have* to come here."

"Alec!" It was a cry from Stephanie's heart. "Don't you see I want to help you—I want to believe you. Darling, I don't understand—you're hiding something. *Why* don't you tell the truth?"

"I *am* telling the truth," said Alec, sullenly.

"Then where did the car break down?" Max persisted.

"It was by the church in Longford Lane," said Alec.

"All right. Twenty minutes is a long time. People must have passed. People coming home from work. People in the houses near by must have heard your engine turning over. Didn't anyone offer to help?"

"I didn't see a soul," said Alec.

"Too bad," said Max. "It looks as though you haven't an alibi after all. . . . So you got to the pub at ten past seven, and you played a rotten game of darts because you were upset about the car. Is that right?"

Alec hesitated. What *didn't* the fellow know? "I suppose so," he said finally.

"And not because you'd just murdered Hilda?"

"No," shouted Alec. "Damn you, no! Why should I want to kill her?"

"You know that better than I do," said Max, "though I can guess. What were your real feelings about Hilda?"

Alec looked from Max to Stephanie and back again. "I told you," he said. "Nothing very much at all."

"You told me you weren't angry when Hilda badgered Stephanie. Is that true?"

"Stephanie knows how I felt," growled Alec.

"Exactly," said Max. "Stephanie knows. You told *me* a pack of lies, but Stephanie knows the truth. You pretended to me that you didn't care one way or the other, but Stephanie knows you were beside yourself. I put it to you that you hated Hilda for getting in the way and upsetting your life with Stephanie. That was why you killed her."

"It's a lot of nonsense," said Alec.

"Oh, Alec," cried Stephanie, "you know it isn't *all* nonsense. You surely remember how you talked to me about Hilda, after she came to my place? You were livid. I don't understand why you have to pretend like this."

"You're imagining things," said Alec. "I was annoyed; I wasn't livid, as you call it."

Stephanie gazed at him wide-eyed. "You know that's not true," she said.

"Oh, go to hell!" shouted Alec. "You're on his side."

"You've no right to talk like that," Stephanie flamed. "I came here because I believed you'd be able to explain everything. I tell you I'm trying to help you. Oh, Alec, you're making me so wretched. I've never seen you like this before. Do tell the truth.

There must be something you're keeping back. Why are you?"

"I've said all I'm going to say," said Alec. "I'm fed up with all this chatter. You two have got hold of a lot of idiotic ideas, but they won't get you anywhere. I'm going to the pub. You can do what you like."

"Just a moment," said Max. "It isn't going to be as simple as all that. Sit down—I haven't finished."

Alec sank back. "Well, you'd better get it over quickly. What is it?"

"Before you rush off," said Max, "I'd like to give you an outline of the case against you."

"There isn't any case," said Alec, shortly. "You've no proof at all."

"There are a lot of very suggestive circumstances," said Max. "You knew Hilda when you were young—you're one of the very few men in her life. Your account of your relationship with her at the time has never seemed convincing—you've been less than frank, but the facts will come out, you may be sure. For a long time you didn't see her. Then you met Stephanie and were dead keen to marry her. Yes, you were crazy about her, in a selfish sort of way. Hilda turned up and began to make a nuisance of herself. She was threatening your relationship with Stephanie."

"Pure imagination!" said Alec.

"There's plenty of evidence," said Max. "We needn't go into that again. On the night of the murder, there are forty vital minutes that you can't account for except by a car breakdown that nobody noticed. In that time you could have killed Hilda. Sometime after that night—perhaps the very same night—you drew sketches of Hilda of a kind that you couldn't have drawn if you hadn't killed her. Ever since then, you've behaved like a guilty man. You've lied and gone on lying. You can't think of a consistent story because you're all twisted up. Just how long do you think you'd last in a witness box, with what you've got on your mind?"

"It won't come to that," said Alec. "This case of yours wouldn't convince anyone. It's just a flight of fancy from beginning to end. There isn't a single scrap of evidence that I was at the house that night, and there can't be."

"I wouldn't be too sure about that," said Max. "You're a child in these matters, Forbes. You're a blunderer, you know that. You've made three or four mistakes already—bad ones. How many more are there that haven't come to light yet? I've talked to the inspector in charge of this case, and he's put ideas into my head. I wonder, for instance, what shoes you wore when you went to Hilda's. The inspector has a collection of footprints, and he's looking for a shoe that fits. I wonder what clothes you wore? You say you've never been to her house. Suppose there's a fiber of her carpet or her dress, or one of her hairs, adhering at this moment to some portion of your suit or your overcoat? You never thought of that, did you? Something the police could positively identify! Are you certain there isn't?"

"There can't be," said Alec, in a hoarse voice. Specks of moisture glistened on his forehead. "I tell you I wasn't there."

"You might just as well admit it," said Max, inexorably. "You know you did it. You know, and I know, and Stephanie knows. The knowledge is in your heart. You can't conceal it. What are you going to gain by waiting? The police will turn you inside out. They'll question and probe, and you'll twist and turn, and in the end they'll bring it home to you. Don't underrate them, Forbes. You may think now that the evidence is thin, but they'll build it up, item by item, and in the end they'll get you."

"You can't frighten me," said Alec. "I tell you I didn't do it."

"An innocent man is going through hell this very minute, Forbes, because of you. You can end that tonight. It won't help you, but you'll have a black sin off your conscience. Christ, have you no compassion?"

Alec clenched his jaw. "I didn't do it," he said.

Max got up. "Very well, it's up to the police. You didn't dare ring them. I'm going to." He went over to the telephone. "Do you want a couple of minutes to think it over? I mean a couple of minutes? *I'm* not bluffing."

Alec suddenly cried, "Wait!" His heavy face was drained of color. If only he could think clearly! How strong *was* the evidence? How strong was *he*? What would the police find, and what would they ask? Suppose they arrested him on suspicion? Suppose they just watched him, so that he couldn't get away? Oh, God, he was tired. What did it matter? But it mattered that he shouldn't be shut up in a cell—it mattered that he should be able to make his own choice. To make a break for it or—die his own way. Not to be shut up for weeks and then hanged by the neck.

He said, "Come back here, Easterbrook. I want to talk to you."

"Well?" said Max.

Alec made a desperate effort to pull himself together. "You want to save Lambert, don't you?" he said. "More than anything else?"

"Yes."

"Do you think you're going about it the best way—by ringing the police?"

Max sat down. "What else can I do?" he asked quietly.

"You said the other day that you thought the case against him was very strong. You must know, in spite of all your talk, that the case against me *isn't* very strong. It's a pretty thin motive, don't you think? And I'll be able to explain the drawings, don't you worry. I'll think of something. There isn't a scrap of evidence and you know it. Do you really believe that the police will abandon their case against Lambert on the strength of what you know? You haven't a hope."

"Then," said Max, "you've nothing to worry about, have you?"

Alec shrugged. "I wouldn't say that. I didn't do it, but that doesn't mean I should be very happy having the police around."

"What exactly are you driving at?"

"Couldn't we do a deal?"

Stephanie, who had been sitting wide-eyed, watching them both, called sharply, "Alec . . . !"

Max's look imposed silence on her. He got up and began to pace the room. "What sort of deal are you thinking of?" he asked.

"I'm admitting nothing," said Alec, "but if I were to give you a confession, here and now, which you and Stephanie could witness, you'd be sure of saving Lambert."

Stephanie gave a little moan.

"And in return. . . ?" asked Max.

"You'd hold it for a week. That's all. You'd take no action of any sort against me in that time."

"Do you think you can trust me?" said Max.

"I think I can trust Stephanie—if she promises. And you, too —if she promises. Perhaps I've not much choice."

"No," said Max, "perhaps you haven't." He sat in painful perplexity, thinking of George and Lucy and Jane. He thought of having a confession in his hand—something that would guarantee absolute certainty and absolute safety. Alec might get away, but it wasn't Max's job to avenge Hilda. Hilda meant less than nothing to him. If the law wanted retribution, it was up to the law to exact it. So far, the law was just blundering. An unpleasant phrase sprang into Max's mind—"accessory after the fact." There might be trouble if this bargain were made— trouble for Stephanie, too. No, surely not for Stephanie—they wouldn't bother about her. Trouble for himself? Perhaps.

What was the alternative? To hand over Alec now, without a confession. But suppose no one was willing to receive him? Suppose the skeptical Haines came along and went over the evidence and decided there wasn't any case? Then Alec would get away, and George would be hanged. The evidence *was* thin. It wasn't the evidence that was driving Alec to the bargain— it was his own sense of guilt.

If Alec were to slip away now and George were hanged, Max would never forgive himself. He had no right to take the risk. Surely it was more important that an innocent man should be saved than that a guilty one should be punished?

He turned to Stephanie. He could not see her face. He said, "What do you say, Stephanie?"

Stephanie had been thinking, too—unbearable thoughts. She had been fond of Alec—she would probably have married him. And he was a murderer—a cold-blooded murderer! Was it possible that one could be so ignorant of a man's real character after so long an association? How *could* he have done it? It was horrible—it was vile. She ought to hate him, to loathe him. Perhaps she did. He deserved to be punished. He had no right to expect sympathy or help. . . . But they might hang him. Alec hanged! It was unthinkable. He'd been close to her—he'd made love to her. She recoiled from him now, but she must help him if she could. It must have been partly Hilda's fault. Not that that made murder right—but perhaps there was a little excuse. Hilda must have provoked him. But still—a murderer! It made her sick to think of it. All the same, she didn't want him to be hanged. If she could help him get away, she would. If George Lambert were free, nobody would suffer.

She looked up, tortured with doubt and misery.

"Well?" said Max, gently.

Stephanie gave a little nod.

Alec stood up. In spite of all, at that moment he somehow dominated the room. He said, very distinctly, "You swear by everything you hold sacred that you won't let anyone set eyes on this confession that I shall give you and that you won't tell anyone what has passed between us, until a week from now? You swear to keep this agreement in the letter and the spirit?" He looked at Stephanie.

She gave a little shudder. "I promise," she said.

"Easterbrook?"

"You'll never get away with it," said Max, "but I promise."

A look of infinite relief came over Alec's face, a look almost of happiness. Incredibly, he smiled. "Better get some paper and start writing," he said. "I've wanted to get this off my chest for a long time."

❦ THIRTEEN ❦

THERE WAS a moment or two of complete silence. The atmosphere of the room had suddenly become unreal, almost macabre. Stephanie sat with her head bent, so still that she seemed scarcely to be breathing. Her thoughts were in a turmoil. It was all incredible. *Surely* people one knew didn't kill!

Max looked at her anxiously. "You're sure you're all right, Stephanie? If you'd like to go home, I can manage here. You can just witness the signature later on."

"I'll stay," she murmured, without looking up.

"Then we'd better get started," said Max, making an effort to sound normal. "Can you find me some paper, Forbes?"

Alec produced some sheets of foolscap from a bureau. Max sat down at the table, and Alec resumed his seat by the fire. In comparison with the others, he seemed almost nonchalant.

"Better go slowly," said Max. "There'll have to be rather a lot of detail, you know."

Alec nodded. "I'll start right at the beginning," he said. "Twenty years back. What I told you before about my affair with Hilda was all rubbish, of course. There was nothing platonic about it—on my side, that is. It may seem unbelievable to you, but I really did fall for her in a big way. The reasons don't matter now. Perhaps I was young and just spoiling for an affair—perhaps I was carried away because she was so obviously in love with me. . . . Am I going too fast?"

"I'll tell you if you do," said Max.

"We were never formally engaged because her people were against it, but we were both keen to get married right away. Hilda's mother was the stumbling block. Hilda was completely dominated by her mother and always had been. From the beginning, I wasn't looked upon with favor. I was hardly more than a youth. I hadn't any visible means of support or any obvious prospects, and I didn't conform in any way to the family's pattern of behavior. I expect that's what attracted Hilda. She had a passionate nature, and I think she'd have loved to break out of the family strait jacket. Her mother knew that. I believe she looked on me as a dangerous rival. Anyhow, I disliked Hilda's people from the moment I clapped eyes on them, and they felt the same about me."

Alec was following the movement of the pen. When it stopped writing, he went on: "You know what a persistent, strong-willed woman Hilda was. Well, her mother was the same, only more so. She really worked on Hilda. Her idea was that we should wait a year or two 'to make sure.' It was fatal, of course. I was impatient, and Hilda was very emotional. We ought to have married right away, when we wanted to. Instead, we started to have interminable arguments. Sometimes we argued alone, sometimes her parents took part. It was a bloody poor substitute for love, I can tell you. . . . You needn't put all this down if you don't want to. It's just background."

"Leave it to me," said Max. "We'll sort it out afterward."

"Well," Alec went on, "I began to get exasperated. There was one wretched scene after another. At first I was sorry for Hilda—I looked on myself as a sort of knight-errant rescuing a damsel in distress. But it wasn't as simple as all that. Gradually, I began to realize that, in some odd way, she was getting a kick out of the situation. She was completely repressed, and I had to suffer, too. I think she liked seeing me all steamed up. She enjoyed the cat-and-mouse stuff. She enjoyed emotional sessions —they were her substitute for going to bed. I soon got fed up, of course. Our relationship became pretty sticky, and after a particularly violent quarrel, I went away for a weekend with another girl, and Hilda found out. There was hell to pay. There was a blazing family row, and I told them all I was clearing out. I'd had several drinks, and that put the finishing touch to it as far as her people were concerned. I didn't see them again."

"And Hilda?"

"Oh, she didn't let go, not immediately. The situation was meat and drink to her—it kept her in a state of almost continuous nervous excitement. She kept saying she still loved me, but that it was now all the more necessary to wait and make sure. She wouldn't marry me, but she didn't want to lose me." Alec gave a mirthless laugh. "She wasn't very smart. If ever a woman messed up her own life, she did. She wrote endless letters, and she kept ringing me up and going off the deep end on the telephone. We saw each other several times more, but we never got anywhere. I was absolutely sick of her by this time. I couldn't stand the scenes and the frustration. Finally I went off to Paris to paint, and I stopped answering her letters. Three months later I heard that she'd married Lambert. I felt tremendously relieved. I'd got her out of my system, and I was damned glad she'd done the same."

"But she hadn't, of course?"

"No," said Alec, "she hadn't. But I never suspected that at the time. I hardly gave her another thought. I went my own way. What happened in the years that followed isn't of any interest. . . . Then I met Stephanie." He looked across at her, and the lines of his face softened. "I don't need to tell you about that. Stephanie knows that I've been crazy about her from the first moment we met. I was happier than I'd ever been in my life. We were both happy—weren't we, Stephanie?"

She looked up, her eyes full of anguish. "Oh, Alec, if only I'd married you . . ."

"Perhaps it wouldn't have worked out," said Alec, without much conviction. "Anyhow, things were going pretty smoothly with us until the day we ran into Hilda at the show. I knew at once by her attitude and the way she talked that she'd never really got me out of her mind. She'd made the mistake of her life twenty years before, and, inside her, she'd never ceased to regret it. Now she was going to try to make up for it. The way she started wrapping herself round me gave me the creeps. You know what it was like, Stephanie—it wasn't my imagination. She behaved almost as though Stephanie wasn't there. I was appalled. She'd changed enormously—I couldn't see in her any of the things that had once attracted me, and it made me feel sick to think that I'd ever had anything to do with her. But all the things I hadn't liked were more noticeable. She seemed utterly self-centered, and there was a sort of desperate intensity about her that scared me. I felt pretty sure she was going to make mischief, and she did. From the very moment she got in touch with Stephanie, things began to go wrong with us. . . ."

"If only I'd known!" said Stephanie. "If only I'd realized what she was like, when there was still time! If only I hadn't told you about her. . . !"

Alec shook his head. "I doubt if anything would have made any difference as long as we were within her reach. She was a genius at making trouble, and she was determined to ruin our relationship if she could. I saw just what was going to happen. Stephanie would be humiliated, and I should get angry, and we should quarrel, and everything would be spoiled. That was what I feared, anyway, and that was exactly how things began to work out. Perhaps I should have had more faith in you, Stephanie—perhaps I should have waited to see what happened in the end. But when you told me that Hilda had started dripping poison, I was so angry I could hardly control myself. You see, I knew Hilda of old—I knew what she was capable of and what a limpet she could be. It wouldn't have been so bad if she'd telephoned *me* and badgered *me*, but when I saw she was working on you behind my back, I simply had to try to stop her."

"What did you do?" asked Max.

"I decided to have it out with her. There wasn't much hope that an appeal to her sense of decency would have any result, but I thought I might be able to frighten her into keeping out of my affairs. Believe me, it wasn't a pleasant prospect. I loathed the idea of meeting her again, but it seemed the only thing to do."

Max looked at him curiously. "You mean you didn't go with the intention of killing her?"

"No, I swear I didn't. The thought never entered my head. Why should I lie about it now?—it can't make any difference. I simply intended to warn her off—that was all."

"How did you make the arrangement?"

"I rang her up last Wednesday week, in the morning. I said I'd like to have a talk and asked her where we could meet. She got the wrong idea from the very beginning. Even on the phone she made my blood run cold—she was coy and kittenish. She said that her daughter was away and that her husband wouldn't be back till late in the evening, and what about coming round to the house about half-past six? I must have been out of my mind to agree, but I didn't want her here, and if there was going to be a scene, I didn't want it to happen in public. So I said I'd go."

He ran his tongue over his dry lips. "I must have a drink," he said. He poured himself out a whiskey and water and drained the glass. "Where was I?"

"You were going to the house," said Max. "Take your time."

"I want to get to the end," said Alec. "Well, I left the Bradshaws' place a little before six, and I drove to Finchley. On the way I stopped at a pub and had a few double whiskeys to fortify myself. After that, I felt much better. I left the car a little way down the road from the house. The last thing I wanted was any complications with her husband, and I thought if I walked up, it would be less likely that anyone would notice my visit."

"Where exactly did you leave the car?" asked Max.

"About thirty yards up on the right-hand side. I walked

quickly to the house, determined to say my piece and leave before Hilda could start anything. But that was reckoning without her. As soon as I got inside, I wished I hadn't come. Hilda had worked herself up into a frightful emotional state. From the beginning, she acted as though we'd only just broken off our affair, as though the twenty years in between hadn't existed. We'd had a tiff, and now we were going to make it up—that sort of attitude. She was all girlish and intense. It wouldn't have been so horrifying if she'd *looked* attractive, but she was grotesque. She'd dolled herself up and even had her hair waved especially for my benefit. She twirled around in a flirtatious way and said, 'How do you like my new hair style?' as though she were a bloody mannequin! Her face was loose and fleshy, and she flopped about and hung around me as though she expected me to embrace her. Ugh!" Alec shut his eyes.

For a moment there was no sound in the room except the scratch of Max's pen.

"I told her I wasn't going to stay," Alec went on. "I didn't even take my coat off. I wanted to get it over and clear out. I said I could say what I had to say in two minutes. She pretended that she was terribly hurt. She said that she'd looked forward to having a long cozy evening with me. She said that, after all, we *had* been almost lovers once! Every word that she said, every look that she gave me, made me want to vomit. I took a grip on myself and told her in plain words that she was being an unmitigated nuisance, that I didn't want to have anything more to do with her in any way whatever, and that in future she'd better leave me alone."

Max wrote steadily. "How did she take it?"

"I might just as well have talked to the fireplace for all the effect it had. She was incredibly exasperating. She didn't get angry—I wouldn't have minded that. She just smiled, as though she thought I needn't be taken seriously. She was sitting on the arm of the settee, swinging a vast haunch and showing acres of underclothes. She said, 'But Alec, dear, when two people have loved each other as we did, I don't believe they can ever really stop loving each other, do you?' I told her I loathed the very sight of her; that I couldn't find words to tell her how much. She looked completely uncomprehending, and she said, 'How can you talk like that when you know we really belong to each other—spiritually if not physically?' Yes, those were her actual words. 'At least,' she said, 'we must always be friends.' I told her that she'd got the wrong idea entirely, that I had no intention of being friends, and that I just wanted to be rid of her. I told her that I was going to marry Stephanie and that she'd better keep out of our way. She put on that mulish look of hers, and she said, 'Well, dear, there's no reason why I shouldn't be friends with Stephanie. After all, that's nothing to do with you, is it?' Before I could say anything, she started telling me that she'd grown to like Stephanie very much and that she was sure Stephanie liked her. 'You can't stop me seeing her,' she said. 'And I think it's good for her to have an older woman to give her a little advice—after all, Alec dear, I ought to know how to handle you, and she *is* very young. I'm sure I can help her.' "

Max, fascinated, stopped writing. Once again he felt his own gorge rising as the egregious Hilda was conjured up before him. If ever a woman had asked for it. . . !

Alec was on his feet, pacing the floor. His face was a mask of hatred. "I lost my temper. I called her all the foul names I could think of. I could hardly keep my hands off her. I wouldn't have believed I could hate anyone so much. She began to snivel and came up close to me and put her head against my shoulder. Her hair reeked. I pushed her away. Suddenly she gave me a crafty smile through her tears, and she said, 'You might just as well face it, Alec—you'll never get rid of me.' I knew she was right. I knew that now she'd started again, she'd go on pestering me as long as there was breath in her body. I lost all control of myself. When she bent down to pick up her handkerchief or something, and I saw her neck all bare, I couldn't resist the impulse to hit her. I lashed out at her with the side of my hand

—a sort of rabbit punch. Like this." He struck viciously at the air.

Stephanie moaned.

"It was bad luck for me that the blow landed in the most vulnerable spot. If I'd tried for it, I couldn't have been more exact. It knocked her clean out—she just crumpled up on the floor without a sound. I didn't feel sorry—I was glad I'd shut her up. Then, as I looked at her, I realized that I'd only made things worse. There'd be a frightful row when she came to—a scene with her and trouble with the husband and, perhaps, trouble with the police. She'd have a new hold on me. I could see her enjoying herself, telling you all about it, Stephanie, and giving you more good advice. I could see her being understanding and forgiving with me, wanting to 'make it up,' coming after me, nattering and babbling forever and ever. I stood over her, loathing her guts . . ."

He stopped pacing. Beads of sweat glistened on his forehead.

"The idea came to me in a flash. She was unconscious—I could do what I liked with her. Why should she ever regain consciousness? I could kill her without any trouble at all, and she'd never bother me again. It was so simple. At the time it didn't even seem wrong. I *hated* her, and I wanted her dead, and I felt she deserved to be dead. I didn't stop to think anything out. All I thought was how easy it would be. If I put her head in the gas oven and turned the taps on without leaving any fingerprints, it would look like suicide. And that's what I did."

"It didn't occur to you," said Max "that there might be bruises?"

"No, it didn't. At that point, I wasn't capable of rational thinking at all. The whiskey must have had something to do with it. I did realize I'd have to be careful about fingerprints—that was all. The main thought in my mind was that there'd never be another opportunity like this."

"What exactly did you do?"

Alec's voice dropped so low that it was all Max could do to hear him. "I took hold of her and half dragged, half carried her into the kitchen. I opened the oven door with a cloth and took out the things inside. I fetched cushions and put them under her, because I seemed to remember that suicides usually made themselves comfortable. I turned on all the gas taps with the cloth, and I wiped the things that I'd touched. It was all terribly simple. The windows were shut, and the room was soon full of gas. Hilda was quite unconscious, and I knew that in a few moments she'd be dead. I was glad."

Stephanie's eyes were fastened on Alec, and there was such horror in them that he winced. "Don't look at me like that, Stephanie," he pleaded. "I know how you feel. I've felt that way ever since."

"What did you do then?" Max broke in.

"I shut the kitchen door from the hall, with a handkerchief round the doorknob. I looked round the sitting room to make sure that everything was tidy. We'd been there such a short time that there was nothing to clear up. I hadn't even sat down, I made sure I hadn't dropped anything or left any traces. Then I went out by the front door. There didn't seem to be anyone about. I crossed the road and walked a little way in the darkness. Then I stopped and waited a few minutes. I wanted to be sure that no one went in before Hilda was dead. Then I rushed down to the car and drove like hell to the Bush and Kettle. I didn't imagine I'd ever need an alibi, but it did seem to me that the sooner I was with other people the better. . . . As you said, I played a lousy game of darts."

"And then you went home?" said Max. He paused. "How did you feel?"

"I didn't feel anything that night," said Alec. "By the time I got home, I was pretty drunk. But the next day was ghastly. I couldn't believe that I'd done it. Wherever I looked I could see Hilda lying on the floor. I didn't know what to do. I was terrified—terrified of myself. It didn't occur to me then that

I'd be found out. I tried to justify myself. I tried to persuade myself that Hilda had made me do it—that it was just the same as though I'd hit her, and she'd died. I knew it wasn't, but I tried. I kept telling myself that now it would be all right about Stephanie and that I'd soon forget what I'd done. I had dinner with her that night, and every time I looked at her, I saw Hilda's face. We quarreled. I knew things would never be the same again."

"When did you do the drawings?" asked Max.

"I suppose it must have been that night. I couldn't sleep. I don't remember doing them, but I remember sitting at the table with a pencil, churning everything over in my mind. Then they arrested Lambert. I couldn't believe he'd ever be found guilty, but I read the evidence when he was committed, and I was staggered. I swear I'd never have let them hang him. I'd have given myself up or confessed in some way. Stephanie, whatever you think of me, you must believe that."

Stephanie gave no sign. Max said, "It hardly matters now, anyway."

"You don't believe me," cried Alec. "Of course, you don't. Why should you? But it *is* true. I couldn't get him out of my mind for a moment. When you told me, Easterbrook, that you thought he'd be hanged, I was appalled. I didn't know how to talk to you, what to say to you."

"It doesn't matter," repeated Max. "I think we'd better break this up as soon as possible. There's really nothing more to be said, is there? Except for one point. When eventually I hand over this document to the inspector, he'll want to know for certain that the confession is true. I'd like a bit of internal evidence. Can you tell me something that you couldn't have found out afterward—from me, for instance, or from the newspapers. Something that'll convince the inspector you were there."

Alec sat thinking. "I can tell you about Hilda," he said. "I remember what she was wearing—a long-sleeved green frock and a string of pink beads that clashed with it. And she had round rubber heels on her shoes. They were the last thing I saw before I closed the door on her."

"That should do," said Max. He studied his long manuscript. "I suppose it never occurred to you that the gas taps might have been wiped clean?"

Alec shook his head. "I made a mess of it, didn't I? I took it for granted that Hilda's own prints would be on the taps."

Max nodded. "Well, we'd better have this thing signed," he said. "I think I've got everything that's necessary. It convinces *me*—I hope to God it'll convince the police." He gathered up the papers. "You'd better read them," he said. "And sign each sheet." Now that the murder was out he felt sick of the whole affair. It was pretty squalid, however you looked at it. It made him angry to think that Stephanie was in any way mixed up in it. He felt her misery as an ache inside himself. The best thing that could happen now would be for Alec to clear off right away. She was bound to feel like hell until he'd gone.

Alec didn't seem to be reading the pages through—he gave each one an indifferent glance and then signed it. Well, it was his lookout—probably he didn't care any more. Max took the pen from Alec and handed it to Stephanie. White-faced, but with a steady hand, Stephanie added her signature, and Max followed suit.

Alec got up. "Well, that's that," he said. "I have an odd feeling that we ought to celebrate. It's a great relief to have got it all down."

Max regarded him curiously. Whatever the fellow was feeling, he was putting a good face on things.

Stephanie said, "What are you going to do, Alec?"

He looked at her in a rather lost sort of way, as though he hadn't thought of doing anything particular. "I don't know," he said. "I did have some plans, but they don't seem very practical. What would you do, Easterbrook?"

"God knows," said Max. He shrugged. "Get to the Continent,

I suppose. In seven days you should be able to cover your tracks. I don't feel I can advise you."

Alec ran a hand through his thick hair. "It's my problem, I know. I don't really want to go anywhere, but I expect I'll think of something."

"You must do something quickly," Stephanie said. "You'll be all right—you can make a fresh start."

"Without you?" said Alec, his dark eyes resting for a moment on the silver-blond hair that he'd loved so much.

"I can't come with you," said Stephanie. "Can I? You'll be safer alone."

"Of course, you can't," said Alec. He gave a harsh laugh. "Even I wouldn't suggest that. I don't know why you're bothering about me at all. You must loathe me."

"Oh, Alec, I don't. Please don't say that. I—I don't know what I feel. I don't think I've got any feelings left. All I know is that I want you to get away. I don't care what you've done— I want to know that you're safe. Hilda's done enough damage. I couldn't bear it if . . ."

"Don't worry," said Alec. "I'll see you don't have to visit me in the condemned cell. Perhaps there's a plane out tonight." He went to the telephone, and Stephanie heard him ringing the airways terminal.

Max lit a cigarette and stood staring out of the window into the darkness. Poor devil!—there wasn't much of a future for him. Not these days, with radio and all the rest of the police gadgets. He wouldn't have much of a chance, except in the sort of place where no man would choose to live. He'd probably do better to throw himself into the river. It would be easier for Stephanie, too, in the end.

Alec finished his telephoning. "There's a plane leaving for Marseilles at nine," he said. "They're keeping a place for me. If I drive straight to the airport, I think I can just make it."

"What about your passport?" asked Stephanie.

"Oh, yes," said Alec. "I'd almost forgotten it." He collected it from the bureau.

"Have you got enough money?"

"I shall manage," said Alec. "I've got enough to pay my fare to Marseilles, and after that, I'll have to work my way, I suppose." He gave a faint smile. "I dare say I may have time to arrange for my foreign holiday allowance before the balloon goes up."

"Oh, Alec!" Stephanie turned her face away.

Max said, "Hadn't you better be packing a bag?"

"Of course," said Alec. He went upstairs to the bedroom.

"Oh, God," breathed Stephanie, "I hope he gets that plane." Her features had become almost haggard. Max ached to hold and comfort her.

"It's hell for you," he said. "I wish I could help. Shall I get you a drink?"

"No—I should be sick. Oh, Max, what a nightmare this is! I can't believe it. . . . Do you think he'll get away? I'm so afraid."

"He'll be all right," said Max, putting as much confidence into his voice as he could.

"I feel it's partly my fault," said Stephanie, miserably.

"That's nonsense. You've got things out of focus."

"I don't know . . . *Ought* I to go with him, do you think?"

"For God's sake!" Max exploded. "Stephanie, you're not serious?"

"I—I just don't know. I can't think. If it would help him . . ."

"You can't sacrifice yourself out of pity for him. That's what it is, isn't it—pity?" Max searched her face. "It's not that you feel you can't live without him. If it were, you wouldn't hesitate."

"I suppose you're right," said Stephanie. "But he'll be so lonely. . . ."

They waited, each occupied with private thoughts. Max was cursing the role that fate had assigned him. Cursing fate itself—for letting him meet the one girl who had ever really interested him, throwing them together in circumstances that brought them incredibly close, and yet making it impossible for him to do anything about it. A man could hardly make love to a girl when he was, at the same time, practically hounding the man *she* loved to the gallows.

A footstep sounded on the stairs. Alec came down, carrying a small bag. He got his overcoat and scarf and put them on.

"Well," he said, "this is it." He stood by the door, the shadow of a smile on his powerful face. "I feel I ought to say some famous last words, but I can't think of any. Goodbye, Easterbrook. I don't bear you any malice. You did what you felt you must—and it would have been all the same in the end."

"Goodbye," said Max. He met Alec's eyes and once again was conscious of something attractive in the man. "Good luck, wherever you go," he said.

Alec turned to Stephanie. Without a word she went up to him and laid her head on his shoulder. Now that he was going, she was remembering only the things she had loved about him—his sensitivity, the way his tempers would suddenly give place to laughter, his happy moods when he was working hard, the ridiculous things they had done together and enjoyed. She sobbed, and Alec put his arms around her. "Don't mind too much, Stephanie," he murmured. "Perhaps it had to be like this. We've been happy, haven't we? And it mightn't have lasted, you know. Not with my foul temper." He stroked her hair. "Try to forget me, it'll be the best thing for you. But if you think of me, remember that I *did* love you. In my fashion. And now, goodbye." He turned her face up to his, kissed her, then thrust her from him. He picked up his bag, the door slammed, and he was gone.

Stephanie stood looking at the door for a few seconds, biting her lips. Then she threw herself on to the settee and cried unashamedly.

❧ FOURTEEN ❧

STEPHANIE'S SOBS gradually subsided, and a stillness fell on the room. Max glanced diffidently at the crumpled figure on the settee and went to the sideboard. As the chink of glasses reached her, Stephanie sat up.

"I'm sorry to have let you in for this," she said with a wan smile. "I'd better go and make myself look a bit more human." She disappeared to the bathroom and Max poured out two stiff drinks.

He was sipping his own, thoughtfully, when she returned. The ravages of her outburst had been expertly repaired, but the shadows under her eyes told their own tale.

"Feeling better?" asked Max, with deep concern.

"Much better, thank you. Yes, I could do with a drink now." She took the glass, but sat staring into its amber depths.

Max said, "I don't know what you want to do, Stephanie. I'll take you home if you like, but perhaps there's someone you could go and stay with. I'd feel happier if you were with a friend."

"You needn't worry," said Stephanie. "I shall be all right—now. And I haven't the vaguest idea what I want to do."

"I'm terribly sorry about it all—you know that."

"It wasn't your fault."

"I was afraid you might confuse the instrument with the cause."

"I know you couldn't have done anything else," said Stephanie. But she added, with a touch of bitterness, "You should be feeling jubilant. Everything's worked out wonderfully for you."

"I feel like hell," said Max. His nerves, as well as hers, were stretched almost to breaking point. "You're mistaken if you imagine I'm bubbling with joy inside. I'm glad for George's sake, and I won't pretend I'm not, but the last thing I would have wanted was to make you unhappy. It simply couldn't be helped."

"You needn't concern yourself about me," said Stephanie. She was making such an effort to control herself that she sounded distant. "I'll be all right if Alec gets away. You do think he will, don't you?"

Max avoided her eyes. "I think he has quite a fair chance," he said finally. "If he makes good use of his long start, he should be on the other side of the world by next week."

Stephanie clutched hopefully at the straw of comfort. "Yes, and then he can begin afresh. He's very capable, and he isn't *so* old. Forty's quite young for that kind of man. Professionally, he isn't even in his prime." She looked at Max as though for further encouragement, but finding none in his expression she turned away. "I think I'll go out for a little while," she said. "I need some air."

"Shall I come with you?"

"No, thanks, I'll be better on my own. I won't be long. And then you can take me home, if you will."

"Anything you say," said Max. He helped her on with her coat. "But if you're not back soon, I shall worry." She went out, and the studio seemed strangely desolate.

Max, left to himself, paced moodily up and down the big room. He wondered if he would ever again see Stephanie as she had been on that first gay evening when they'd met. From now on, she'd be bound to associate him with misery and tragedy. She'd probably be glad to see the last of him, he reflected bitterly. Admitting to himself that he loved her, he realized that he must be the last man on earth she would willingly have anything to do with. He wondered what she was feeling about Alec. The man had never been good enough for her, of course, even supposing he was a genius, and Max didn't think he was that. In a way this present situation must be worse for her than if Alec were dead—his departure was just as final, for he could never come back. And yet he wasn't dead. Stephanie must always be haunted by the knowledge that by making a physical effort she could be with him again.

Max churned this thought over in his mind. It seemed to him there would be no end to the matter. Stephanie would continue to worry about Alec. He might even write to her one day, if he succeeded in finding sanctuary somewhere. The thing might drag on and on. Stephanie was altogether too warmhearted, in Max's opinion. Imagine even thinking of going away with the fellow. . . !

A sound between a groan and a sigh escaped from his lips. How happily he could skip the next few weeks! The sooner he was back again in Germany and at work, the better. It had been a ghastly leave. . . . He checked himself on the edge of self-pity. At least it hadn't been a wasted one. It would be grand to see old George looking his cheerful self again. That would make up for everything. Well, for almost everything.

His reflections were suddenly interrupted by the sound of a car drawing up outside. Now who the devil could that be. Not Alec returning, surely? As footsteps crunched on the gravel, Max went quickly to the door and opened it. A man was standing there—a man in a soft felt hat and a raincoat—a man whose eyes twinkled under bushy gray brows.

Of all people, Inspector Haines!

"*Hello*, Inspector!" said Max.

"Good evening . . ." began Haines and stared. "Well, bless my soul, if it isn't Mr. Easterbrook! I must say I didn't expect to find you here."

Max struggled to control his rising panic. "Yes, I'm ahead of you for once, Inspector."

"You certainly are," said Haines, in a puzzled tone. "Is Mr. Forbes at home?"

"He's not, as a matter of fact," said Max. A fluent and rational explanation seemed called for. "He had to rush off soon after I got here—some friend of his was taken ill. He won't be long—he asked me to wait."

"Well," said Haines, pleasantly, "I don't suppose he'll mind if I come in and wait, too." He entered through the aperture which Max reluctantly widened for him. "Ah, it's nice and warm here." The inspector threw off his coat and went over to the fire, rubbing his hands together. He seemed to be in quite a good humor. "How's the inquiry going, Mr. Easterbrook?" he asked, with his old quizzical gaze. Something in Max's face caught his attention. "You look as though you've been missing your sleep."

"Yes," said Max, "I have been pretty busy. I'm afraid I haven't made much progress, though." He was trying not to look at the table, on which Alec's confession lay in a hideously prominent position. If only he could conceal it somehow without attracting Haines's interest!

"I hardly expected you would," said Haines, stumping slowly round the room and examining the pictures. He looked at the Laocoön, stopped for a moment in front of the easel. "Still searching for the needle in the haystack, eh?" His eyes swept the table—and passed on. "How did you come to contact Forbes?"

Max, his forehead damp with sweat, forced himself to be casual. "Oh," he said, "Jane Lambert happened to mention someone who put me on to him."

"H'm!" Haines didn't look too pleased. "The day I saw her she hardly uttered a sound. . . . Anyway, have you found Forbes helpful?"

Max shook his head. "Not so far. Most disappointing, in fact, like everyone else in this business. Actually, Inspector, I doubt if it's worth your while waiting for him."

Haines smiled grimly. "Still running the police force, eh? What a chap you are! I think I'll stay, if you don't mind."

Max shrugged. "Just as you like, of course. It's nothing to do with me. Make yourself at home. If you want to wash, it's the first door on the left upstairs."

"I'm very comfortable, thank you," said Haines, settling into a chair. "How long did Forbes think he'd be? Where's he gone, anyway?"

"Somewhere quite near—I don't know the address. He thought he'd be about an hour, and he's been gone some time already. By the way, Inspector, how did *you* get on to Forbes?"

"Still asking questions, too, Mr. Easterbrook?" Haines had a sardonic look. "Well, I suppose there's no harm in telling you that." He felt for his pipe and began to fill it. "As a matter of fact, a parcel was delivered at the Lamberts' house yesterday morning. We've been keeping an eye on the place, and one of our chaps took delivery. Just a precaution, you know."

"Very commendable," said Max. "And what was in it?"

"It was a small framed picture, addressed to Mrs. Lambert. I traced it back through the firm that framed it for her to Mr. Forbes. Apparently it was a picture that Mrs. Lambert purchased at a private exhibition of his paintings some weeks ago. A girl in the showroom remembered seeing her talking to Forbes as though she knew him, so I thought I'd better have a word with him. But as you say, it's not likely to lead anywhere. I'm afraid I still think Lambert's our man." The inspector cocked his ear as footsteps sounded once again upon the gravel. "Ah, that must be Forbes . . ."

The door opened and Stephanie came in, a much more tranquil look on her face. "Max . . ." she began. Then she caught sight of his companion rising from a chair. She stood stock-still, staring.

"Oh, Stephanie," said Max, trying desperately to signal a warning with his eyes, "this is Inspector Haines of Scotland Yard. Inspector this is Miss Franks, Alec Forbes's fiancée."

"How do you do?" said Haines, with a benign smile.

Stephanie looked from Haines to Max and then—by a process of reasoning which to Max was only too plain—to the telephone. Her eyes narrowed. Max had a fierce, intense expression which she took for defiance. She walked quickly up to him, her eyes blazing, and slapped his face. "How *could* you?" she cried. "You contemptible cad!"

Haines could hardly believe his ears. "What exactly is going on here?" he asked, his voice taking on the sharp edge of authority. "Miss Franks, will you kindly explain?"

"As though you don't know!" Stephanie flung at him. She was pale with anger. "I suppose you've read the whole thing already."

"Stephanie!" cried Max.

"Read *what* thing?" asked Haines, with quick curiosity.

Stephanie stared at him, and suddenly realized that she had blundered. Her eyes fell to the table where Alec's confession lay, and with a gasp, she moved toward it. Haines, following her movements, was across the room with astonishing agility for a man of his years, and in a moment the manuscript was in his hands.

Max dropped wearily into a chair. "The inspector," he said to Stephanie, "looked in quite accidentally for a harmless little chat with Alec. Thank you for your confidence."

Stephanie uttered a long-drawn "Oh!" and put her hands over her face.

Haines, having given the document a preliminary inspection, settled down with deeply knitted brows to read it through. No one interrupted him. When he had finished it, he looked up with a face like granite. "This is an astonishing piece of work," he said. He looked at Max. "Who wrote it?"

"The text is mine," said Max, curtly. "As you can see, Forbes signed it, and Miss Franks and I witnessed his signature. He dictated the confession."

"And where is Forbes?"

Max said quietly, "I'm afraid, Inspector, your bird has flown."

Haines's tough old face slowly turned a dark red. "Are you trying to tell me that he dictated this confession this evening, in your presence, and that you let him go?"

"That is the incontrovertible fact," said Max.

"I'm astounded," said the inspector. There was nothing benign about him now. "In thirty years I've never heard anything like it. Easterbrook, you'll live to regret this."

"Your assurance that I shall live is comforting, Inspector."

"Bah!" Haines rammed the document into one of his capacious pockets. "May I ask *why* you let him go?"

"It was the condition on which he agreed to confess," said Max. "I can explain everything . . ."

"I very much doubt it," said Haines. "For the moment, that can wait—the first thing is to find him. Do you know where he's gone—either of you?" He looked sternly at Stephanie.

"You'll have to do your own searching," said Max. "We're not in a position to help you."

"So you intend to obstruct the police! Very well, my lad, I'll deal with you later on. Miss Franks, what was Alec Forbes like? Describe him!"

Stephanie stood like a statue.

"You see, Inspector," said Max, "you'll have to count us out."

"I'll count you out, all right," said Haines, grimly. His quick eye ran round the room and settled on the bureau. . . . In a few moments he had the contents turned out on to the floor. Suddenly he pounced on a photograph and held it up to Stephanie. "Is this your boy friend? All right, I can see it is." He gave Max a derisive glance and left the studio with a rasping "Stay where you are, both of you."

As the door banged, Stephanie dropped into a chair. "How *could* I have been such a fool?"

"The damage is done now," said Max, coldly. His face was smarting, and his pride was hurt. A word of regret would, he felt, have been appropriate.

"What will they do?" asked Stephanie.

"About us?"

"No, about Alec."

"Oh, to hell with Alec!" as Max snapped the words out he saw the look of pain on Stephanie's face and made an effort to curb his irritation. After all, the fellow was on the run now—it wasn't reasonable to expect her to think of anything else. He said, gloomily, "They'll send out a description to every police unit. There's a radio car out there now—at this very moment there are tickers at work all over the country." He looked at his watch. "They'll probably get him at the airport. It's touch and go—he should be taking off in about ten minutes. Even if they don't manage to stop him at this end, he'll be on the passenger list, and they'll get him at Paris or Marseilles when the plane lands. You may as well face it."

"I can't bear it."

Max lost patience. "Why won't you be realistic?" he said in a hard voice. "There's no real hope for him, anyway. I understand how you feel—it's natural, but it won't help. Damn it, Stephanie, face the facts. Whatever he meant to you once, right now he's a murderer. A brutal, callous murderer. You don't seem to have grasped that yet. You're just being sentimental. He can't escape the consequences of what he's done. He's finished, whether he gets away or whether he doesn't—and he probably knows it. If he escapes the law, he's got to live with himself, and that may be worse than being hanged."

"How *can* you say that?"

"It's the truth, and being an ostrich won't alter it."

"As long as he's alive, there's still hope for him," said Stephanie.

"Don't you believe it. What sort of future do you think there is for him—going into hiding, changing his name, skulking in some benighted place at the back-of-beyond, always afraid, always wanting to get back, always regretting. . . ? For heaven's sake, haven't you any imagination? That's not life, it's a living death. The kindest thing you can wish for him is a quick end."

"Oh!" gasped Stephanie, "how I hate you!"

The door opened, and the inspector came in, flinging instructions back over his shoulder to someone outside. He turned to Max. "I think we shall have your friend within a very short time," he said. "And now, Mr. Easterbrook, you'd better start that explanation."

"By all means," said Max. "It's really quite straightforward. You've read the confession—you've seen what's in it. The point is that when I came here this evening I had very little of that information. What I had was highly suggestive, but not conclusive." He explained to the inspector about the sketches. "There were a few other things, but they didn't amount to much. I was convinced that Forbes had killed Mrs. Lambert, but I couldn't prove it. Miss Franks and I put our cards on the table—or shall I say, I put the cards on the table and Miss Franks watched. When they were spread out, neither Forbes nor I liked the look of them very much. He thought they were too good for his comfort, and I thought they weren't good enough for Lambert's. So after a lot of talk, Forbes agreed to sign a confession on the understanding that we'd take no action for a week."

"You had no right whatever to make such a bargain," said Haines, sternly. "It was a most improper proceeding."

Max flushed with anger. "That's an ungrateful attitude, Inspector. I'd like to point out that *your* contribution to solving this case has been rather less than nothing. You rushed in and arrested the wrong man, you dug your toes in and wouldn't listen to argument, you neglected to make obvious inquiries, you virtually told me to go to the devil, and here I hand you the answer on a plate and you complain. You may not have the murderer, but at least you've got the truth."

"We're fussy people," said Haines. "We like to have the murderer as well."

"Well, you'll probably get him," said Max, "thanks to Miss Franks. I don't give a damn any more. All I'm saying is that working on your own, you wouldn't have got either the truth or the murderer. Why, you'd never have got on to Forbes at all except for a stroke of luck over the parcel."

"Be fair," said Haines. "You had a stroke of luck yourself with Jane Lambert."

"All right. But suppose we'd started even, where would you have got? I tell you there wasn't enough evidence to bring the thing home to him, except by the sort of bargain I made."

"That bargain," said Haines, "makes you an accessory after the fact. The three of you have deliberately conspired to defeat the ends of justice, and you'll have to answer for it."

"I'll answer for it anywhere," cried Max. "Suppose I hadn't made the bargain—suppose I'd rung you up, as I could have done, while Forbes was still here and invited you to cast your eye over the exhibits? Believe me, I haven't forgotten our last conversation. You weren't exactly co-operative, were you? How did I know you wouldn't decide the evidence was thin? As a matter of fact, I think that's just what you would have done. It *was* thin. And then what would have happened? You wouldn't have been able to hold Forbes—he'd have cleared off, and that would have finished Lambert. And you talk about defeating the ends of justice! What ends—hanging an innocent man?"

"This is all very eloquent," said Haines. "But I've only your word for it that the evidence you had wasn't sufficient. It might have seemed very different after Forbes had been questioned." He looked keenly at Max. "You see, Mr. Easterbrook, I can think of another reason why you and Miss Franks should have made the bargain. You may have thought that it was a good way of saving Lambert, and of saving Miss Frank's fiancé at the same time. That *is* a possibility, isn't it?"

"Miss Franks has had very little to do with it," said Max, quickly. "All she did was to listen and to witness the signature. I don't know what her motives were—that's her affair! I don't think she wanted an innocent man hanged any more than I did, and if she wanted to save her fiancé—well, it may be unlawful, but it's natural. As for me, I didn't care two hoots about Forbes.

I was sorry for Miss Franks, but if the evidence had been good enough I'd have handed him over, and Miss Franks knows I would. I had only one idea in my mind, and that was to make certain of getting Lambert out of the place you put him in."

"And you think you've done that?"

"Well, haven't I?"

"It remains to be seen," said Haines. "This document . . ." he tapped his pocket, "this document may seem to you a very fine piece of work, and so it is in some ways. It contains a great deal of very useful information, and if we can get hold of Forbes, we can check it. But by itself, and without Forbes, it's a very different proposition. It's not even a sworn affidavit—legally, it's of very doubtful value, if any. Forbes could repudiate it tomorrow. Unless he turns up, you may find you've not been nearly as clever as you imagine."

"I don't imagine I've been clever," said Max, savagely. "This isn't a game I'm playing. I tell you again, I'm doing the best I know in order to get Lambert out of jail. The best I can. I never imagined that that confession was a sewed-up, watertight, legal document, but surely to God, it's good enough for you to with-draw the prosecution against Lambert."

Haines sighed. "It depends, Mr. Easterbrook. To you, con-fessions are no doubt very impressive, but they're no novelty to us at the Yard. After a well-publicized murder, I've known them come in by almost every post. People confess to murders they haven't done for all sorts of strange reasons—to save someone else, to gain notoriety, to earn money, or perhaps just because they're cracked. The point is that every confession has to be checked—and it's very difficult to check a confession when the confessor has run away. That always throws doubt on its genuineness."

"But this document tells the whole story," cried Max. "The whole thing's there from start to finish—motive, machinery, everything—all in detail. Surely you can tell for yourself that it rings true."

"Oh, it's got a ring about it," Haines conceded. "The question is whether it's the ring of truth or the ring of literary composition. I never have underrated your abilities."

"But the facts are there," said Max, earnestly. "Facts that Forbes couldn't have known about if he hadn't been the murderer. The description of what Hilda Lambert was wearing, for instance. He couldn't have found those things out from me—he must have seen them."

"Lambert knew," said Haines. "He saw the body."

"I never talked to Lambert about it."

"That's what *you* say. Again, I've only your word for it. And then there's another possibility. Forbes could have visited Mrs. Lambert and noticed these things without having killed her. The real murderer may have gone along afterward."

"Forbes would hardly have seen the soles of Mrs. Lambert's shoes in the course of a social visit!"

"That depends," said the inspector, dryly.

Max gave an exclamation of impatience. "In any case," he said, "if you examine the timetable you'll find there just wasn't time to fit anyone else in after Forbes—not convincingly."

"H'm," said Haines. "You may be right—we shall have to go into that. All I'm saying now is that I'm not satisfied there's anything in this document that you and Forbes and Miss Franks couldn't have cooked up here in this room, if you had any reason for doing so. I'm not suggesting you had. All I'm saying is that the document isn't conclusive—at the moment."

"At least," said Max, "if you're so damned reluctant to believe what's written on that paper, you can hardly accuse us of being accessories after the fact. According to you, there wasn't a fact. You can't have it both ways. I must say, I think you're being extremely unreasonable, Inspector. You blamed me for being dissatisfied with what evidence there was before the confession, and now you've got both the evidence that I had *and* the confession, you're still doubtful whether it's sufficient. I give up!"

"That may be a little premature," said Haines. "Suppose we

wait and see what happens? I feel quite confident that within the next few hours we shall have news of Forbes. Once he's in our hands, the whole position will be changed." He turned to Stephanie. "I'm afraid I must ask you to wait for a while, Miss Franks. I realize all this must be very distressing to you."

"Don't mind me," said Stephanie. "I'm past caring."

The evening wore slowly on. Nobody wanted to talk, for there seemed nothing more to say. The inspector spent some time out at the car. Max half-heartedly suggested food, but Stephanie wasn't interested. She smoked interminably. Nothing could rouse her from the apathy into which she had sunk. Max's anger had faded, and he wished he could make his peace with her, but she was clearly not in the mood. Ten o'clock struck. Surely they ought to know by now whether Alec's name had been on an air passage list or not!

"It looks as though he's given you the slip, Inspector," said Max.

Haines shook his head. "I doubt it."

Another half hour passed. Stephanie lay stretched out on the settee. Her eyes were closed, but she was wide awake. Max was pacing backward and forward again—he couldn't keep still. The waiting was agony. He was about to suggest to the inspector that news before morning was unlikely and that an eye could be kept on them just as easily at home when there was a sharp rat-tat at the door. Haines leaped up, and Max caught a glimpse of a uniformed officer as he left the room.

He was away for about five minutes. When he came back, it was clear from the look on his face that he had news.

"Well, Inspector, have you found him?"

"Yes," said Haines, "we've found him."

Stephanie said, "Oh, God, now it all begins again. I *can't* bear it."

Haines shook his head. "On the contrary," he said, "it's the end. I'm sorry, Miss Franks, but Forbes is dead."

"Oh, no," cried Stephanie. *"No!"*

"I'm afraid so. Apparently he was on his way to the airport, but he didn't get there. He ran into a lamp standard on the North Circular Road . . . he was killed instantly. The identification has just come through. They found his passport."

Stephanie got up slowly, her face blank. "Well, that seems to be that, doesn't it?" she said in a harsh, unnatural voice. She was too tired to think or feel any more. It was finished, that was all she could realize now. She said, "May I go home, Inspector?"

"Of course," said Haines. "I don't think we shall have to trouble you again for a bit."

Max looked helplessly at Stephanie. If only there were something he could do for her. The words that sprang to his lips were trite and not worth saying. The only thing that could help her at this stage was a sleeping tablet. He said, "You'll let me see you home?"

"There's no need," said Stephanie. "I'd rather go by myself."

"Very well—I'll ring for a taxi."

"No—I want to walk. I'll pick one up somewhere."

He looked at her with deep anxiety. "Stephanie, isn't there anything I can do?"

"Haven't you done enough?" she said. "Goodbye." She nodded to the inspector and walked out of the house.

Haines sighed and sat down. "You don't seem very popular, my lad."

"No," said Max. "She's had a hell of a time."

"H'm. I should think she was well rid of him. Best thing that could happen, if you ask me."

"Yes," said Max, "but try telling her." He lit a cigarette. "Well, what happens now, Inspector? Doesn't this make a difference?"

"It might," said Haines, cautiously.

"I suppose it *was* suicide?"

"That's what it looks like. We'll know better when the full report comes in, but apparently there's a witness who says Forbes suddenly accelerated to about seventy and drove straight for the post."

"He had guts, anyway," said Max.

Haines puffed thoughtfully at his pipe. "Of course," he said, "if a man commits suicide immediately after signing a confession of murder, it does strengthen the confession enormously."

"Surely it lets Lambert out," said Max.

"I can't guarantee that. We shall have to look into everything very carefully—including your behavior, Mr. Easterbrook. It wasn't right, you know, it wasn't at all right." The gray eyes twinkled. "However—speaking quite unofficially, I don't *think* I shall have to arrest you."

Max gave a tired smile. "That's generous of you, Inspector." He got up. "I hope you'll forgive all the hard things I said in the heat of the moment. It's been a pleasure to work against you! Will you join me in a drink?"

"Well," said Haines, "without prejudice, I think perhaps I will."

❧ FIFTEEN ❧

MAX STOOD gloomily watching his luggage being put into the airways bus. Nearly a fortnight had passed since that momentous evening in the studio, and his leave was over.

He'd done what he'd set out to do. George had been able to keep his appointment, and he and Lucy were both on top of the world. Ironically, the only flaw in George's happiness now was Max's own distress. Well, there was nothing to be done about that.

Max ground out the stub of his cigarette and glanced up at the clock. George and Lucy were running it pretty fine. His gaze swept the busy waiting room.

Suddenly his heart gave a leap. A slim, familiar figure was hurrying toward him, almost running. A moment more, and she was in his arms.

"*Stephanie!*"

"There was a traffic block," she said, breathlessly. "I was so afraid I should be too late. How long before you leave?"

"Ten minutes. . . . Oh, Stephanie, I thought you were never going to forgive me."

"I've behaved very badly," she said, looking up into his face. "When I got your letter I was still all tied up inside. I simply couldn't answer it. I knew I was being unfair, but I couldn't help it."

"Never mind, now. You're here, and that's all that matters. How did you know I was leaving?"

"George rang me up. He told me he and Lucy had arranged to see you off, but he suggested I should come instead. In fact, he said quite a piece." Stephanie smiled, but her eyes were moist. "Max, he's terribly nice. I don't wonder you feel as you do about him. . . . I'm glad things have turned out all right for them."

"Let's not talk about it," said Max. "I want to forget all that now."

"I want to forget it, too, but there's something I must say first. . . . Max, I'm so sorry about so many things."

"Don't, darling. Please don't. We both said things we didn't mean. It was a ghastly position for you."

"But I ought to have trusted you. When I think of what I did, I'm ashamed. I lost my head completely, and instead of blaming myself, I blamed you. And you were so patient. Can you ever forgive me?"

"I don't know what you're talking about," he answered, gravely. "You know I've always thought you perfect, ever since I saw that you hadn't got horns and a tail!"

"Oh, Max!" she said, laughing a little but with tears in her eyes, "that isn't the right answer at all. I ought to grovel. . . ."

"It wouldn't suit you a bit," said Max, firmly. "Stephanie . . ." A loudspeaker cut him short. "Oh, damn, that's for me. I'll have to go, and there's so much I want to say."

"Won't you be back?"

"Yes, in the spring. I could try to get a job here. Would that be a good idea?"

"It would be a wonderful idea."

The passengers were converging on the bus. Max took her hands. She was very close to him and very sweet. As she looked up and smiled, he bent and kissed her.

"Goodbye, Max," she said. "Safe landing, darling!" She waved as he climbed into the bus, and as it moved off, she called out, "Till the spring!"